GHOSTS KNOW

GHOSTS KNOW

RAMSEY CAMPBELL

TOR®

A TOM DOHERTY ASSOCIATES BOOK

NEW YORK

GHOSTS KNOW

Originally published in the United Kingdom by PS Publishing Ltd.

A Tor Book
Published by Tom Doherty Associates, LLC
175 Fifth Avenue
New York, NY 10010

www.tor-forge.com

Tor® is a registered trademark of Tom Doherty Associates, LLC.

Library of Congress Cataloging-in-Publication Data

Campbell, Ramsey, 1946–
    Ghosts know / Ramsey Campbell.—1st ed.
        p. cm.
    "A Tom Doherty Associates book."
    ISBN 978-0-7653-3633-0 (hardcover)
    ISBN 978-1-4668-2786-8 (e-book)
    1. Radio talk shows—Fiction.   2. Psychics—Fiction.   3.   Paranormal fiction—
Fiction.   4. London (England)—Fiction.   5. Psychological fiction.   I. Title.

    PR6053.A4855G48 2013
    823'.914—dc23

                                                                2013022124

First U.S. Edition: October 2013

Printed in the United States of America

0 9 8 7 6 5 4 3 2 1

For Jeremy Dyson—

here's to keeping it Northern!

Now, their spirits were standing on the very streets they [the Kray brothers] used to rule over . . .

"Give me some proof that you're here," I said in my mind to the brothers.

"Tell the reporter someone else was supposed to join you today. His fingers are missing."

"What a strange message," I thought, but I relayed it to Laura.

Her face flushed. "The photographer was supposed to be here to take pictures," she said . . .

We rounded the next corner and were both taken aback when we ran into the cameraman: he was wearing fingerless gloves.

Joe Power, *The Man Who Sees Dead People*
(as told to Jill Wellington)

GHOSTS KNOW

1

ON THE AIR

"And another thing about all these immigrants," Arthur from Stockport declares. "You won't want anybody hearing about the factory that's had to change its name."

"You're here to enlighten us, Arthur."

"Don't patronise me, Mr Wilde."

I've never had a caller make my name sound so much like an insult, though he's had plenty of competition. Beyond the soundproof window of the studio Christine twirls one finger in the air. "You've got just a minute, Arthur," I tell him. "We're nearly at the news."

"You always put anyone who thinks like me on last, don't you, Mr Wilde? Bob from Blackley, he's another. You haven't let us on for weeks and now I've not got time to say what I came on for."

"You're using up your minute, Arthur."

"It was a muslin factory till the lot who took all the jobs said it sounded too much like Muslim. They didn't fancy the idea you could make those in a factory, so they told the boss they'd get him done for being racist if he didn't call it a fabric manufacturer."

"Where did you hear about that, Arthur?"

"It's well known, Mr Wilde. Just try talking to a few people that live in the real world. And before you ask, the factory's somewhere in Lancashire. Pakishire, we'll have to call it if they carry on like this."

"You mustn't use words like that on here, Arthur."

"It's all right to call us Brits, but they won't let us call them—"

"That's all from Wilde Card for another lunchtime," I say not quite fast enough to blot out his last word, and flick the switch to cut him off. "Here's Sammy Baxter with the news at two o'clock."

I take off my headphones as Christine switches the output to the news studio. I'm leaning back in the swivel chair to wriggle my shoulders and stretch when Rick Till blunders in, combing his unruly reddish hair at the same time as dragging his other arm free of his leather jacket. He's always this harassed when he's due on the air, even though he isn't for five minutes. "All yours, Rick," I say as he hangs the jacket on the back of my chair.

Samantha's newscast meets me in the control room. "Kylie Goodchild's mum made an emotional appeal . . ." The fifteen-year-old is still missing, but we don't hear just her mother's voice; it's underlaid by the kind of tastefully mournful music that films use to demonstrate they're serious. I'm so offended by the artificiality that I yank the outer door open and demand "Whose idea was that?"

Christine comes after me and lays a hand on my shoulder. "Graham . . ."

Some of the reporters and presenters in the large unpartitioned newsroom glance up from their desks, and Trevor Lofthouse lifts his head. He shakes it to flip back a lock of hair and adjusts his flimsy rectangular spectacles but doesn't otherwise respond. "Do we really think we have to manipulate the listeners like that?" I'm determined to establish. "Do we think they won't care otherwise?"

"What are you saying is manipulation?" Lofthouse retorts.

"Calling it an emotional appeal. What other kind is she going to make? Who needs to be told?" As the news editor's spectacles twitch with a frown I say "And calling her the girl's mum. What's wrong with mother? It's supposed to be the news, not somebody gossiping over a fence."

"You're off the air now, Graham. No need to start more arguments today." Before I can retort that I never manufacture them he says "Why are you so bothered?"

"Maybe I hate clichés." I sense that Christine would like me to leave it at that, but I resent the question too much. "Can't we even broadcast an appeal without some music under it? We mustn't think too highly of our audience if we think they need to be told what to feel."

"It's from Kylie Goodchild's favourite film."

Lofthouse doesn't tell me so, and Christine doesn't either. Paula Harding has opened her door and is watching me across the length of the newsroom. Even though she needs heels to reach five feet, it's disconcerting that I didn't notice her until she spoke—I've no idea how much she overheard. "Which film?" I suppose I have to ask.

"*To Kill a Mockingbird*," says Trevor. "Her class are studying the book at school and they were shown the film."

I'd say it was an unusually worthy favourite for a girl of her age, but Paula calls "Can we talk in my office, Graham? I've just heard from one of your listeners."

Christine gives my arm more of a squeeze than she ordinarily would at work, and I lay my hand over hers for a moment. As I head for Paula's room everyone grows conspicuously busier at their desks. They're embarrassed to watch me, but I suspect they're also glad I've been singled out rather than them. Even Christine doesn't know what I'm thinking, however. If Paula means to lecture me or worse, that may be all the excuse I need.

2

HOW TO EARN SWEETS

As I close the door of Paula's office Rick Till speaks from the computer on her desk. "Here's Rick Till Five on Waves in Manchester," he says in a voice so suavely confident that I can hardly believe it belongs to the discomposed man who ousted me from the studio. He plays the station jingle—"We're the station that makes waves"— before starting to chat like a cross between a comedian and a chum who's dropped in. "It's Friend A Faith Day, so cuddle a Christian or snuggle a Sikh or hug a Hindu, or you could embrace an Evangelical or squeeze a Shintoist or make your own arrangements . . ."

The name of the day is the reason I've had two hours of calls like Arthur's and a few more moderate. Paula perches on the cushion that adds stature to the chair behind her desk and plants her stubby hands on either side of the screen. "Let me just give you Rick's Trick for today," Till is saying. "What was the name of the ship in the Anthony Hopkins film of *Mutiny on the Bounty*? That's the Tony Hopkins one, not Charles Laughton or Marlon Brando." He doesn't simply say the names but adopts a version of the actor's voice for each. "Yesterday's winner was Annie from Salford, and the question was what were Fay Wray's first words to King Kong . . ."

I hope Paula doesn't expect me to learn from his example, and my gaze drifts to the window behind her desk. Beyond the double glazing the canal glitters with sunlit ripples as a barge slips into the shadow of a bridge. The vessel is losing a race with a train on the left side of the canal and an equally elevated tram on the other, a contest that would be silent except for Till. "Time to rock with Rick. Here's the Gastric Band from Oldham with their new single, 'Eating Up the World' . . ."

Paula turns him down at last. "Park your bum, Graham," she urges.

The low flabby leather chair I sit in gives a nervous fart on my behalf. Paula leans forward, but her straight black hair has been so thoroughly sprayed it doesn't stir. Chopped off straight at chin level, it lends her pale face the look of an Oriental mask. She's resting a hand next to a glass bowl of sweets, and perhaps I'm meant to be aware that she hasn't offered me one. "So what do you think of our Rick?" she says.

"I expect he's what people want to hear after two hours of me."

"We need to speak to all our audience." Paula sucks at a bottle of Frugen ("the trigger of vigour") and wipes the nipple before saying "Anyway, I heard from Arthur Mason."

"I don't think I know him."

"You were talking to him before you came out to complain about Mrs Goodchild."

"I wouldn't have said anything if I'd known it was her idea. You don't need me to tell you I hope she finds her daughter. I expect the girl's just gone off somewhere for reasons of her own. Girls that age often do, don't they?" In case Paula thinks I'm avoiding the reason that she called me in I say "I didn't know his name was Mason."

"He says he has to ring up dozens of times to get on the air, and you always put him on at the end. That'll be Christine's decision as your producer, will it?"

I don't want Christine to be blamed for any trouble I've stirred up. "Somebody has to be last. He had nearly five minutes."

"He's not the only one, he says. Does Bob from Blackley come to mind?"

"He used to be a regular, but we haven't heard from him for a while as far as I know."

"Mr Mason says that's because of how you dealt with him last time. Do you think we should listen to you, Graham?"

I've time to wonder if she's questioning my honesty before she takes hold of the computer mouse to bring up my voice from Learn Another Language Day, weeks ago. It sounds even more detached from me than it always does in my headphones. "And now here's Bob from Blackley . . ."

"Get it right. There's no Blake about it."

"I believe it's always been pronounced Blakely, Bob."

"About time they called it black and have done with it. If that lot want us learning new words there's one for them."

"Which lot would that be, Bob?"

"The lot that has the law on us if we say anything they don't like, and it's the tax we've paid that pays for them to do it. It's getting so you won't even be able to say you're white."

"Why on earth would anybody want to stop me? As it happens I am."

"Half the time you don't sound it. It's the likes of you that want to stop us being proud of it. Where's White Pride Day with all these other days?"

"It might sound a bit like a kind of sliced bread, do you think?"

"More like you're scared to say there ought to be one. They wouldn't like it, the lot that's driving us out of our own country."

"Who's being driven, Bob? Whites are the largest group where you live." While speaking to him I'd found the statistics for Blackley online. "Less than four per cent black people, and—"

"Never mind your figures. You want to come and walk along the street here. You'd love it. It's full of the lot of them."

"You still haven't said which lot you mean."

"The Sicks and the Shites and the rest of their sort. You can't hardly move round here for refugees."

"It's Shiite, Bob, and how can you tell by looking? It's a religion, not a race."

"Don't talk to me about religion. That's their excuse for everything they get up to. I ought to tie a curtain round my head and then I could ride a bike without a helmet. Or I could say I'm an Islam or a Mohammed or whatever they like to be called and then I'd be able to tell the wife and the girl to hide their mugs and shut their gobs because Allah says so. Mind you, that'd be a blessing."

"Haven't you any faith of your own, Bob?"

"I've got plenty of that and it's all in myself. And I'll tell you what else I believe in, this life and that's your lot. The life these Islams and the rest of them want to rob off us." He's interrupted by a screech that puts me in mind of a butcher's circular blade. "I'm on the fucking radio," he shouts. "Close that fucking door or I'll fucking—"

"I'm sorry, you can't talk like that on the air. Gussy from Prestwich, you're live on Wilde Card."

"The things you have to deal with, I think it's time they had Presenter Awareness Day."

"I'm not going to argue with you about that."

"Sometimes what you think shows through, Graham," Paula says as she stops the playback.

I have the disconcerting sense that my voice has returned to me. "I wouldn't want to think I'm just controversy for hire."

"What do you think the new bosses would say if they heard all that?"

If she's decided I don't fit in now that Waves has become part of the Frugo empire, I'm glad. I almost retort that I may have had a better offer, but instead I say "What do you?"

"That you could have been sharper with him. You let him get away with those comments about women. Your show isn't called Gray Area any more. Remember your slogan."

"It's a phone-in, not a drone-in." I've played it so often that it starts up like a recording in my head. It was among my more desperate attempts to impress her with a brainstorm, and I barely managed not to laugh when she said it was the one she liked. "You want me to go on the offensive," I say but don't necessarily hope.

"If you feel it say it, Graham. Don't go too far but as far as you can. You know what Frugo tells everyone who works for them."

"I don't believe I've heard it," I say without wanting to know.

"Everything you do and say at work should be an ad for where you're working. Just do everything you can to make certain you're one, Graham. They'll be listening to our output before they come to visit. Let's make sure they know we're the ones making waves."

She sits back to end the interview. As I stand up, drawing a sound that might be a sigh of relief or resignation from the chair, she says "It's about time Bob was on your show again. Tell Christine to put him on next time he calls." This halts me long enough for her to ask "Was there anything else?"

I won't mention Hannah Leatherhead until we've had more of a word. I'm turning away when Paula says "Aren't you having your sweet?"

I'm reminded of visiting the doctor's as a child or of being rewarded with a sweet for some other unpleasant experience. Wrappings rustle as I rummage in the bowl and find a lemon drop. "Thanks," I say, mostly for the sweet, and hear Paula's keyboard start to clack as I reach the door.

Nobody in the newsroom seems to know whether they should look at me. I unwrap the sweet into my mouth and drop the cellophane in the bin beside my desk on the way to the control room. Christine spins around in her chair as I ease the door out of its rubbery frame. "Was it bad?" she murmurs.

She's enough of a reason for me to keep working at Waves—the eternal valentine of her gently heart-shaped face framed by soft spikes of black hair that's cropped to the nape of her long neck, her slim lithe body in a black polo-neck and matching jeans, her eyes alert for my answer, her pink lips parted in anticipation. "It isn't going to change my life," I say, which makes me aware that I've yet to mention Hannah Leatherhead.

3

STAGING THE ANCESTORS

It's Walk To Work Day, but every workday is for me. As I step out of the apartment building, where the massive lintel over the tall thick door still sports the insignia of a Victorian broker, the gilded nameplate of Walter Belvedere's literary agency glints above my handwritten cardboard tag. Perhaps he can place my novel if I ever finish it. A train swings onto the bridge over the street with a screech of wheels on the curve of the track, and I'm reminded of the noise that made Bob from Blackley lose control. Though the sun is nearly at its peak, the street is darkened by office blocks—you could imagine the shadows are their age made visible, more than a century of it. Sunlight meets me on Whitworth Street, where a man in shorts with a multitude of pockets is parading the biggest and certainly the bluest poodle I've ever seen. Along Princess Street girls are cycling in the first-floor window of Corporate Sana ("We mind if your body's healthy," says the slogan), but Christine isn't in the gym; she's producing the food and news show, Currant Affairs. As I pass her flat on Whitworth Street I glance up at the windows, but there's no sign of an intruder.

Where Oxford Street turns into Oxford Road a Palace faces a Palace. The one that isn't a hotel displays posters for an American psychic, Frank Jasper. Early lunchers are taking sandwiches or sushi down the steps to eat by the canal. They make me feel later than I am, and I hurry along the western stretch of Whitworth Street to Waves. The guard at his desk nods to me as the automatic doors let me in, and a lift takes me to the fourth floor, where Shilpa at Reception is on the phone, attempting to explain that there's no prize for solving Rick's Trick. My badge on its extending wire unlocks the door to the newsroom, where Trevor Lofthouse is playing back a television newscast on his computer. I'm making for my desk when I see the name Goodchild on the screen.

It's a press conference with Kylie Goodchild's parents and a teenager. At least it isn't using any music. Mrs Goodchild is a redhead, rather too plump for the unbuttoned jacket of her grey suit. Her husband is even broader and a head taller, and resembles a pugilist despite his tie and dark suit, mostly because of his large flattened nose. To judge by the name tattooed on the teenager's neck, he's Kylie's boyfriend. He's warning anyone who may have abducted her, in language so ferocious it blots out his mouth—censorship does, at any rate. Mr Goodchild jerks a hand that isn't quite a fist at him, and a journalist takes the chance to ask "Is it right you're bringing in a psychic?"

As Goodchild gives a nod so fierce it looks defensive, his wife says "We'll do anything we've got to that will bring our Kylie back."

In the control room Christine meets me with a smile and a wave as if we didn't part just a few hours ago. The news gives way to my signature tune, and a girl's even brighter voice chirps my slogan as I don the headphones and read the screen. "First up is Margaret from Hyde," I say. "You're calling about Kylie Goodchild, Margaret."

"I'm praying for her and her parents. I feel in my heart they'll find her now Frank Jasper's helping them."

"What makes you say that?"

"He's meant to be marvellous, isn't he? One of my neighbours went to see him last night at the Palace and she said he was."

"Did he tell her what she wanted to hear?"

"He most definitely did." She's either unaware of my irony or ignoring it. "He was in touch with her father."

"I take it the gentleman's no longer with us."

"He died a couple of years ago. Mr Jasper knew that and he knew his name was John."

"That's unusual."

"He told her a lot more than that." By the sound of it Margaret has spotted my skepticism. "He knew she used to worry about her father but he says she needn't any longer," she insists. "And he knew her grandchild's having some problems at school but they'll be sorted out before long. And her father's glad she's been able to have some work done on her house and take a holiday she's been wanting to take."

I've found Jasper's web site. *Frank Jasper—Your Psychic Friend*, the opening page calls him. He's holding out his hands as though to bless his audience or to offer them an invisible gift, unless he's inviting donations. His ingratiating chubby face is topped with a shock of hair so pale that it may have been bleached by the sun that bronzed his skin, or else all this is as artificial as his wide-eyed look. I think he's trying to appear alert and welcoming and visionary too. His denim shirt is almost the same watery blue as his eyes, and its open collar displays a bright green pendant nestling among wiry golden curls on his chest. We're told he has advised police on investigations in America and helped recover stolen goods. His customers are promised that he'll tell them the name of their spirit guardian; supposedly we all have one of those. All this makes me angry, and so does Margaret's account, though not with her. "Did she really need her father to tell her any of that?" I ask as gently as I can.

"That wasn't all. He said her father was standing by her shoulder."

"Don't say he said her father was her spirit guardian."

"That's exactly what he did say. How did you know?"

"Maybe I'm as psychic as he is."

One reason I've grown confrontational is that Paula has appeared in the doorway of her office. "Did he say what the lady's father looked like?"

"Just like her favourite memory of him."

I don't want to risk destroying this, even if there's no reason to assume Margaret's neighbour is listening. "And he doesn't only tell people what they want to hear," Margaret says with some defiance. "He told one couple their son killed himself when they thought he died in an accident."

Paula is advancing across the newsroom, but I don't need her to tell me how to feel. "Well," I say, "that must have done them some good. Cheered them up no end, I expect."

"He has to tell the truth when he sees it, doesn't he? He said their son had found peace."

"I hope the parents have despite Mr Jasper."

"Why do you say that? It was because of him. He said now their son is always with them."

"He's never turned into their spirit guardian."

"Wouldn't you want him to? Don't you believe in anything?"

Paula has come into the control room to stand at Christine's shoulder like a parody of the subject under discussion. "I believe Mr Jasper is a stage performer," I inform anyone who wants to hear.

"If you think you're as good as he is," Margaret retorts, "why don't you have him on your show and see who's best?"

I'm close to declaring that I hope I'm better in several ways when Paula grabs Christine's microphone. "That's what you need, Graham. Let's have him on."

"Excuse me a moment, Margaret. I've got our manager in my ear." I take myself off the air to ask "What are you saying I should do?"

"Bring him in and question him as hard as you like and let your callers talk to him."

"Margaret, we'll see if I can grant your wish. Keep listening and you may hear Mr Jasper."

"I'll tell my friends," she says, not entirely like a promise.

Christine's microphone is still open, and I've been hearing Paula say "See if you can book Graham to watch him on stage before he comes in."

I play a trail for Rick Till Five so as to speak to Christine. "Don't say who you're booking for. Just reserve a seat as close to the stage as you can and I'll pay cash."

"All right, Mr Devious. You sound as if you've already made up your mind about him."

"Haven't you?"

"I'll leave it till I've seen him."

"Go ahead, book two seats. I expect Waves can stand the expense." I should have asked if she wanted to come, not least in case she might notice details I overlook. "The more eyes the better," I say and go back on the air.

4

AN ACT AT THE THEATRE

"Now there's a Jay down here in the stalls," Frank Jasper says and advances to the footlights, which intensify the golden glow of his tanned face. "I know they mean a lot to someone. I'm getting a sense of some unfinished business. Is it J for Jo? Somewhere in these first few rows? Jo something, is that what I'm being told?"

He's stretching out his hands in an appeal you could take for an offer. His intent gaze passes over Christine and me in the fourth row, and I'm tempted to respond. If I claim to be Joe, how will he carry on? Perhaps Christine guesses my thoughts, because she rests one hand on my thigh before giving me a tiny frown and an equally private shake of her head, at which point someone speaks—an elderly woman in the aisle seat beyond Christine. "Is it Josie?"

"You're absolutely right. That's what I've been hearing, Josephine."

"We mostly called her Josie."

"I know you did. She wasn't older than you, was she? Pardon the personal question."

"She was our aunt, mine and my sister's."

"I need you to know I wasn't saying you were old. Now don't tell me, didn't she have a lot of grey hair?"

"There was still a bit of red in it."

"Sure, that's what I'm saying, it was mostly grey. Okay, don't say anything, let me hear this now. I'm getting something about glasses. Some glasses that were broken."

"We did have a pair mended for her."

"She didn't always wear them, though."

"Sometimes she forgot and we had a big argument about it."

"She wants you to know you mustn't blame yourself for anything you said, because now she can see fine. We all will when we're where she is. Wait now, I'm hearing something else. She likes to talk, Josie, doesn't she?"

"She didn't say a lot. Half the time if we asked her anything she'd just sulk."

"That's why she's talking so much now. She wants to pass on all the stuff she didn't get to say. Don't you think she was like that because of her illness?"

"I suppose that must have been part of it."

"I guess she suffered some, didn't she? But she wants you to know how much you helped. Now what she was saying before, is she going to be concerned about a will?"

"She didn't leave one."

"That's what Josie's telling us. There's no need for anyone to be concerned about it. You should all share whatever she's left for you."

"There's only me and my sister."

"She seems to think there's a partner as well."

"My sister's married. I'm not."

"That's what Josie's saying. She won't mind if they share with your sister."

"Are you sure? Josie didn't get on with him at all."

"That's why she's saying this now. She's at peace with it and she wants you all to be. Wait, there's something else she wants you to know. What was it that was very valuable to her? Don't tell me, she's trying to show me. Something bright. Are we talking about jewelry?"

The elderly woman nods once more. "It was a brooch her mother gave her for her twenty-first."

"That's it, her birthday brooch. And then was it lost? Josie thought it had been stolen, didn't she? She accused someone of stealing it. She said you had."

The elderly woman dabs at her eyes. "She accused all of us."

"That's right, her very words. Well, now she knows you didn't take it, and she wants whoever finds it to have it. You haven't yet, have you?"

"To tell you the truth, we've been too upset to look."

"Believe me, Josie doesn't want you to be. She's promising to do her best to help you find it. She'll always be with you. She's at your shoulder now."

"Well," the woman says and for a moment seems unable to continue. "Thank you, Mr Jasper."

"Call me Frank. That's what I am."

If it weren't for the contents of my pocket I don't know whether I'd be able to keep my anger to myself. Jasper has begun to range along the edge of the stage, so slowly that I've time to wonder what he's looking for. "We're still down here at the front," he says, and I glance about for clues he might plan to build on. He's only holding out one hand now, which could mean he isn't so sure of himself, but more likely he's devising his next trick. His face lights up as he steps closer to the pit and extends his other hand. "I'm getting an uncommon name."

The more specific he is, the more it will betray he's obtained the name beforehand. "Is it Delbert?" he says and frowns at someone, presumably himself. "Or Hubert? No, wait, I'm getting it now. Is there a Herbert here?"

I wouldn't be surprised. Surely others in the audience have

noticed that the names are growing less unusual. When nobody reacts he tries another ploy. "It's his grandfather who wants to get in touch with him, an old man with a stick."

Does he really expect anyone to think this is out of the ordinary? Too many of his fans will believe what they've paid to believe, but the price of the tickets is simply inflaming my rage. "He wants you to remember he was on your side," Jasper says as if this isn't true of any number of grandparents and their grandchildren. "Was it when you were in some kind of trouble as a child? He's telling me it involved the police."

I'd like to glance around and see how many people are finding this applies to them, but I don't want to draw his attention. "Was it your father who called them?" he's saying. "He accused you of something and your grandfather put them right. Didn't your father say you'd attacked him?"

It's becoming uncomfortably personal. I can't imagine that most of his listeners would want to claim it for their own, at least until Jasper says "You were only standing up for your mother." I expect some of the audience would be happy to have that said about them, but Jasper carries on. "Your grandfather was always defending you both, wasn't he? Otherwise you'd have been treated worse."

I grip the edge of the seat with both hands to ensure I don't inadvertently shift and catch his eye. "You were still treated bad, weren't you?" he says as if it's practically unknown for anyone to think that of their childhood. "Didn't your father lock you and your mother in the flat when he went out for a drink?"

I'm unaware of shaking my head until Christine turns to look at me. As I shake it more tersely and fiercely to warn her against singling us out, Jasper says "He didn't like your grandfather visiting, did he? Wasn't there something he used as an excuse to tell him not to? Wait, he's showing me. He used to smoke a pipe and your father said it made him sick. Didn't you think it looked like a pipe in an old magazine?"

He's good at his act, I'll give him that. Until you analyse them some of these details seem uncannily precise. "Hey, you thought it made him look like Sherlock Holmes," he says. "That's why you figured he'd sort things out for you and your mother."

This isn't going to reach me. I'm not paralysed, I'm just keeping still so as to stay unnoticed. "Now he's showing me somewhere with a whole lot of tenements," Jasper says, which could refer to quite a few districts of Manchester. "That's where all this happened, isn't it? Don't tell me what it's called," he says as if I would, and I swallow a laugh at the idea that he's addressing the voice in his head. "It's Hulme."

Christine peers at me, although surely I didn't react. Is that what's obvious—my determination not to? "He remembers the balcony outside your apartment," Jasper says. "What happened there, that's why he made things right with the police."

I won't look at Christine, and I wish I didn't have to face him either just now. I do my utmost not to blink or to display any expression as he says "You were trying to protect your mother. Your father dragged you out and hung you off the balcony by your feet, and the neighbours had to make him stop."

"No."

If I say this aloud it's surely under my breath, but Jasper gazes straight at me. "He knows you find it hard to believe," he says, "but he wants you to know he'll be by your side whenever you're ready to acknowledge him."

He steps back from the footlights and raises his eyes while Christine keeps hers on me. "Now there's someone in the balcony," he says. "Who's the lady who recently went into hospital? I'm hearing about one of several children . . ." If he's even slightly psychic he ought to be able to sense my glare on him. He'll need a spirit guardian by the time I've finished with him. He won't know what he's dealing with until tomorrow.

5

SECRETS

As I unlock the hefty Victorian door of my apartment Christine says "What's actually wrong?"

"All right, that was me. It was all me."

She waits outside Walter Belvedere's agency until I turn the knob that brings up the light in my hall. "What was, Graham?"

"The boy with Sherlock for his grandfather and a staggering drunk for a dad."

"I didn't know," Christine says and shuts the door as if she's making sure we won't be overheard. "Frank Jasper didn't just say that, though. Didn't he say Herbert? That isn't your name."

"It used to be."

W. C. Fields is exchanging looks with Jackie Coogan across the hall. The eyes of all the vintage film posters are easier to ignore than Christine's scrutiny, which follows me into the kitchen. "You never told me," she says.

"It was my father's. I don't need to tell you why I dropped it."

She looks mostly reproachful. "Is there anything else I should know?"

"Not a thing. We're done with it. That isn't me any more." Any guilt I feel is for not having visited my mother or even called her on the phone for weeks. I've turned the kitchen light up full, intensifying the blackness of much of the room—the cupboards, the furniture, the work surfaces, the tiles on the floor and walls. "Are we having coffee?" I propose rather than ask.

"If we want to stay awake."

"I need to think before tomorrow." Filling the percolator doesn't seem to help, and as it starts to creak with heat I say "He had to know that name in advance. Someone must have tipped him off."

"Who are we talking about, Graham?"

"I don't mean you, not consciously anyway." Nevertheless as I sit on a spindly chair I say "Are you absolutely sure you didn't give them anything he could have used?"

"I don't see how when I didn't know your name," Christine protests and sits opposite me at the round black wafer of a table. "I said the tickets were for Francis and you saw I paid cash at the Palace."

"Maybe the name was a bit too clever. You rang up from Waves, didn't you? That's it, of course," I say and almost take her hand. "That's where you called from to arrange our interview as well. He'd have traced the number and put the two together, and he had hours to find out all about me."

"That can't be it, Graham."

I'm disconcerted by how much I resent this. "Why not?"

"Any calls we make from Waves, the number's automatically withheld."

"Then someone must have recognised me at the theatre. That's why I wanted to get there as near to the start as we could, to give him less time to check up on me, him or whoever's working for him. I wish I'd sent you to pick up the tickets. You could have given me mine and I'd have got there late."

"Don't you think you're being a bit too suspicious?"

"No, I think I wasn't nearly suspicious enough. It's a good job I was careful with this." I unbutton my collar and unclip the tiny microphone before lifting the recorder out of my pocket. "If he tries to deny anything he said," I tell her, "here's the proof."

"I didn't know you had that."

"I didn't want you to." This time I do take her hand. "If you knew you might have given it away," I murmur. "I know you wouldn't have on purpose."

My attempt at gentleness isn't helped by the need to raise my voice in competition with the robust burbling of the percolator. Christine pats my hand before opening the cupboard above the glass hob to take out a brace of mugs. She gives me Not Drowning, my suggestion for a Waves slogan Paula didn't like and I suspect didn't understand, and then resumes her seat with On Your Wavelength, her slogan, which Paula chose. She sips her coffee until I have to say "Is it my turn to ask if something's wrong?"

"Are there any more secrets you've been saving up for me?"

"Those weren't secrets, they were just things that aren't worth knowing. We all have a few of those."

"I didn't think we had any. You know everything about me."

"I know you're my cute producer and a psychologist as well."

"I've got a few letters after my name, that's all. Good at writing essays but who knows if I'd have been much use at the job."

"You're good with all kinds of people, Chris. There are too many graduates to go round, that's the trouble. You said you saw someone from your graduation year working in a supermarket."

"We'll all be working for Frugo soon."

I need to get back in touch with Hannah Leatherhead. I haven't mentioned her to Christine yet, but I will once I've learned if there's a definite offer. Instead I say "I do think with all your knowledge—"

"I ought to be making more use of it and not hiding away from the public."

"I was only going to say I'm surprised you can't see through the likes of Frank Jasper."

"Maybe there's more to see than you want to think, Graham."

"It sounds as if you'd like there to be. That's not like you," I say but have to add "Is it?"

"I don't believe psychology can explain everything. There has to be more to all of us than that." With a hint of reproach Christine says "He found out more about you than I had."

"I told you how." Having left her unconvinced brings me close to rage, certainly only with him and his tricks. "Tomorrow I'll prove it," I assure her. "And honestly, now you know everything you'd want to know."

"Well, here's something you didn't know about me." Christine takes rather more than a sip of her coffee as a prelude to saying "I told you Oliver started knocking me about and that's why I left him. He'd lash out if he couldn't win an argument, and I'd got tired of letting him win." Another swallow of coffee lets her say "He kept telling me he'd had an abusive childhood as if that was an excuse. He even tried to make me feel it was up to me to understand him."

"You know I'd never do that. I hope you know." When Christine only gazes at me, at least without disagreeing, I add "And see, you had a secret after all."

"It isn't the same, Graham. It wasn't about me."

I know better than to argue under all the circumstances. She finishes her coffee and glances at the recorder lying dormant on the table. "If you're going to be busy with that," she says, "I'm off to bed."

I don't need to be psychic or even a psychologist to read her mind. "It can wait till the morning," I say, and soon we're on top of the quilt in the bedroom. The subdued light is all I need in the way of mystery. Her firm cool fingers on my back and her legs around my waist feel like forgiveness as well as the delicious messages they're sending to my nerves. We don't need words when we're so close. I'm deeper inside her than any question could take me, and surely she feels united with me. We can forget about false spirits, as if there's any other kind, and even about investigating them while I have Christine in the flesh. At last we gasp, sharing our breaths, and as we grow peaceful in each other's arms I remember wondering as a boy why people called it the little death. This kind of dying I can live with, and before long we come back to life.

6

A SCAR AND AN INSIGHT

"Police are appealing for anyone who's seen Kylie Goodchild since the twelfth of May to contact them. Remember that was Diversity Dividend Day . . ."

The twelve o'clock news is cranking up my irritation while I wait for Frank Jasper—not the content of the newscast or even Sammy Baxter's chummy tone, but the way she links each item with the next. "Meanwhile in Baghdad a car bomb has killed at least twenty people . . ." What does she mean by meanwhile? It reminds me of captions in old cinema serials and makes me feel as if she's trying to bundle the randomness of the world into a narrative that will lend it sense. One of the injured came from somewhere not too far from Manchester, which apparently renders the carnage more significant, though not for long in terms of airtime. "And now in sport there's rumours of new blood at Manchester United . . ." I might be tempted to broadcast some wry comment once the news ends with the weather, but my jingle intervenes, and the Wilde Card slogan reminds me why I'm here. "Wilde is right," I say. "Graham Wilde here, the Wilde man of Waves. Today I've got a special show for you. Clairvoyant Frank Jasper has agreed to leave the stage and take questions. Can he predict what's coming? I'm hearing a voice in my head that tells me he's here even though I can't see him."

Christine widens her eyes and cocks her head in a gesture that might be on the way to a rebuke, and then she lets go of the microphone and leaves the control room. I've asked her to say as little as possible to Jasper, and nothing he can use. As I tell the listeners that I saw his show last night she reappears with him. When she lets him into the studio I lean across the console and give his hand the briefest shake. "Welcome to Wilde Card, Mr Jasper."

He's wearing white slacks and an equally white T-shirt, which is emblazoned with the slogan **SEE THE TRUTH**. Perhaps we're meant to see him as modelling innocence. He sits opposite me and raises his gaze like a promise of honesty. His eyes are intent on looking both alert and gentle, positively sympathetic. His faint smile may be meant to appear relaxed and amiable, but I'd call it smug if not secretly amused. "The name's Frank," he says. "This is a surprise."

"I wouldn't have thought you'd want any of those, Frank."

"There's not a whole lot I like more than surprising people."

He's going to play more of his word games, is he? That's fine if the listeners notice. "Do I call you Gray?" he wonders—says, at any rate.

"I didn't think you'd need to ask." When he leaves that unanswered I say "Try Graham. What were you calling a surprise?"

"Finding you're running this show. Didn't I give you a reading last night? That was at the Palace, your listeners should know. I'll be giving readings there all week."

"Are you having to ask if you gave me one, Frank?"

"I don't have that great a memory. It isn't necessary for what I do. If the spirit world speaks directly through me I may not remember what I said."

"Then here's a reminder," I say and switch on the playback.

There's silence for a moment and then for another. The recording was more distant and muffled than I liked, and I fiddled digitally with it, as much as it could take. Jasper clasps his hands together and parts his lips, just in time for his voice to be heard. "Now there's a Jay down here in the stalls . . ."

"Gee, you did show up prepared," Jasper says and looks reproachful. "Did you check with someone if it was okay to record?"

I've paused the playback so that he can't blot it out. "Wouldn't you want anybody to?"

"I'm just concerned about whoever got the reading."

"I don't believe it was too personal. Would you like me to edit out everything she said?"

"Hey, it's your show. You do whatever you feel you have to."

I have to glance past him, because Paula has come to her door. As I meet her eyes she gives a single nod. "I will," I say and let the playback loose.

"Is it J for Jo? Somewhere in these first few rows? Jo something, is that what I'm being told?" When at last the lady in the audience rewards him with Josie's name I stop the playback. "What would you say about all that, Frank?"

"I'd rather hear what else the lady has to say."

"You can't take a guess at her name."

"I'm not always told those. The spirits let me know when I've found who they're seeking. That's what counts."

"Didn't you say Josephine was at the lady's shoulder? I wouldn't call that far to seek." As Paula shuts her door, presumably content to let me deal with him, I point out "Somebody cynical might say you didn't tell her as much as you seemed to. They'd say you knew there was a good chance there'd either be someone with a name like Jo near the stage, so you could be that specific, or somebody who knew someone with that kind of name. And once you got a response you started trawling for the full name or a surname."

"Well, that's a whole lot of words just to try and take away the lady's comfort."

I won't respond to that except by reviving the playback. He

gazes at me while we listen to several of his exchanges with the lady's niece, and then I cut off his voice, which the digital improvements have left a little thin and shrill. "Everything you said to her could mean something else."

"But it didn't, Graham, did it? You heard the lady say so herself."

"You weren't even sure what colour Josie's hair was until you were told. Glasses could be spectacles or glassware, and it's an easy bet that some of those would have been broken in the past. You claimed Josie liked to talk and when her niece told you she hadn't you made out she'd changed in the afterlife."

"I guess you're paid to think that way." Jasper's gaze has grown infuriatingly tolerant. "I just wonder," he says, "what your listeners think."

"Let's find out, shall we?" Christine has entered a caller's details on the monitor. "Martine from Longsight," I say. "You've a question for Frank Jasper."

"First of all I want to say I'm shocked how rude you're being to your guest. Did Mr Jasper know this was how you were going to treat him?"

"I'm sure Frank did some research." As he shakes his head I say "Go ahead and speak to him."

"I'm not finished with you yet. You're trying to twist things to discredit him. He didn't just say the lady's aunt's name before the lady said anything. He said her aunt meant a lot to her and there was unfinished business, and that turned out to be the will she didn't make."

"The way he phrased it, Will could have been somebody's name."

"Oh, Mr Wilde, how determined you are not to believe anything you aren't paid to believe."

"It's got nothing to do with money." Rather than say this despite the provocation, I ask her "Are you ready to talk to my guest yet?"

"I'm here for you whenever you're ready," Jasper says, "and please do call me Frank like all my friends do."

"Well, thank you very much." At first the privilege seems to have robbed her of words, and then she says "Do you think some people have a gift like yours even if they don't know?"

"It could be everybody has if they search deep enough within themselves."

"Would you want that?" I wonder. "You'd be out of a job."

"It isn't just a job, Graham."

"Maybe you could run courses for budding psychics." His wistful expression as much as his comment has provoked my retort. "Any other questions?" I ask the caller.

"Do you think you have the gift, Martine?" Jasper intervenes.

"I'd love to find I did. Can you tell over the air? Would you be able to give me a reading now, Mr Jasper, Frank?"

"He can't do that, Martine, sorry."

Christine gazes at me through the window as Jasper says "How come you're speaking for me, Graham?"

"I'm saying you can't do that on my programme."

Perhaps he sees why, though I don't know whether Christine realises he could have planted Martine to ask for the reading. "Okay, Martine," he says. "When can you come to the Palace? Name your night and I'll fix up free tickets for you and a friend."

"We don't do that on here either."

Christine frowns, because we've given away tickets to shows in the past. This time Jasper doesn't protest, perhaps for fear I'd point out that he could research Martine's background—there can't be many people of that name in a single district of Manchester. "Then just tell the front of house I sent you," he says, "and there'll be tickets."

"Thanks for your call, Martine. Shall we hear some more of your performance, Frank?"

"Sure, let people make up their minds."

I let the playback run until he tells Josie's niece her aunt is with her. "What would you say you were doing there, Frank?"

"Just exactly what everyone heard."

"You told the lady her aunt had lost something valuable. Not much of a deduction when she'd told you her aunt was careless with her spectacles. And you could have seen from her face they'd been accused of stealing it, the family you weren't sure about until she said who was who. Someone cynical might say she told you more than you told her."

"I don't know why anyone that cynical would come to see me. Don't you have callers waiting in line?"

I glance at Christine, who nods at the monitor. In a moment details of two callers appear on the screen, and I'm infuriated by the notion that Jasper is more capable of picking up cues from her than I am. "Answer me one question first," I say. "Is it a chummy place, the afterlife?"

"That's kind of an English way of putting it. Can you say what you mean?"

"Are all the dead on first-name terms? Whenever you said you were in touch with somebody you never gave their whole name. Do we forget our last names once we're dead?"

"Most people forget stuff as they get older, don't they? It's part of the process of becoming what's essential about each of us. All that matters is it never dies and we find peace."

I meant to show up another flaw in his performance, but I've handed him a notion he may not even previously have thought of. I need to be more alert, and I feel as if I've already overlooked some remark of his or something else about him. "Are we taking more calls?" he says.

"In a moment." I don't want to be distracted from identifying whatever I failed to notice. "Let me ask you this," I say to gain time. "Why did the lady get Josie for her, what's the phrase you use, her spirit guardian?"

"Don't say you wouldn't want it, Graham."

"I'm asking why she'd be favoured and not her sister."

"There's no time and space in the forever. I'm sure Josie is with both of them."

Perhaps I can recognise the clue while he's dealing with a caller. "Now we have Vic from Crumpsall," I say. "What would you like to ask Frank Jasper, Vic?"

"Do you reckon you're clever?"

Jasper's sad smile doesn't falter, and so I say "Frank?"

"Not him, you," says Vic. "How many more silly tricks are you going to play to try and make him look bad?"

"What tricks do you think you've been hearing, Vic?"

"The lot of them. Don't fret, Frank, anyone with half a brain can see what he's up to. The likes of him should keep their gobs shut while you're helping the police. You don't want to be put off finding the lass that's disappeared. You're doing it for nowt, he might like to know."

"Is that right, Frank? You aren't charging a fee?"

"I hope you didn't think I would, Graham."

"I just wanted to tell you we're all with you, Frank," Vic says. "You do whatever's wanted to find the girl, God protect her."

"Thanks for your contribution, Vic." I don't know if this sounds ironic; my voice in the headphones seems too remote for me to judge. "Harry from Harpurhey, you're on the air."

"Let's be hearing you, then." He gives me a moment to feel encouraged before he says "Let's hear what he said to you at the Palace."

For just an instant I think Jasper isn't anxious for it to be broadcast. I'm very much hoping to discover the reason as I set off the playback. "I'm getting an uncommon name . . ."

There's no question that he knew my discarded one but didn't want to seem too obviously informed. Of course, he would have prepared for the interview by looking on the Waves web site, and he'd have recognised me at the Palace from my photograph. I let his monologue run to the end, stopping it just short of the single word I blurted. "What did you think of that, Harry?"

"What do you? It's meant to be all about you."

I could question whether it's accurate and challenge Jasper to prove it is, but I'm goaded to enquire "How do you think he does it then, Harry?"

"How he says. That's if it's true, and you're not saying different."

I'm tempted to deny it is, not least because Jasper's gaze is insufferably confident, but I could be shown to have lied. Am I really so desperate to expose him? Surely I haven't run out of legitimate options, even if I'm reduced to asking Harry "What do you think is so accurate?"

"You tell us. Herbert's your real name, is it?"

"It was one of them. It isn't now."

"He got that, then, and the things that went on when you were a lad. He even knew you lived in Hulme and all about your grandpa."

"Not all about him. Not quite your usual style, is it, Frank?"

"You'll need to tell me what you mean, Graham."

I'd like to let him wonder for a while and demonstrate he's less perceptive than he wants his audience to think, but I can't leave a silence on the air. "You never said his name. Don't say he's forgotten that when you said he could remember so much else."

"Maybe he figured he didn't need to mention it," Jasper says. "Like you said, he told you so much that you recognised."

I'd be more infuriated by his deftness if I hadn't thought of a trick of my own. "Can you ask him now?"

"That isn't how it works, Graham. I'm just the receiver. The spirits choose when they want to get in touch."

"You said yourself he wants me to acknowledge him." I wish I'd let the playback reach that point. "You said he's at my shoulder. I just need him to confirm his name."

"Gee, you sound like you're running a security check on your own grandfather," Jasper says, holding up his hands. "Do you really want me to try and raise him now he's at peace?"

He might be trying to look like a saint displaying stigmata—there's even a scar on his left palm. I'm about to authorise him to rouse my grandfather when the sight of him seems to pinch the world into sharper focus, and I recall what he said earlier that I didn't fully grasp. It feels as though I've discovered a talent quite as psychic as his, and I say "Do you think I could do it?"

"It might take a while. If you want me to give you some tips—"

"I thought you said everybody has the gift."

"Sure, but you need to develop it. If you've had no experience—"

"I think I may be having one right now. It seems as if I'm being told something about you, Frank."

A hint of wariness fades from Jasper's eyes. "Looks like you could be, sure enough."

"He means my headphones. I'll say goodbye, Harry, but keep listening," I say and perch them on top of the console. "Now they're off and you'll hear if any messages are coming through them, Frank. Do you want to keep an eye on the window to make sure nobody is signalling somehow?"

He turns his chair halfway around as Christine gives me a bemused look, and I push his microphone closer to him. "It seems as though I'm hearing about that scar on your hand," I tell him. "Didn't it happen when you were a boy?"

"Sure, that's why it's healed so much."

"I'm getting that it was made with a knife." When this earns me only a tolerant gaze I say "Was it your knife? Didn't you do it to yourself?"

"I've grown up a whole lot since."

"No more than I have, Frank. Now I'm being led to believe your parents didn't want you to have a knife."

"I guess not too many parents would."

"Yes, but we're talking about yours. I'm hearing it was your father in particular. Didn't he have a special reason to be concerned? I'm getting the impression it has to do with his job," I say and watch Jasper's unresponsive profile. "Wait, I'm seeing some kind of uniform. Was he in the police?"

Jasper doesn't face me. "He may have been."

"Surely you'd know, Frank. He wasn't in the secret police, was he?" When Jasper still doesn't glance at me I say "Now I'm seeing you in the open, at a table in the open. Was it under a tree? Wasn't it an oak?"

"I guess most of us have been someplace like that."

"That's where I see you playing with your knife. Wasn't it by a playground? You mustn't think I'm blaming you. As you say, you were young. About twelve, would you have been? That's the number I'm seeming to hear. And the friends you wanted to impress were that age."

"Don't you think a lot of boys that age played with knives back then?"

"You mean we can say things about people that sound more personal than they really are." While his head jerks almost imperceptibly at this, his eyes are nowhere near meeting mine. "Let's see if this is more specific to you," I persist. "What are you saying, Frank?"

At first he doesn't react, and Christine frowns through the window at the silence. After some seconds he looks at me, though his eyes display no expression. "What do you mean?"

"Maybe it conveys more to you than it does to me. Something about a clown and a pup?" As Jasper shakes his head slowly enough for a reproach I say "No, wait, I'm hearing down and up. It's down, it's up, only you're saying it so fast the words are blurred. You're saying it as fast as you're stabbing with the knife. You'd been doing that between your fingers on the table and then you started on either side of your hand and kept turning it over. And then your hand slipped or the knife did."

As I don the headphones Jasper stares at me as if his stiff face is striving to hold his eyes blank. "No need to say anything if you'd rather not," I tell him. "I can see it's all true. Maybe I should thank my grandfather." Jasper says nothing, and so I say "Harry? Oh, he's gone. I was going to ask him what he thought of that, but I'll ask you instead. Can you tell the listeners how I did that, Frank? Maybe I'm as psychic as you are."

7

SHOWING HOW

Most of the callers seem to blame me for fooling Jasper. More than one accuses me of duping him, even if they don't know how. Only the skeptics ask me to reveal the trick, and I refer them to Jasper, who tells them he can't say. Hilda from Miles Platting assures him that she's bought tickets for his show, which she hadn't known about until she heard him on the air, while Gerald from Mickle Trafford condemns me for giving Jasper publicity and warns me I'll be in his prayers. At last Sammy Baxter brings us the news, and I can't help hoping it will include Kylie Goodchild—I'd like to watch Jasper's face if Sammy mentions that he's involved in the search. "Okay," he says at once and shoves back his chair. "I guess my hour is up."

"Aren't you staying for the second half? You might think of something else you want people to hear."

"I'm fine with what I did. I trust them to know what they heard."

He holds my gaze while he leans across the console and extends his unscarred hand to shake mine so loosely and tersely that I could imagine he's ensuring my clairvoyance doesn't grasp any more of his secrets. Christine escorts him out of the control room as the news goes by again. At least Sammy Baxter doesn't mention him. I'm undecided how to handle any questions about my reading of his past, but stories about ghosts along with calls ridiculing them dominate my second hour. Eventually the two o'clock news reminds us once again about Kylie Goodchild, and I'm taking off my headphones when Shilpa calls through from Reception. "I've a lady on the line for you, Graham."

The door judders open and Rick Till rushes in, almost missing his breast pocket with the comb he's just inexpertly used. "I'll take it at my desk, Shilpa," I say and give Christine a quick smile in passing, which she doesn't seem to feel is enough of a response to whatever questions she has for me. I dodge between the desks to pick up the extension on mine. "Put her through, Shilpa."

"Is that Graham?"

I ought to recognise the voice. "Nobody else," I try saying.

"It's Hannah Leatherhead. We met the other evening."

"I remember."

"I'm Derek Dennison's producer."

I would have said so if it mightn't have been overheard. "I know."

"I was just listening to your interrogation."

"Which one was that?"

"You're right, wrong word. Your investigation of Frank Jasper. I'm wondering how you knew so much about him."

"I think you'd have to ask the expert, and that's him."

"That's your way, isn't it, Graham? You're careful with your words." As I wonder how much she intends this as praise she adds "Don't give away too much for nothing. I wouldn't ask you to."

"I didn't think you were."

"I'm in London for the next few days. I just wanted to let you know you're quite an asset to broadcasting. When I'm home you might think of giving me a call if you like and we could meet for a chat. There are things about your kind of show we could discuss."

"I'd like that. Where should I call you?"

"Here is fine."

I can't help feeling as if my perceptions that fastened on Jasper are receding at speed. "Sorry, where's here?"

"The BBC, where else?"

"I was only making sure."

"Still being careful what you say? I understand. Must run now, but I'll be waiting to hear from you."

"You will. Thanks, Hannah," I say and plant the receiver on its stand. I'm about to leave my desk for the day when Paula Harding says "Well, Graham."

I've no idea how long she has been at my back. I could have done with being at least slightly psychic. I work on controlling my expression if not stowing it away as I turn to face her. "Well, Paula."

"How would you say that went?"

"The programme." When she only gazes up at me I say "My programme, you mean, obviously. I think it made its point, do you?"

"I expect your guest does. I'll be sending it to the new management if they didn't hear it. I think they should."

If Hannah admires me for guarding my language, she ought to try talking to Paula. "Why's that?" I have to ask.

"You had them in mind, didn't you? You remembered what was said."

"About how we're all an ad for them, you mean."

"You need to play more of those unless you want the management to think you aren't happy working for them." Having searched my eyes for happiness, Paula raises her voice. "Just in from Frugo, everyone. At least four advertising breaks per hour in future. Before you head off, Christine, tell Rick, could you?" she says and turns back to me. "Apart from that, Graham, I'd be surprised if they aren't pleased with the effort you've made."

I wasn't aware of making one. "You think they'll want more episodes like that."

"Never be shy of an argument, and here's a new slogan for you. Speak your mind but make sure it's worth hearing."

I'm not sure how directly this is aimed at me. "Are you saying I should use it in my trail?"

"Have some imagination, Graham. Think how it fits. Now here's Miss Ellis to spirit you away."

Christine is waiting just not close enough to appear to be trying to listen. She gives Paula a smile so flattened it barely is one and heads for Reception as soon as I leave my desk. Behind us Paula is telling Sammy Baxter "No need to be so formal with the weather forecast. Let the listeners hear how you feel about the weather." A woman with a signed photograph of Rick Till—a good deal more composed than the tousled fellow I vacated the studio for—has called the lift, and nobody speaks while we're all in the windowless box. Outside the building Christine crosses the road the moment the traffic lights turn red, and a driver planning to ignore them has to halt with a screech of brakes. Once I join her on the pavement she swings round to scrutinise my face. "Who was on the phone you didn't want Paula to know about?"

I feel ambushed. "Was it that obvious?"

"It was to me."

This sounds like a rebuke, which her eyes make more evident though not clear. "Just someone from the BBC up the road," I tell her.

"Am I going to have to guess what they wanted?"

"Of course you aren't, no more than I am, anyway. Maybe they wanted to talk about a programme."

"Any in particular?"

"I can't say yet. I mean, I don't know." More defensively than I care to feel I add "You know I don't like to talk about things until I have a proper sense of them."

"Not even to me?"

"More to you than anybody else."

I'm not sure how much this placates her as she makes for the nearest steps down to the canal. When I follow her onto the towpath, beside which a barge garlanded with cartoon flowers is waiting for a lock to fill, she says "Are there any more secrets you've been keeping?"

"I wouldn't call that one. I was going to tell you as soon as I had something worth telling."

Two joggers give us a wary glance and dodge around us. Christine doesn't speak again until we've passed under the road heavy with traffic. As we come alongside the block with Waves on the top floor she says "So did your caller have a name?"

"A lot more of one than the people Jasper says he talks to." No doubt that's as irrelevant as she clearly thinks it is. "Hannah Leatherhead," I tell her.

"Am I supposed to know who that is?"

"I didn't till I met her. I'd stopped off for a drink on the way home and she came over to ask how I was finding Waves."

"And how are you?"

"We might want to discuss our options now that Frugo's taken over, do you think?" This sounds like Jasper's style of question, and perhaps that's why it goes unanswered, obliging me to say "She produces Derek Dennison."

"She's not looking to replace him, is she?"

"Why wouldn't she?"

Christine blinks at me or at the glittering of sunlit ripples. "I've listened to him now and then. He has his points."

"He's fine for anyone who wants to be told what to talk about. That's all he seems to tell his callers half the time he's on the air."

"Graham, you don't always let people decide for themselves as much as you may like to think. You were so eager to prove Frank Jasper's a fake that you set up that trick in advance."

"I didn't tell you about it first, you mean." We're walking under Oxford Street, and the bridge turns my voice hollow, detaching it from me. "That's because I didn't set anything up."

"Then how did you manage to tell him so much about himself?"

"Exactly the same way he did it to me."

Christine gives me a sad look rather too reminiscent of the ones Jasper kept producing in the studio. "If that's another secret—"

"It really isn't much of one." With an effort that seems greater than the revelation warrants I say "For a start, his name isn't Jasper, it's Patterson. Pattercake, some people used to call him at school."

"How do you know all this? If it's online—"

"I'm sure he's kept it off. It isn't on his web site." If I let her have time to deduce the truth she might think I'm being secretive, and so I say "I was at school with him."

"Where?"

"In Hulme, just like he said. Don't let the accent fool you the way it fooled me. He must have been in the States long enough to pick that up."

"But then when did you recognise him?"

"Not until I had him in the studio. We weren't in the same class at school. I mightn't have known him except for the scar. I saw him doing that one night when I was on my way home. Maybe it's why he decided to go in for a different kind of trick."

"So you think he recognised you at the Palace. Wasn't he taking a risk that you'd say who he was?"

"Unless he believes in himself so much he's convinced nobody could see through him."

The backs of offices wall in both sides of the canal, and Christine heads for a wrought-iron gate that brings us back to the streets. I sense she's disappointed, with the truth about Jasper or with me if not both. "I still don't quite understand how you dealt with him," she says.

"Just how you saw and how I told you I did."

"But why didn't you tell everyone who he was?"

"It must be because I let people make up their own minds after all." As the roar of traffic greets us at the end of the cobbled side street I take her hand. We're in sight of the Palaces that corner two sides of the crossroads, and I'm happy to turn my back on the theatre. "Somehow," I say, "I don't think we'll be seeing Mr Jasper again."

8

THERE WAS NO GHOST

Although it's past ten in the morning, a mist is lingering outside the Palace. Has it drifted up from the canal? Somebody gullible might even imagine that Frank Jasper has arranged for it to add to his mysteriousness, any that remains. I'm alongside the theatre before I realise the grey cloud was left by a bus held up in traffic. As I make to cross the junction I catch sight of Jasper.

He's on the front steps of the theatre, and talking to several people. I'm tempted to wait for him to notice me so that I can watch his reaction, but haven't I done enough by now? Surely it would be malicious to confront him in front of his fans, however deluded they are. I'm both amused and angry to find myself hoping to go unnoticed while I wait for the lights to let me cross the road.

A train on the elevated track paces me like a patrol car but speeds ahead before I arrive at Waves. I've just stepped into the lift when the street doors reopen and a woman hurries over to the guard at his desk. I don't hear what she says to him, but he calls "Mr Wilde." I jab the button to hold the lift, too late. The lift doors meet as she lurches at them, and I can't prevent it from carrying me upwards.

Christine is producing Currant Affairs. I swap greetings and he odd rudimentary joke with colleagues on the way to my desk. I've just sat down when the phone on it rings. "Graham, there's a lady here for you," Shilpa says.

It can't be Hannah Leatherhead, can it? She said she was going away. I hurry out to find a woman in at least her fifties, who is perched on the sofa opposite the lifts. "Here he is," Shilpa says.

"I know." The woman weighs her words down with a reproving look in my direction. "Don't you know me, Mr Wilde?"

"Sorry, I do." When her large wrinkled somewhat pendulous face withholds any response I put more regret into adding "Forgive me. I couldn't stop it."

"I don't expect they pay you to."

"I couldn't stop the lift when this lady wanted to get in, Shilpa. Believe me," I tell our visitor, "we aren't paid to upset the public."

"Aren't you?" Even more accusingly she says "I don't think you know me at all."

"I'm really very sorry. I'm not sure what else—"

"I'm Cheryl Needham."

I have to assume she's a recent caller to Wilde Card, though I can't remember a Cheryl. "Good to meet you," I try saying.

She looks disappointed if not worse. As I wonder if I have any option other than admitting ignorance she says "Josephine Hull was my aunt, Mr Wilde."

For just another moment I'm bewildered, and then I recognise her from the Palace. "You mostly called her Josie."

"I don't suppose you'd remember if you hadn't got me taped."

"I hope you don't mind too much. I couldn't really have asked you in advance."

"You didn't afterwards, and you put me on your show when Mr Jasper said you shouldn't."

"I don't think he quite said that. It's not like him to be that precise." When she only stares I say "If you'd like to hear exactly what was said I can play it back for you."

"I never listen to your show, and from what my friend says who did I'm glad," she retorts before turning to Shilpa. "Your Mr Wilde wants to think a bit less of his job and a bit more of other people's feelings."

"Miss Needham was at Frank Jasper's show the other night," I feel driven to explain.

I don't see why this antagonises her—at least, not until she says "It isn't Miss."

"Forgive me, you did say there was just you and your sister."

She gazes at me as sadly as Jasper did. "I lost my husband last year."

How could I know that? I'm tempted to point out that Jasper should have if he were what he claims to be, but she's saying "Maybe now you can understand how much it meant to hear from someone who's gone over."

That sounds like being unable to keep your balance, a thought I suffocate with all the sympathy I can muster. "I do, Mrs Needham."

"Then why did you make fun of my feelings on your show?"

"I honestly don't think I did. If you can bear to listen—"

"I've listened to you long enough. It's like my friend says, you can't bear hearing anybody but yourself." Her wrist grows shaky as she levers herself to her feet, and she bats me away with the back of her other hand as I make to aid her. "I won't be wasting any more time," she says, "talking to anyone here."

"If you'd like to speak to the station manager—"

"He lets you get away with what you do, does he? Then I wouldn't want to know him."

I poke the lift button on her behalf, earning a nod that I'm not sufficiently unwise to mistake for approval. She stares up at the ruddy numbers until a lift arrives with a thin ding of its electronic bell. Once the doors have shut behind her Shilpa murmurs "I expect she said all she wanted to say."

I don't even know whether I'm entitled to hope that's the case. I should have been aware of trespassing on her emotions when I put her on the air, but how much more cynically did Jasper use them? I mightn't have broadcast the recording if Paula hadn't told me to be more confrontational. Or am I blaming her and Jasper to avoid taking all the blame I should? I'd like to talk to Christine about it—I feel as if I'm keeping a secret from her as I return to my desk. While she's busy in the control room, perhaps I should mention the incident to Paula; suppose Cheryl Needham decides to complain to our new owners? I'm pushing back my chair when a face looks in from the reception area. I clamp my hands on the sides of the desk and rise slowly out of a crouch as I see I'm not mistaken. It's Frank Jasper.

9

A HESITANT ASSERTION

I don't know if Jasper saw me. He's beyond Shilpa's counter, and moves away to speak to someone—Cheryl Needham, I'm instinctively sure. He was surveying the newsroom the way he used to look around at school, searching for somebody to use or to impress. That's what he did before playing his trick with the knife. The similarity is one more reason for my fists to close while I stalk across the room to ease the door wide.

Cheryl Needham isn't out there, but several people are with Jasper. There's a man tall and broad enough to guard the entrance to a nightclub. He's wearing a suit, unlike the teenager in a singlet that exhibits how he's worked on the muscles of his brawny arms. I feel as if I ought to recognise the men and their companion, a small pale fleshy woman with red hair. I saw them recently—saw them with Jasper outside the Palace. They must be fans he's brought along to witness whatever routine he intends to perform, and I speak to Shilpa because I don't immediately trust myself to be polite to him. "Any problem, Shilpa?"

"We've not been any, have we, love?" the large man says and simpers at her.

I don't need to be psychic to identify the redhead as his wife, since she seems to think he's making too much of Shilpa. Perhaps that's why Jasper intervenes. "Robbie and Margaret," he says before turning to the almost neckless teenager. "And Wayne, let me introduce you all to—"

"Allow me. I'm Graham Wilde."

The woman seems about to speak, but her husband shakes his bulky head. It's Wayne who says "So?"

"Didn't Frank mention me? I was a subject of his. The one with the grandfather who didn't have a name."

The large man looks ready to defend Jasper. He's beginning to put me in mind of a bodyguard, not least because his flat crooked nose looks like a result of a punch. "We don't know anything about that, chum," he says.

"You just missed another of your subjects, Frank. The lady whose aunt didn't make a will was complaining about the show."

Jasper adopts his saddened look. "I hope she wasn't complaining about me."

"Give over distracting Frank, will you." Wayne is giving me a red-eyed glare. "We're here for my girlfriend."

However unlikely the idea seems in a number of ways, I can only ask "Is she working here?"

"Are you having a fucking laugh?"

"It's all right, Wayne," the woman says more indulgently than I find appropriate. "He's not going to know."

"Then he fucking should. They all should."

"Cover your lugs if you need to, love," the large man tells Shilpa. "I reckon you're not used to our kind of language."

"Don't be making out it's mine," says his wife.

"Someone should be with you very soon," Shilpa assures them all, unless she's warning them.

"Thought that's what he was for."

Apparently Wayne has me in mind. As he shows more displeasure by turning his back on me, I catch sight of the tattoo that occupies much of the left side of his short neck. So I didn't recognise him and his companions just from seeing them outside the Palace. "Forgive me," I murmur.

Wayne swings around to stare at me, and the girl's name comes with him. "What for?"

"I didn't realise you were here about Kylie Goodchild."

His eyes narrow, which appears to squeeze them redder. "What's it got to do with you?"

"Nothing personal. I just saw her on your neck."

I'm making her sound like a love bite, which may well have been in the area. Perhaps that's why Robbie Goodchild looks uneasy, dragging the fingertips of one hand across his forehead, and I make a bid to divert his thoughts. "Who are you here to see?"

Margaret Goodchild seems glad to have the subject changed. "Whoever Mr Jasper says we should."

"It won't be me."

"Why not?" Wayne demands, touching the name on his neck as if it's some kind of charm.

If they're here to broadcast an appeal the news team will handle it, and I'm about to say so when Christine opens the door behind me. "One minute, Graham."

That's how soon I'm on the air. Once we're on the far side of the door Christine says "What's he doing here?"

"Jasper? Someone must have encouraged him," I say loudly, but nobody in the newsroom owns up. "I assume he'll be claiming he can find that couple's daughter."

"I hope someone does soon."

"Obviously I do, but they won't with his kind of help."

Christine frowns at me as if I'm willing him to fail, but it's simply that I know he's bound to. As I sit at the studio console Sammy Baxter predicts a week of increasingly sultry heat in the tone of a housewife passing on the good news to a neighbour over their garden fence. I'm donning headphones when Paula Harding strides down the newsroom and disappears towards Reception. I wish I could hear how she deals with Jasper, but I'm on the air.

It's Play A Blinder Day, which sets the rest of us the task of learning how it feels to be blind. I tried wearing a blindfold designed to help passengers sleep on planes and groped all the way through my apartment, an adventure that took most of an hour. Although I managed not to break anything I missed Christine, not least whenever I imagined rediscovering each other just by touch. Perhaps we can do that tonight, though the callers to Wilde Card are starting to make me feel guilty. So far all of them are blind, and they don't think much of their dedicated day—one finds the idea offensive, and another says the whole idea is patronising, while the third contributor objects that it simply lets people believe they're aware of the blind and then forget about them for the rest of the year. I feel awkward for arguing with any of these callers, but isn't my reluctance condescending too? As I'm reduced to suggesting that a token reminder is better than none, Paula reappears outside the control room.

Her back is to the window. She may be addressing the newsroom, since all the staff raise their heads. They're looking not at her but towards Reception, and in a moment Margaret Goodchild comes into view. I'm trying to concentrate on my latest caller—he thinks a new tax ought to finance aids for the disabled—when she's joined by Frank Jasper.

Is he talking about her daughter? She and Paula and my colleagues are all watching him. As he takes a couple of tentative steps towards the nearest desks I see that he's holding an object in both hands—a large thin book. He extends it as though he's mistaken it for a dowser's wand, and his progress grows more confident. He's almost striding as he reaches the nearest unoccupied desk. It's mine.

What trick is he trying on now? I think the spectacle has deafened me to the voice in my headphones until I realise the caller is waiting for me to speak. "That isn't how taxation works, Peter," I say as Jasper turns away from my desk. He's gazing at the book he holds at arm's length. His mouth moves as he advances towards me, but I can't read his words. Paula watches him pace past her, and doesn't intervene even when Margaret Goodchild opens the door of the control room for him.

As Jasper glides through the doorway without a sound I could imagine that he's talking to the book, since he doesn't lift his gaze from the leafy Oriental pattern on the cover. I'm about to put Peter on hold when Wayne and Kylie's father step into the control room. "Stay on the line, Peter," I say and set off an advert for Frugoway Holidays. "What's going on in there, Chris?"

"I'm not sure," she says, and the headphones also bring me Jasper's voice. "I feel closer to him," he's saying. "I feel he has something to tell us."

I'm able to doubt his intentions until he ventures forward as if the book is leading him—as if he wants everyone to think so. He might be holding it out to somebody he can't or doesn't need to see. As a jingle ("There's less to pay with Frugoway") brings the advert to an end Paula waves to attract my attention, and I wonder why she doesn't follow Jasper—indeed, why she let him come this far. Instead she nods at the microphone, presumably to remind me that controversy is meant to sell. She can have her wish, and I say "Peter, can I call you back?"

There's no sound in the headphones apart from my own flattened voice. I could feel like Jasper, sending a question into the void to somebody who isn't there. "Peter's had to leave us," I say, "but here's a surprise guest. Frank Jasper must have felt welcome when I had him on the other day, because he's back with us."

I'm expecting some response, but he's intent on the book. "I'm being told," he says, "it's somebody who had a lot to say to her."

"Who are you talking to, Frank?"

"Don't distract him." Margaret Goodchild clasps her hands

together and hurries into the studio, letting the door thump shut. "Please don't," she murmurs. "That's our Kylie's book."

"I have to let the listeners know what's happening, Mrs Goodchild. We're live." She seems to find some of this encouraging, and so I say "Kylie Goodchild's parents have enlisted Frank Jasper. That's right, is it, Mrs Goodchild? He offered you his services?"

"My husband went to him," she says in a whisper entirely too awed for my taste.

"And Frank says he isn't charging you."

"He says he never does."

Is this just when the police are involved? I wonder if it's for fear of being investigated. I don't like to interrogate Kylie's mother, but as I withhold a question her husband shoves open the door into the studio. Paula steps into the control room as Robbie Goodchild mutters "What's he saying?"

"He wants to know if we're paying Mr Jasper."

"I'd give Frank everything we've got if he can bring our Kylie back." Robbie Goodchild scowls at me and looks away. "I don't mean what this lad's saying. How's it any of his business?"

His wife raises a finger without quite touching her lips. "We're being broadcast, Robbie."

"That's his lookout. I'm asking you what Frank said."

"He says somebody here was talking to Kylie."

"He didn't name anyone," I point out to the listeners as well.

Wayne looks ready to shove Kylie's father aside. "Which fucker else is he going to mean?"

"You mustn't say things like that," Margaret Goodchild pleads. "You'll be getting us thrown out."

"What doesn't he want folk hearing?" her husband demands just as Jasper says "He saw her recently. That's what I'm getting now."

I won't let this go unchallenged. "I'm sure that's true of somebody in here."

"Sounds like he's fucking talking about you," Wayne shouts and glares at the book, which Jasper appears to be pointing at me. "Is he in her fucking album?"

"I'm sorry, that's got to be all," I say and interrupt the broadcast with a Frugohome insurance advert. "I'm going to have to ask you to leave."

"Please look in Kylie's album first," Margaret Goodchild begs. "See if you're there."

"Forgive me, Mrs Goodchild, but I can tell you I'm not without looking."

"Then you won't mind fucking doing what she wants," says Wayne, "will you?"

No doubt he's concerned for his girlfriend, but his aggression seems a little studied. I suppose he'd feel unmanly to let his actual emotions show. Paula strides out of the control room, and I think she's off to call security until she halts at Trevor Lofthouse's desk. Meanwhile Margaret Goodchild takes a small framed photograph out of her handbag. "Here she is," she says as if she's trying to pretend she has no reason to sound anything but proud. "Please don't be sure till you've had a proper look."

The photograph shows the head and shoulders of a slim pretty teenager with long hair not nearly as red as her mother's and a smile that looks as though the camera had to take it by surprise. I take time to scrutinise it before saying "I'm really sorry, Mrs Goodchild, but I've never seen her that I can remember."

I don't see what else I can do besides looking sympathetic, no easy task while I'm furious with Jasper for offering her hope that's no better than a trick. The advert is coming to an end, and I'm finding another to keep Wayne off the air when Paula ushers Lofthouse into the control room. "Take everyone outside, Graham," she says. "Trevor will sit in for you."

I'm not far from feeling driven off the air. As I let Trevor have my place at the console, Kylie's mother hustles Wayne and her husband out of the studio. She's still displaying the photograph, which

Christine gives more than a glance. "Here's Trevor Lofthouse fill-ing in for Graham," Lofthouse says as I follow Jasper out, and Paula is about to speak when Jasper halts. "Wait, there's something else," he says.

He's facing Trevor's desk. The hubbub of the newsroom subsides to not much more than a murmur. Now that he has his audience's attention he says "I'm nearly seeing her."

Kylie's mother swallows so hard that wrinkles dig into her throat. She's barely able to ask "Is she here?"

"Not now." For a moment I take him to be urging silence, and then he says "She's under something, or she was."

Kylie's father drags his nails across his forehead. Before the marks can fade he mutters "Don't say she's under the ground, for God's sake."

"I'm not seeing that. I feel she was under a bridge."

Is he playing with the possibility that she has run away from home to sleep rough? Kylie's father stares at him, but the perfor-mance seems to be over. He takes the photograph none too gently from his wife and holds it above his head. "Come on, some of you saw her. You must of been here when she came."

Everybody gazes at the photograph, and then heads begin to shake. Once they all have Paula says "You might try asking Shilpa at Reception."

"She's the girl I was talking to before."

I suspect Paula hoped to ease him and his companions out of the newsroom, but she isn't as skilful as Jasper with tricks. Good-child is still elevating the photograph when his wife gives Jasper a beseeching look. "Can you see anything else, Mr Jasper?" she says with not much of a voice.

"I don't believe I'm going to be told any more just now."

"She's all right, right?" Wayne insists. "You told Marg she wasn't here like the ones you reckon you talk to."

"She wasn't speaking to me, no."

As I refrain from commenting that he's told the truth twice on the run, Kylie's mother says "Then could we see about her album?"

"It's all yours, ma'am."

Patterson is trying to sound more American than ever. When he passes her the album Kylie's mother holds out both hands as if to cradle it. He seems to think she wants it opened, and he spreads it wide at two pages near the middle of the book. The left one is occupied by a childish drawing of a bearded leering fellow in a turban—I suspect he's meant to be Mohammed—and its neighbour bears an inscription framed by cartoon flowers. A sheet of paper that marked the place slips out and flutters face down to the carpet. "I'll get it, Marg," says Wayne.

He's still in the last of his crouch, which makes him look ready to lunge at someone, when he mumbles "What the fuck." As he straightens up he trains his raw gaze on me and turns the page away from him almost violently enough to tear the cheap but glossy paper. It's a photograph from one of the stacks on the reception counter, pictures of the station personnel. It's of me, and I've signed it to Kylie Goodchild. "Seen it before, have you?" Wayne says so fiercely he sprinkles me with saliva.

"Somebody has." The rage I've been withholding is nearly uncontrollable now. "What's the trick this time, Frank?"

"There's no fucking trick," Wayne shouts and swings around to exhibit the photograph to my colleagues. "See what it says? 'Have a good life, Kylie,' and it's him saying."

"Mr Goodchild, Mrs Goodchild," Paula murmurs. "I'm going to have to ask—"

"Don't try getting rid of us," Wayne warns her. "We're not on any fucking show now."

"Give me a moment, Paula." I don't want them to leave until I've exposed Patterson's trick to everyone. "Mrs Goodchild, you must have seen what happened," I say as gently as I can. "Your friend Frank made it look as if he was being led to me when he knew that was there all the time."

"He didn't, Mr Wilde."

"I really do find that hard to believe."

"Don't you fucking call Marg a liar."

"Wayne," she pleads, but he looks unwilling to be calmed, and Paula lifts the phone on Trevor's desk. "Will you send someone up to Waves, please?" she says. "There's a disturbance."

"Mr Wilde." Kylie's mother seems as anxious to resolve the situation as I am. "Mr Jasper didn't know your picture was in Kylie's album," she says. "Nobody did."

"Kylie had a rubber band round it when we got it from her room," her husband says. "Mr Jasper wanted something she'd had a long time."

"There's no band on it now," I have to point out.

"It snapped in my bag." Mrs Goodchild seems to grow aware of the caricature of Mohammed, and hurriedly closes the album. "It was shut like this when I gave it to Mr Jasper," she assures me, "and he never looked inside."

I'm sure she must believe this. Her husband plainly wants me to, but Wayne looks eager for me to deny it. Instead I say "I'm sorry, I honestly can't remember her at all."

"If you ever met her you'd remember," Wayne protests, "and you fucking did."

"Mr Wilde," Kylie's mother says, "could you have sent her your picture?"

"Nobody's ever asked for that, I'm sorry."

"I knew you hadn't," says Jasper—says Patterson.

This is so blatantly opportunistic that I turn on him. I've clenched my fists and opened my mouth before Paula hurries to let in two uniformed security men. I could almost feel they're here to restrain me—that's the effect they have, so that I succeed in saying only "If I remember anything about your daughter I'll be in touch."

"Fucking make sure," Wayne mutters.

Paula watches the security men usher him out, followed by Patterson and the Goodchilds. As soon as the door closes she says "Better not keep the listeners wondering what's happened to you, Graham."

"I'm sorry if I was responsible for any of that."

"I expect Waves will survive," she says and waits until I hurry into the control room. Did Trevor or Christine see the photograph of Kylie Goodchild? I haven't time to ask, and perhaps this isn't the place either. "Thanks for filling in, Trevor," I say to the microphone as well as to him. "I've just been trying to help Kylie Goodchild's parents. I wish I could have done more, but I've nothing to be ashamed of."

10

ON THE SITE

We're crossing the road by the Palaces when Christine says "Can you still not remember her, Graham?"

"That's right, I really can't remember."

"No need to shout at me."

I've only raised my voice to be heard over the howl of a police car. I don't even know why she was reminded of Kylie Goodchild, since Jasper's posters have been replaced by advertisements for a production of *Carousel*. The police car overtakes on the wrong side of the road, spattering my feet with a remnant of this morning's rain, as I say "I said I remembered the class from her school. There was nothing to single her out, that's all."

"Slim and getting on for my height with long hair."

"How many girls would that be? Anyway, you don't need to tell me what she looked like."

"She had a lot to say for herself."

"Give me some examples." When Christine shakes her head I say "There you are, you don't remember as much as you think."

"I know she had plenty to say to you. She seemed to want to talk to you more than anybody else."

"If I didn't know better I'd say you were jealous."

"You should know better." Christine falls silent while a second police car races past, flashing its disco lights, and then she says "I expect her boyfriend would have been."

"The thug with one word on his mind?" The thought of Wayne prompts me to add "He wasn't with her class that day that you remember."

"I don't believe so. He'd have seen you sign the photo for her, wouldn't he?"

I don't seem to have wanted this answer. As we reach Waves a train worms its way around an elevated bend, so that the photographs below the windows look as if they're being folded up. The lobby doors sidle aside, and the guard at his desk gives me a sharp look—perhaps he's more on the alert since he had to deal with Wayne. I'd show him my badge if he didn't know me well enough.

It's Obesity Obliteration Day. The jingle and the slogan for Wilde Card shut me into my headphones, and then my voice does, never quite conforming to how it sounds inside my head. It's flatter, more Mancunian, and is that what everybody except me hears when I speak? "Just water for my lunch today," I'm saying. "That's my gesture for the occasion. I hope nobody thinks it's a rude one . . ."

This is my bid for the style Paula thinks our new owners would prefer, and I think it makes me sound like a Frugo cashier chatting at a checkout. The callers want to argue, though not about this. Dave from Mostyn objects that the name of the day is offensive— that we ought to say overweight, not obese. Julie from Withington thinks it isn't offensive enough—that the greedy are offending the rest of us by eating too much of our food and expecting us to pay for their bad health and just by making us have to look at them. Hilary from Whalley Range maintains that parents of corpulent children should be required to wear T-shirts saying **I'm A Fat Kid's Mam** or **Dad**. It's time to play an ad for Frugoliath exercise equipment, after which we have Peter from Didsbury. He's so outraged by all the comments he calls weightist that he sets about broadcasting his glandular history at length. I'm about to cut this short, since I think he has more than made his point, when Christine says in my headphones "Do you want this next call? It's about Frank Jasper."

"I don't need protecting from him, Chris."

"Only it's the lady you recorded at the Palace. Cheryl from Droylsden."

I gaze hard at Christine, not least because I didn't mention that the woman came to Waves. "Let her at me," I say and go back on the air. "Thanks for all that, Peter. Now here's Cheryl from Droylsden on quite another subject, aren't you, Cheryl?"

"You didn't tell me you were going to invite Mr Jasper back."

"I didn't invite him, he came unannounced. Anyway, you had another chance to hear him."

"I didn't." Just as resentfully she adds "My friend says you wanted to get rid of him."

"Not for a moment, Cheryl. If he'd like to get in touch I've a few more questions for him."

"My friend says you only have him on to make him say what you want everyone to hear."

"I don't think I could force Frankie to say anything. That's his trick." I nearly lost control there—Frankie was the name he disliked at school—and so I don't pause before saying "When he was on yesterday—"

"My friend says you cut him off."

"Somebody he brought was using language we can't broadcast."

"She thinks you used that for an excuse."

"Is she there, Cheryl? By all means put her on."

"I'm on my own." This reminds me she's recently widowed, but before I can apologise Cheryl says "She wouldn't talk to you anyway. She says you won't let people have their say if you don't agree with them."

"I really don't think—"

"See, you're doing it now, and she says you did to Mr Jasper. She says you didn't want anyone to hear what he had to say about you."

I can't let rage make me speechless. "By all means tell everybody what that is."

"He was saying you were mixed up with the girl they're looking for."

"Her name's Kylie Goodchild, Cheryl. Everyone should keep a lookout for her, but I don't think there's any use looking round here. At me, I mean, or anybody else here for that matter."

"Mr Jasper wouldn't have come without a reason."

"I signed a photograph for her, that's all. I did for half her class when they came on a school visit."

I think Cheryl had no answer to that until I hear a muffled sound. She has put her hand over the mouthpiece. I feel as if I'm being forced to believe in an unseen presence—as if Jasper has brought off one of his tricks. In a few moments she declares "My friend says—"

"I thought she wasn't supposed to be there."

"She's just come in." As I refrain from wondering aloud if the friend even exists, Cheryl tells everyone "She says you said you never saw the girl at all."

"Honestly, nobody needs to be scared of me," I say with all the calm I can produce. "Your friend's more than welcome to speak up for herself."

"I told you, Mr Wilde, she won't come on your show. It's a pity you didn't mention the photo while Mr Jasper was there."

"Frank knows all about it, trust me, and so does everyone else who was here."

"Maybe you should hope that's all he knows."

That's at least one innuendo too many, and my rage breaks loose. "Unlike our Frankie, I've nothing to hide."

Christine blinks at me through the window, but I'm glad I said that. At the end of a silence sufficiently intense to belong to more than one person Cheryl demands "What are you saying about Mr Jasper?"

"For a start he was brought up in Manchester, and he's gone to some trouble to see his public doesn't know."

"He's never from round here." I can't judge whether Cheryl is proud that he's local or far too belatedly skeptical about him, even when she objects "How would you know?"

"Not from the Internet. He's covered his tracks there. Your friend heard me read his past, though, didn't she? The scar I was talking about, he got that in Hulme."

Cheryl muffles the mouthpiece again before retorting "She wants to know how you can say that."

"Because it's true. If anybody thinks I played some kind of trick by recognising him you'd have to wonder if he—"

"Graham." Christine is holding up a hand as well. "Look at his web site," she says urgently in my headphones. "Go to the sidebar."

I type Patterson's false name in the search box and bring up the site. There he is, baring a sample of his bronzed chest and opening his eyes wide as if they're as guiltless as ever. I find the sight not much worse than irritating, even when my gaze shifts to the sidebar—and then I have an unwelcome suspicion. I click on the button that says **LIFE**, and up comes his biography. **Frank Jasper, born Francis Patterson in Hulme, Manchester.** I know that wasn't there last week, but now the site spells out details of his boyhood.

11

IT WAS WRITTEN

"It isn't as new as you think, Graham."

"Believe me, it is."

"But if you look at the date—" Christine says and brings up the properties of the biography page on her monitor.

"I nearly fell for that myself. All it says was that the page was made a year ago. I'm telling you it wasn't on his site last week."

"What was, then?"

"It must have said the page was under construction. Don't you see what he did? He made the page and stored it till he had to put it on his site."

Wilde Card has just ended, and we're at her desk. Before bidding me a sad farewell Cheryl from Droylsden hoped I'd open my mind long enough or wide enough to see the truth. I thought she might have attracted more of Patterson's supporters onto the air, but the next caller thought obesity should be taxed and the parents of the roly-polies in particular, which provoked enough arguments to fill up the rest of the hour—all of it that wasn't occupied by ads for Frugold jewellery and Frugoggle spectacles and the Frugodsend charity card. Now Christine says "Why would he want to do that?"

"So he could put it up if anybody found him out and say he never hid the information in the first place."

I'm attempting to keep my voice down, but perhaps it reaches further than it needs to, because Paula Harding says across several desks behind us "Are you two conducting a post mortem?"

"I think the subject's dead," I say, "and I'm the murderer."

Perhaps she wasn't joking as much as I took her to be, if at all. "Let's continue it in my office," she says, and when Christine makes to follow me "I'm talking to Graham."

I overtake her just in time to hold open the door of her office. She perches on the cushion that adds stature to her chair and switches off Rick Till or at least hushes the computer. Her head sinks—she might be miming some kind of confirmation—as I lower myself onto the flatulent leather chair. "Well," she says, "this is getting to be a regular event. One of your listeners has been in touch."

"Should I guess which one?"

"Cheryl Needham from Droylsden."

"She's changed her mind, then. She said she wasn't going to bother you, bother speaking to you, I mean. She thought you'd just be on my side."

"I listened to your show." Paula lets this and her gaze gather weight before she says "You're getting edgier, Graham."

Is she referring to how I feel just now? I do my best to match her ambiguity by saying "So long as it's what's wanted."

"Cheryl was right, I'm afraid."

I'm hearing Hannah Leatherhead's invitation as I say "Right about what?"

"No need to go for me, Graham. I'm not one of your contestants." She pauses as if she's searching for a more accurate term and says "She was right that I'm on your side."

"Oh, I see." This seems inadequate, and so does "Well, thank you."

"I told her it's the style you're known for and I didn't think you'd actually been rude to her, but obviously it's her privilege to take it further if she really wants to. I think whatever you said to her about Frank Jasper would have been wrong."

"You won't hear any argument from me."

"So long as I do when I switch you on." Paula lets me glimpse a smile that can hardly signify a joke and says "It's true he never said he was local. He does his best to sound as if he's not."

"He's saying he is now on his web site."

"I expect you must have made him. Anyway, he should be proud to admit it." Paula leans forward, which doesn't disturb so much as a strand of her cropped glossy hair, to murmur "You knew each other, didn't you?"

"That's it. The whole truth."

"I don't know if you should give it away on the air. Keep people guessing," she says and sits back. "It's just a pity you didn't remember signing Kylie Goodchild's photograph while you had Jasper on the air."

"I might have except for dealing with her boyfriend. You couldn't have known what he was going to be like."

"I don't suppose Jasper did either."

"Patterson," I can't help saying. "Too busy talking to my nameless grandfather again, maybe."

Paula lets out a sound that falls short of a laugh. "What was his name, by the way?"

"My grandfather? Wilfred."

"Not that unusual," Paula says as the phone shrills on her desk. "Yes, he's here," she says after listening to someone as inaudible as Jasper's sources and extends the receiver to me. "It's somebody about your show."

"Do you want me to take it here?"

"Why, would you prefer not?"

"It's your office," I say and lurch almost onto all fours in my haste to seem eager instead of defensive. The leather cushion sends a whoopee in my wake as I grab the receiver and step back. "Hello," I mutter. "Graham Wilde."

"Gosh, I can barely hear you, Graham. It's Hannah Leatherhead."

"Oh, hello." I need to find somewhere to look other than at Paula—along the canal beyond the window behind her desk. "Wasn't I going to call you?" I say not much louder.

"Hold on just a second." In little more Hannah says "Is that better?"

It isn't for me. She has switched her phone to loudspeaker mode, rendering her voice close to painful in my ear. I can't hold the receiver at a distance in case Paula hears something she shouldn't—I want to be sure of the situation before I reveal it. "We ought to talk soon," I tell Hannah.

"We should. I was just calling to say I'm back in town sooner than expected."

I don't know if Paula is watching me, but I can sense her attention, which feels as if a security camera is focused on me. If psychics existed, perhaps this is a taste of how they'd feel. It seems to turn the rest of my surroundings less substantial, especially a line of figures standing on a footbridge against the glitter of sunlight on the canal. The best response I can give Hannah is "Glad to have you back."

"So whenever you feel like a chat, I'll be around."

"Well, not right now."

Do I need to avoid using Hannah's name in front of Paula? Before I can decide Hannah says "Am I being slow? Can someone hear?"

"She might."

"Oh, what a clot." A silence leaves me thinking Hannah has ended the call until she returns unamplified. "There, I've turned myself down," she says. "Shall I wait to hear when you're ready?"

"Whenever you're free."

"I am today if that's any use."

I feel driven by the situation, but I don't see how this can be bad. "What about now?"

"Now would be stupendous. Where?"

"Where we met?"

"Nowhere better. When?"

"As soon as I can walk to it if you like."

"I'll be there," Hannah says and rings off.

The identity parade on the bridge has disappeared along the towpath, beside which fragments of ripples resemble a digital message. I take a moment to prepare a neutral smile for Paula before handing her the phone. "Thanks for that," I feel bound to say.

"Any time, Graham." This seems unlikely, and she takes the receiver so loosely that I'm afraid she'll drop it. I have to keep hold while she says "Was that someone anybody shouldn't know about?"

I feel as if she's using the receiver to capture my hand. "Anybody such as who?"

"Graham." She shakes her head—I could imagine she's testing her hairdo for stiffness. "Christine," she says very much in the tone of a rebuke.

"Good heavens no. Not a bit of it. Absolutely not, believe me."

Is this too much? Paula scrutinises my face for a protracted moment before grasping the phone. I'm turning away when she says "Graham."

It sounds like the threat of a reprimand. That's at least one too many, and I'm ready to respond along those lines as I confront her. "Don't you think you deserve a sweet today?" she says.

"If you do."

I could have made that less ambiguous, but I feel guilty, all the more so as I reach in the glass bowl like a child taking a reward for having told the truth. I grab a mint striped like a beetle and leave Paula's office without glancing back. I'm unwrapping the humbug as I reach Christine's desk. "Can you spare me till tonight?" I murmur.

She blinks at the cellophane I drop into her bin as if she thinks it's intended as some kind of token. "What's Paula's idea now?"

"Nothing to do with her," I say and lower my voice further. "I'm meeting somebody you know about."

"Good luck," Christine says under her breath, "if that's what you want."

She means I'm not supposed to be superstitious, of course. A lift is waiting beyond Shilpa's desk, and I suck the humbug as the floors climb by. As the lobby doors glide apart I step into the sunlight, which is so fierce it almost seems to weigh me down. Then my teeth meet through the carapace of the mint with a crunch that resonates through my skull, and a cold sharp taste fills my mouth as Kylie Goodchild's boyfriend steps into my path.

12

NEAR THE WATER

Wayne is wearing shorts patterned like a chessboard and chubby trainers and a T-shirt hardly large enough for him. While his broad chest and brawny arms seem designed to impress, his stomach looks like the product of many a Frugoburger. His eyes are even redder than last time, and I smell herbal smoke on his breath as he demands "Where you going, boy?"

I'm about to enquire what this has to do with him when I realise that his lurch at me has reopened the automatic doors at my back. He must think I'm retreating, but I won't do that from him. "Nowhere at all," I assure him.

"Waiting for the bouncers to see me off again?"

As Wayne glares past me the guard calls from his desk "Everything all right, Mr Wilde?"

"Nothing I can't handle, Charlie, thanks."

When I step around Wayne the doors falter open before shutting with a padded thud. He darts ahead and turns on me, walking backwards. "Don't want to talk to me, right?" he says not far short of my face.

"I'll talk to anyone," I retort, but I don't need Hannah Leatherhead to see me in this kind of argument. She's just a few minutes away, and the prospect makes me ask "Shouldn't you be at school?"

"Want rid of me as well, do you?" By way of explanation he adds "They've thrown me out of that fucking place."

"Anyway, I've an appointment. You'll have to excuse me."

"I won't be doing that, boy," he says as if he's determined to reduce my age to his and glances at a group of office workers who are taking a smokers' break. "Think I can't talk if there's people about? Have another fucking think."

"I'm sure it would take more than that to shut you up." At least I've thought how to avoid encountering Hannah in the street. "I'm going down by the canal," I inform him. "Then you can swear all you like."

"I won't just be fucking swearing."

I don't know if this is a threat or a boast about his vocabulary. As he swaggers down a ramp to the canal I'm made aware how short his legs are. His scalp looks like a translucent dome preserving the black roots of his hair. I don't know how any of this can have appealed to Kylie Goodchild, and I catch myself wondering how I may have struck her. On the towpath Wayne swings around to demand "Why'd you say you never saw Kylie?"

"With no disrespect to the young lady," I say, which makes me sound like my grandfather, "I didn't think I had."

"You're disrespecting me as well," Wayne says and rubs the name on his neck until the skin turns red. "You're making her sound like any other fucking tart."

Rather than argue I stride past him. As he overtakes, crowding me towards the water, I say "Tell me what I should remember about her."

"What's she got to do with you?"

Is this possessiveness run wild? With an effort I say "We want the same thing as her parents, don't we? To find her safe and sound. If you tell me what to look for I can put it on the air."

Ahead the towpath is deserted apart from a small gathering of the homeless, who are sitting on the stone edge with their feet in the canal. While one woman sucks on a bottle of wine her companions glance up as if they think we're on our way to join them. She looks away when Kylie's boyfriend narrows his eyes as though he wants to squeeze them redder still. "What stopped you copying her picture if you wasn't meant to know what she looked like?"

"I hadn't thought of describing her then. Never mind, it doesn't matter."

Wayne grinds his knuckles against the name on his stubby neck. "What fucking doesn't?"

The woman hoots with laughter and tips the dregs of wine into her mouth before shying the bottle into the canal. "If you can't be bothered giving me the information," I tell Wayne, "I expect the police can. Do we know how the investigation's progressing?"

"Wouldn't you like to know," Wayne says, and his skin twitches his eyes thinner.

Was I ever this irrational at his age? His fierce grimace prompts me to ask "Aren't you fond of the police?"

"They're the law. They fucking think they are, any road."

"They're more likely to track down your girlfriend than Frank Jasper is."

"Never mind trying to make out he's useless. He found you and nobody's forgetting."

"Do you really believe that? I thought you were a little more intelligent."

"Stop sounding like a teacher or you'll be in the fucking hospital."

"Aren't they on your list of friends either?" A backward glance shows me that the drinkers are out of sight around a bend in the canal. We're alone all the way to the bridge at Oxford Street, but I'm not about to put on speed—I won't have Wayne thinking I'm afraid of him. "Believe me," I say, "Frankie knew about my photograph."

"Don't call him that. He's not your friend, and I saw Marg give him Kylie's book."

"Can you honestly say you watched him every single minute after that?" When the boy's lips work as if he doesn't know whether to spit or speak I say "Remember you're dealing with a professional."

"I know you're one of them. You got us thrown out of your show before Frank had a chance to say about your photo."

"Ah, so now you're saying he did know about it in advance." As Wayne bares his stained teeth I say "It was nobody but you who got everyone thrown out, Wayne."

"Don't you fucking try and pass it on to me."

We're nearly at the steps up to the bridge. "I'll leave you here," I tell him.

"I'm not done with you, boy. Nothing like."

Suppose I shove him in the murky water? It's my impression that he's capable of doing that or worse to me. If he attempts to block my way he'll end up in the canal, and I won't be caring whether he can swim. I'm readying myself for a furious lunge when he glances up the steps. "Fucker," he mutters.

He may have me in mind or the policeman who's tramping down from the street. "Better not find out you're hiding any other shit," Wayne advises me before he dodges under the bridge.

"I'd nothing to hide in the first place," I call after him. The policeman watches me until we pass on the steps, and I give him the kind of wearily amused look adults share about children. Perhaps he thinks responding would be unprofessional, since his scrutiny doesn't falter. I'm tempted to send him after Wayne, if only to make it clear where his attention ought to be, but I don't need the police to help me deal with teenagers. I just hope Wayne knows I'm equal to him.

13

WINE WITH A WAG

The Dressing Room feels like an outpost of the Palace. It's a few hundred yards away on Oxford Road. Floor-length curtains are tied back on either side of the long polished bar, behind which footlights magnify the shadows of the acrobatic topsy-turvy bottles on the wall. When I step out of the glaring sunlight I have to blink to be sure Hannah Leatherhead isn't in any of the booths furnished with theatre seats and overlooked by mirrors surrounded by light bulbs, or at one of the circular tables around which upholstered stools sprout like fungi in a pantomime. She isn't at the bar either, where the barman and his ogrish shadow move to greet me. "Same as ever, Mr Wubbleyou?"

He always seems to be understudying the comedians whose posters and photographs are among the multitude that decorate the walls. "You must be psychic, Benny," I tell him.

"Cobber's Piss it is." He pours me a large glass of New Zealand white and leans across the bar. "Here's another one you can't put on the air. What do you call a Pakistani that's been run over by a steamroller?"

"I wouldn't dare to guess."

"A flat pack," he says much louder than he asked the question. "Eh?"

He laughs into my face until I feel compelled to respond with a guilty titter. "Lord help us, Benny, where did you dig that up?"

"Made it out of my own head," he says with a reproachful look.

I stop short of remarking that it's nothing to be proud of, and he's eager to add "What do Muslims buy their dinner in the street off?"

"I've a terrible feeling I'm about to hear."

"The Allah cart," he says with all the pride of a father displaying a photograph of a favourite child. "Eh?"

"That's dreadful even for you, Benny," I tell him, apparently to his delight, and take refuge in a corner booth.

Three girls around a table are sending texts from their phones and saying rather less to one another while they sip drinks in lanky glasses. A rapid tapping like a woodpecker's belongs to a young businessman busy at his laptop. An elderly man with a stick at his side keeps reaching for a tankard in between drawing lines of various colours around words and phrases in a newspaper. Beyond him the street door is outlined by sunlight, which shivers whenever a bus goes by. I'm letting my gaze drift across the display on the walls outside the booths—posters for plays that saw their final curtain long ago, portraits that I could imagine have been browned not just by age but by the historical cigarette between the actor's lips or elegantly elevated with two fingers, comedians feigning lugubriousness if they aren't owning up to their offstage selves—when I see Frank Jasper.

He's between a picture of a clown with an ambiguous mouth and a group portrait of seven dwarfs. Though this suggests he's little better than a circus act, I'm infuriated to find him here at all. What has he written above his autograph? I lurch out of the booth and shove my face close to his as I read his flamboyant script. *For everyone I've read and everyone I have to . . .* I can't help feeling this could be aimed at me. Whatever sound it provokes me to make, Benny calls "Nothing like a laugh, eh, Mr Wubbleyou?"

"Nothing like one is right." I'm still glaring into Jasper's glossy eyes as I say "How did he creep in?"

"You'd have to ask the management. I'm just the lad that mans the pumps. Better than pumping a man, eh?"

"Seriously, Benny, I don't think he does anybody's image any favours."

As I speak Jasper's face takes on a saintly radiance. I'd be enraged by the idea that he's forgiving me, but the glow like a spotlight comes from the street, along with a crescendo of traffic. "He's never messed up your image, Mr Wubbleyou," Benny says.

I'm about to ask whether he heard Jasper on my show when a new voice asks "Is this about your picture, Graham?"

It's Hannah Leatherhead. She's wearing a white lace blouse and a beret of the same material, and equally white slacks that emphasise the generous breadth of her hips. Her face is broad as well, and the tips of her auburn page-boy hair seem to indicate her wide although slightly tentative smile. "What do you think I was saying about it?" I wonder aloud.

"Pardon me, that was intrusive. I won't mention it again." She glances around the room, presumably in case anyone heard her referring to the photograph I signed for Kylie Goodchild. "Where are you sitting?" she says, and almost as immediately "Let me buy you another drink."

Though my glass is far from empty, Benny says "I'll bring it over."

"I'll have the same," says Hannah.

I see him think better of using his name for it. As Hannah sits across from me in the booth he brings us two glasses so nearly full that the feat looks theatrical. "Settle up when you're done," he says. "Is she fond of jokes, your lady friend?"

"Benny," I warn him.

"I wasn't going to say you're one." He keeps up a reproachful look while he says "I was only going to tell her why they call it windaloo."

"They don't, Benny."

"No offence, eh? A bit of fun never did us any harm," he says to Hannah. "I think Mr Wubbleyou's scared to have me on his show."

"I don't believe he's scared to have anybody on." As he ambles back to the bar she murmurs "I wanted to tell you how impressed I was with the way you dealt with Frank Jasper."

"Well, thank you. Some would disagree."

"They must only hear what they want to hear." She sips her wine and says "So what's your game plan, Graham?"

"Which game is that?"

"Your career. Where do you see yourself in say five years?"

"National radio wouldn't be bad. Maybe television if they think I've got the face for it."

"I'd say you had an honest one, and I'm not often wrong. I just wonder if you couldn't put your skills with language to more use somewhere else."

"Don't tell anyone," I say and drain my first glass. "Even my girl-friend doesn't know, but I'm working on a novel."

"You won't want to reveal your plot, I suppose."

"You could say it's about appearances. How nobody's what they seem to be, even to themselves."

"Any publisher in sight?"

"I don't want anyone to see what I'm doing till I've finished."

That's true even of Christine, but I feel guilty over telling Hannah about it before her. As I make a start on my second glass Hannah says "Some of the writers Derek's had on his show say that too."

It's my cue to ask "How do you find Mr Dennison?"

"He's the man for the job."

This is even more unwelcome than it's unexpected, and I try to douse my feelings with a drink. "You're happy working with him, then."

"I wouldn't work with anyone I wasn't. Are you ready for another? This is my treat."

It seems increasingly less like one, and I can't find anything to say while Benny brings me a third glass. Having also given me a solemn look—for all I know it may mirror my expression—he says "Is it time for a joke yet?"

"I've had enough for one day, thanks."

Not much of the remark is aimed at him, but it appears to fall short of Hannah. As he carries off my empty glasses I say "You weren't thinking of some kind of competition for Dennison."

"I don't think I'm with you, Graham," Hannah says and adopts a hopeful smile rather too reminiscent of how Benny waits for a laugh. "We don't go in for those at the BBC."

"This one." I let go of the glass to jab a thumb in my general direction. "I mean me."

"You're the competition, that's true enough."

"And I take it that's how you'd like me to stay."

"Not exactly, Graham. Wouldn't you like to develop your skills as an interviewer? The ones we heard you using on Frank Jasper."

"I could suggest it to our new owners, I suppose."

"What's your instinct about them?"

"None to speak of till I meet them."

"Sorry, I should know by now you don't like to give away too much." Hannah abandons her attempt to prompt a smile and says "Do you think they'll let you be all you want to be?"

"I'll find that out, won't I?"

"If you're happy with how things are progressing that's completely fine, Graham."

I'm starting to feel as though, having lost my way at some stage of the conversation, I'm wandering ever further from it. I don't know whether a drink will help, but down it goes. "And if I'm not?" I wonder.

"Then I'm here."

I won't let myself be tempted to assume too much—I may already have fallen into that trap. "Well, so you are."

"I don't know if you want to share any thoughts about my proposal."

Barely in time I stop myself from saying that I didn't know she'd made one. "Do you mind if I ask what that is?"

"I'd mind if you didn't. I'd think you mightn't be serious." Hannah rests her open hands on my side of the table and leans forward to murmur "An interview show, and perhaps you could take calls from listeners."

"You don't think Mr Dennison would feel I was trying to take over from him."

"You would be. He's of a mind to move on."

I'm astonished that I could have misunderstood so much that she's been saying, and then I'm enraged; Wayne must have left me confused, and Jasper's picture may have made me worse. I have to regain some calm before asking "When is he looking to do that?"

"If it weren't until I have someone who can take our lunchtimes forward, that would be ideal."

Her smile is on the rise again, encouraging me to ask "Do you think you have?"

"That's up to you to say, Graham."

I take a moment to envisage my likely future with Frugo, my programme growing riddled with more adverts while I'm expected to manufacture contention on demand, whatever my beliefs. If I'm partly responsible for promoting this image of myself, that's all the more reason to leave it behind. I mustn't let excitement rob me of caution, and I say "Can we talk about a salary?"

"I'm sure we'd have to tempt you away with more than you're being paid now."

"Well, if that's definite I don't see how I can't be."

"That's prodigious, Graham." Her smile gives up its prudence, and mine does in response. "Let me talk to someone about numbers and then you must come in and see us," she says. "Another glass to celebrate before I go?"

"I shouldn't." Since her smile doesn't waver I add "But I will."

At least she has another one this time. Benny glances at our faces but apparently can't trust what he sees until Hannah says "Go on, Benny. We're in the mood."

Although I'm not responsible for whatever he inflicts on us I say "Careful."

"You don't look like you are," he retorts, presumably about the wine, and turns to Hannah. "What did the boy with the turban say to the nurse who was looking for nits?"

"I'm agog," Hannah says and disconcerts me by adding "I've never been more of one."

"She's a laugh, your lady friend. You want to take a leaf out of whatever you take them out of." I've a sudden uncomfortable premonition that he's going to declare it's a bush, but instead he tells Hannah "Sikh and ye shall find."

"That's painful, Benny," I protest, but he laughs until Hannah gives him enough of a smile to satisfy or at least placate him. As he bears our drained glasses like trophies back to the bar I raise my latest glass and clink it more or less accurately against Hannah's. "Here's to our future," I say. "We'll have to think of a name."

"See if you can come up with a few for our next meeting." She takes a larger sip of wine than usual and says "Could I ask you one favour?"

"No need to stop at one."

"I will for now. Could you keep all this absolutely to yourself until everything's signed and we've announced it officially?"

"Can't I even let my girlfriend know?"

"May I ask what she does?"

"She's my producer at Waves."

"Christine Ellis? She seems like an excellent producer. But in that case no, very much not even her."

I can't throw away this chance, and surely Christine will understand when I eventually tell her. "Here's to keeping secrets," I say and raise my glass again.

"Only ones that have to be kept."

"Like Benny's jokes," I murmur with an apologetic grin at him in case he overheard.

I give Hannah my mobile number while we finish our drinks. "Expect to hear from me very soon," she says and heads along Oxford Road. At the crossroads by the Palaces I look around, but nobody is watching me, not even Jasper now that they've replaced his poster. I wouldn't have minded seeing Wayne once more. My talk with Hannah seems to have given me extra strength, and if he should bother me on the way home he'll be surprised how thoroughly I deal with him.

14

ACHES

"You ought to let Paula know, Graham."

"Can't she wait?" I complain and rub my ridged forehead as if this may speed up the action of the paracetamol. "How many people am I supposed to tell everything?"

"Are you sure you've done that to anyone?"

"If you think I left anything out you tell me what it is."

This sounds irrational, but no more than I think Christine is being. We're at her kitchen table, a rounded glass rectangle on elegant metal legs. Beyond the panes that sandwich air above the piebald marble sink, a bus crosses the junction at Princess Street with as little noise as a coach in a fairy-tale film. "I nearly had to twist your arm to make you own up," Christine says.

"I won't show anyone the bruises." She doesn't seem to think this is a joke, perhaps because after a series of frustrated questions she did indeed start pinching me as though she was determined to wake me up. "You know me," I attempt to persuade her. "I don't like to talk about things that aren't definite."

I don't want to admit having promised not to talk about Hannah, especially since I still haven't mentioned my novel. I rest my gaze on Christine's face and then pick up my mug, which informs me that **THE ANSWER IS THE QUESTION.** Hers is inscribed **THE QUESTION IS THE ANSWER.** My mind can't keep hold of either concept; they seem as evanescent as the zero that fades from the glass surface where the mug stood, and at least as meaningless. I jolt my innards with a gulp of black coffee before saying "Anyway, we were talking about Paula."

"You should at least tell her you've had an offer. You don't have to say who it's from, just that you're considering it. Waves might want to top it now they've got Frugo money to play with."

She's readier to direct my speech than she ever does as a producer. "I expect I could say that if I wanted to."

"Or would you really rather not stay, Graham?"

"This isn't about us, is it? There's more to us than a radio show."

"I hope there is, but if you won't tell me—"

"This could be an opportunity for you to work with someone new as well. It won't do either of us any harm to develop."

Christine sips her coffee and puts down the mug with a muted glassy clank. "You think I'm too settled in my ways. I'm out of new ideas, you think."

"I'm saying both of us, Chris." I reach across the unyielding chilly surface and take her hand. "Wouldn't you say we know each other too well?"

"I don't believe I would."

"At work, I mean, if it's our job to keep coming up with something fresh."

Christine doesn't move her hand away from mine—in fact, it hasn't moved at all. I'm unhelpfully reminded how participants in a séance hold hands to try and conjure up an illusion of contact. "Anyone who didn't know you," she says, "might think you want to work with someone who doesn't know you at all."

I pat her hand on the way to wobbling to my feet, and feel as if I'm being none too efficiently raised by a small dull hook embedded between my eyes. "All right, I'll find out if Paula wants me to stay," I tell Christine, "as much as you do."

She seems disappointed in some way I can't define. We're silent as she follows me along the hall, which is decorated with prints from the gallery up the road—posters for imaginary British destinations. Reminiscence-by-the-Sea consists of centuries of seaside memories merging in a summer haze, while Greater Thorp Than You Think is a village where the cottages grow larger as they recede into misty distance. Beside a poster for Longsleep-in-the-Dell, where a luminous fog is so dense that it's hard to distinguish the shining white edifices from it or to establish their nature, the open bedroom door shows me that the bed we shared last night is as smooth as a blank page. Christine gives me a token kiss that feels wifely if not less than that before opening the door of the apartment. "I'll be along to take care of you," she says.

"Always the professional." I mean this as a compliment, but I'm not sure how it sounds. "I'll tell you everything that happens," I feel driven to promise.

She has half the top floor of the converted office building. A bird is faintly outlined on the Victorian fanlight above the street door, although just now the sun on the scalloped pane blots out the gilded shape. Today is Ignore An Insult Day, and I imagine some of my callers may feel insulted by the notion. Some of the queue for An Evening Of Spiritual Healing at the Palace look as if they might have to ignore an insult if not several. Other people I encounter on my way to Waves seem likelier to hand out a few insults in honour of the day or simply because that's their nature, and I don't suppose the monolithic heat will help.

The automatic doors slip aside, expelling a chill almost as welcome as a drink. For a moment the heat dogs me into the lobby like a fierce breath on my neck. "It's a jungle out there, Charlie," I tell the guard behind the desk, though I just have the tropics in mind.

I'm stepping into the nearest lift when a gust of hot wind crosses the lobby, and two policemen make for the desk.

I shut my eyes while the lift sails upwards, because the red-hot digits above the doors feel capable of snagging my hangover. At last the indicator finishes playing with its splinters and the cage wavers to a standstill. I give Shilpa a smile and drag out my badge. As I fumble to cover the plaque on the wall with my photograph the other lift opens, and the two policemen approach Shilpa. "Is Graham Wilde on the premises?" one says.

"That's me." I swing around rather too vigorously—the hangover drills between my eyes again, making me squint—and let my badge recoil on its wire. "How can I help?"

The policemen aren't much older than I am, but they look resolved to seem it. Both are thin and keen-eyed. One has a long sharp nose, while his colleague's lips are so prominent I could fancy they've been thickened in a fight. The beaky man's mouth forms a line as neutral as his gaze before he speaks. "We'd like a word with you about Kylie Goodchild."

15

AN INTERROGATION

Of all the thoughts that feel like my headache transformed into language, one is so painful that I have to spit it out. "Don't tell me Frank Jasper sent you."

The beaky policeman gazes at me—Nosey from Beak-on-the-Dial, I might dub him. "Is there somewhere we can talk in private, Mr Wilde?"

I'm anxious to learn what they want, however much my headache tugs my brows together. "Is the conference room free, Shilpa?"

"It should be."

"Let me find out," I say and unlock the newsroom door with my badge, only for Lippy from Labia-upon-the-Puss to follow. "I'll come along," he says. "Make sure it's suitable."

Some of my colleagues seem unsure whether I'm in custody as I lead him across the newsroom. I open the door beside Paula's and watch him appraise the conference room, where the long table is attended by a dozen straight barely padded chairs, one more of which has been sent to stand in a corner. A sign on each double-glazed window declares they won't open more than six inches, and could Lippy be ensuring I've no way out? The thought provokes me to go for a quip. "Looks like a good spot for the last meal, don't you think?"

Lippy lets me glimpse a frown as fleeting as a line of invisible ink. "I don't know what you mean."

He needn't think I was condemning myself. "It could be the room for the last supper."

If his face could grow blanker it's clear that it would. I can't tell whether I've offended his beliefs or just his sense of humour. "If you'll wait here, Mr Wilde," he says.

I should tell Paula about the situation—the little I can tell, at any rate. As Lippy heads for Reception I knock on her door. "Advance and be recognised," she calls, which is presumably one of her few jokes—I've certainly heard it before. She gazes over the bowl of sweets as if she thinks I've come to earn one. "Ready for all comers?" she says.

"Just a couple for the moment. I'll be next door having a chat with the police."

"Police." She gazes past me, which seems to attract their tread along the office. "What's brought them here, Graham?"

"I suspect Frank Jasper."

"Well, please keep me up to date."

As I shut her door I'm aware of having neglected to mention Hannah Leatherhead's approach. The suppressed information might be struggling with the painkillers to expand my headache. I dodge to the water cooler and fill a paper cup as the policemen reach the conference room. "Is it drinks all round?" I try offering.

"We don't need anything," Beaky says, and they stand like guards on either side of the doorway until I'm in the room.

When I sit at the head of the table they take the nearest seats on each side. The direct sunlight falls short of my chair, and the air conditioning more or less holds back the heat, but I swallow a mouthful of water that chills my teeth before I feel ready to speak. I'm nervously amused by the idea of blurting out the monikers I've invented for the policemen, and so I say "Can I know your names?"

Beaky looks not far from affronted but says "Rudd."

"Linley," says his colleague.

I'm disconcerted by how much this resembles the name I found for him; some of my listeners might think it proves I'm psychic after all. I don't know what kind of team the duo sounds like—comedians or undertakers? "I always like to know who I'm talking to," I say. "I don't know if you're wondering what I meant about Frank Jasper. He's the character from round here who pretends he's a psychic from America."

"Go on," says Rudd.

"He had a photo I signed for Kylie Goodchild. I couldn't tell you how many I signed for her class when they came for a visit, but he tried to make out it meant something." The policemen are keeping their thoughts to themselves, and I have a sudden unwelcome one of my own. "Is his father still with the police?"

Neither man appears to want the question. After a pause Linley says "Who do you mean?"

"Right enough, his name was never Jasper. It's Patterson."

"Chief Inspector Patterson."

Presumably that's a yes to my question, and it could be a warning too. My headache jabs me between the eyes as if to prod out a response. "I don't suppose you're here to talk about him," I say. "Just tell me how I can help."

Linley sits forward and rests his elbows on the table, but it's Rudd who says "Can you tell us where you were on the night of the twelfth of last month?"

He could almost be reverting to a script from more old films than I can count or name. "I couldn't even tell you what day it is without looking."

"It was a Thursday," Linley lets me know.

"Any particular time?"

"Between nine and eleven in the evening."

"I was working here."

What kind of silence greets this? In a moment Rudd says "You're sure of that."

"I am now I've been reminded. It was the day before Better Luck Day and I was doing some research for my show."

"What sort?" Linley says.

"Just about how many good things have happened to people on Friday the thirteenth. We don't need superstition."

Surely this can't trespass on anyone's beliefs here, but the policemen give me time to wonder before Linley says "How were you doing your research?"

"How does anyone these days? Online."

"Why weren't you doing it at home?"

"I'm not online at home. No need when it's free here."

Whatever they think of that, I'm not expecting Rudd to ask "Are you with anyone, Mr Wilde?"

"In a relationship, you mean? She produces my show."

"Doesn't she have access either?"

"To the Internet, you mean?" I'm increasingly less sure what they're trying to discover, and the uncertainty has lodged between my eyes. "She's got it at her place," I say, "but we don't live together. I wasn't looking at anything I wouldn't want her to see if that's what you're after."

Perhaps they weren't, in which case I've put the notion in their heads. I could invite them to check my computer, or would that sound like a bluff? They can check it if they like—I've nothing to hide—but it's well past time I asked the question my hangover has been obstructing. "What's all this to do with Kylie Goodchild?"

"We have reason to believe," Linley says, "that she was here when you were."

I'm instantly convinced that the source is Frank Jasper, and my headache swells behind my eyes, so fiercely I feel close to going blind. I don't know whether I'll be in control of my words until I hear my voice demand "What reason?"

"She told one of her school friends she was coming to see you."

My headache digs deeper as I see the explanation. "Let me guess. It was Wayne."

Linley produces a notebook but doesn't open it. "Who was that, Mr Wilde?"

"Kylie's boyfriend. He's obsessed with me, and I blame Frank Jasper."

Linley puts away the notebook as if that's an alternative to listening to me. "He has nothing to do with this. The informant was a girl in Kylie's class."

"Well, it doesn't really matter who it was. She was never here." Having leaned forward to take a gulp of water, I stay crouched over the table. I hope this looks like evidence of honesty, though in fact I'm trying to keep clear of the sunlight, which has crept up behind me to settle on my scalp like an extension of my headache. In case my words weren't unambiguous enough I add "Kylie Goodchild, I mean."

"We have a witness to the contrary," says Rudd.

I feel as if the heat has seized me by the neck. "What contrary?" I say before realising how meaningless it sounds.

"He saw a girl of that description here about ten o'clock that night. He's certain it was her."

"Anybody I should know?" My words are falling shorter still of what I want to ask, perhaps because my voice seems more detached from me than ever. "Him, I mean," I say in something close to rage.

"He's an independent witness," Linley says.

Presumably that's a denial and perhaps a warning not to try and find out who. "All right then, just tell me where he was, because I was alone up here."

"He saw her attempting to enter the premises."

"Downstairs, you mean. She wasn't trying to shin up the wall."

They don't appreciate the joke, not that it was much of one. As the heat crawls higher on my neck Linley says "She was waiting to be let in. According to the witness, she appeared to be distressed."

"Why didn't he do something about it, then?"

"He was late for a meeting. He wishes he'd intervened now."

Intervened to prevent what? Rather than demand this I say "You said he saw her waiting. You mean he saw her not being able to get in."

"He didn't see her leaving either, Mr Wilde."

"I don't see quite a lot of things. It doesn't mean they're real." This isn't far from the opposite of the point I want to make, and the heat on my back feels as if it's reaching for my headache. Barely in time I catch hold of a thought. "Hold on," I blurt. "Maybe I remember."

"Take your time," Rudd says as his partner makes to speak.

"Somebody did ring the bell. I suppose it would have been somewhere round about ten."

They plainly think I should offer them more. After quite a pause Linley says "Is there no security at night?"

"He must have been on his rounds." I resist the urge to crouch lower to take the heat off myself—I don't want them to think I'm trying to evade their attention. "If he'd let anybody in for Waves," I say, "he'd have called up."

"According to our witness," Rudd says, "she rang more than once."

"Whoever it was did. A few times, now I remember."

"And how did you respond?"

"I didn't till the last time, and when I looked whoever it was had gone."

"You're saying you went down to look."

"From up here. Wait, I'm remembering." Somewhere between the heat and my headache I'm able to see a figure foreshortened by four storeys, its shadow from the streetlamp lengthening like an arm in search of a prize as it dodges around the corner towards the Palaces. "I saw someone running away," I tell the police. "A man."

"Can you describe him?" Linley says and reaches for his notebook.

"To be honest, I didn't bother seeing how he looked. Too many people think it's fun to ring the bell at night." The heat feels capable of shrivelling my thoughts, but I succeed in retrieving some. "If he wasn't running away he was running," I decide. "You can't see much from up here, but maybe it's worth finding out if anyone else saw him."

Linley has left the notebook in his pocket. "Why are you suggesting that?"

"If the girl was really there, maybe he was why she ran away. He could have been chasing her."

The policemen are silent, and then they stand up so nearly simultaneously that they might have been given a cue. "If you think of anything else," Linley says, "please let us know."

"If I call I'll say I'm helping you with Kylie Goodchild, shall I?"

"If you are," Rudd says and holds the door open like a jailer releasing a prisoner.

I drain my paper cup while watching the policemen cross the newsroom, where most of the heads that are raised to observe them sink very quickly. My mind feels as parched as my mouth, and I refill the cup at the water cooler. It won't do any harm to remind them to question whoever was manning the desk downstairs that night, and I hurry out to Reception, but they're gone. I'm wondering if I should go after them and listen to their conversation with the guard when Paula follows me into the lobby. "Don't say you're making your escape, Graham," she calls, and I do my best to take it as a joke.

16

WAITING TO CREATE

Running Wilde won't do for Hannah Leatherhead, and Going Wilde is just as bad. Wilde at Heart sounds too much like a film. Wilde Man is no better than Wilde Boy, which is no good at all. I'll Make You Wilde and This'll Make You Wilde would be in the bin beside my desk if I'd bothered to write them down, but I haven't even put them on the laptop. Thinking up titles has taken so long that I feel as if my mind is being hindered by a thought I'm not quite managing to have. Of the ideas I've produced Wilde Fire seems to mean most, but will it be enough for Hannah?

I'm in the largest room of my apartment, where the television screen that dominates one wall is even thinner than the disc player, although just as black. They're vying with today's newspaper for attenuation, and the low table across which it's scattered is competing too. Also in the contest are the laptop and the corner desk on which it sits. I chose the location so that nothing in the room would distract me from any work I might be doing at the desk, but just now I feel shut in. I could almost imagine that someone has sent me into the corner—Christine, perhaps.

I didn't tell Paula that another radio station was interested in me. By the time I'd satisfied her curiosity about the police I was due on the air. Christine seemed to think I used this as an excuse to carry on keeping the secret, and even hearing about the police didn't entirely win her over. I tried to placate her by telling her about my novel but stopped short of admitting I've been at work on it all year. Now that she's finished producing this week's Up the Arts I hope she's burning off any resentment in the gym.

The novel's on the screen. The last unfinished sentence has been there longer than I care to think. All I like about the writing just now is the title, *You're Another.* I've thought of a new character who inspires me, but how do I deal with her? I'm tempted to start a new novel about Gladys Savage, except that I'd resent having to abandon months of work. How do I fit her in? Should I make the other characters talk about her? When I scroll through the chapters yet again the sentences seem no livelier than epitaphs. Would she bring them to life, or would they steal hers? Staring at the screen drains me of thoughts, and the sight of the room doesn't help; it seems as scrawny as the thinnest of its contents, too flimsy for my mind to grasp. Perhaps I need to go out for a walk.

In the hall a youthful Judy Garland sends a winsome look to Robert Mitchum's preacher. The corridor outside Walter Belvedere's agency is deserted, but I wouldn't think of mentioning my novel to him yet in any case. Above the glare of the streetlamps the night sky reminds me of a sheet of carbon paper. A train passes over the bridge like a series of illuminated slides through a viewer—should I put that in my novel? If ideas are going to ambush me in the street I ought to carry a notebook.

As I reach the Canal Street bridge I meet a couple climbing the steps from the towpath hand in hand. The younger man gives me a look as if he fears they'll have to ignore an insult if not worse, though I'm simply frowning about my novel. I try on an apologetic smile, but perhaps it looks flirtatious. They plainly don't think much of it, and I hurry down to the canal.

Surreptitious ripples are attempting to wipe out dim reflections of the office blocks that loom above the water. Some floors are lit and some entire buildings, where the rooms remind me of display cases awaiting exhibits. Under Princess Street the bridge is so low that it forces my head towards the restless water. A bat flaps in the dimness and then quacks to reveal it's a duck.

All of this seems to be adding to the mental weight that's suffocating my efforts to think about the novel, and I can't shake off a suspicion that there's something I ought to have told the police. Walking faster doesn't help me leave the impression behind, and strolling fails to let any other thoughts catch up. The backs of office buildings tower above the Oxford Street bridge, beyond which a woman with a vacuum cleaner pauses at each window of a long room as if she's selecting the background against which she'd prefer to be framed. On the far side of the canal discarded plastic bottles are tapping at the bars of a drain to be let in, and a frayed lump of garbage sways with the current as if it's gesturing to me. Ahead I see Waves with all its windows lit against the sky, and I'm making for the next bridge when somebody comes to a window on the floor below the radio station. He's silhouetted against the glare of a fluorescent tube, and although I'm unable to make out his face I can't help feeling watched. On the night the police asked me about I was up there looking down, and now I'm being seen. I feel as if this has something to tell me, and all at once it does. "Yes," I shout and punch the air, neither of which I can recall ever having done before. I've solved the problem with my novel.

I'll tell it from the viewpoint of Glad Savage. She reads people's secrets from their behaviour, and I just need to let her do so from the start, showing how she thinks of herself while inadvertently betraying her real nature. I turn my back on Waves and hurry home. Now that my novel has come alive it seems to bring the world into focus—the jittery ripples that a duck sets off by swimming away from me, a couple in a fifth-floor office switching off the light as if they don't want their assignation to be seen, the terse cry of a siren as a police car halts someone on the street. The plastic bottles are still knocking on the drain, and the tendrils of the lump of pallid garbage give me another wave. In fact they aren't tendrils; they're the fingers of a glove. It doesn't look quite empty; limp though they are, the fingers don't seem as flat as they should. I go to the edge of the towpath and peer across the sluggish murky water. I have to remind myself to breathe, because I'm not sure it's a glove at all.

The idea flares up inside my skull, blotting out my vision. It's so fierce that the glare turns my right eye blind. In a moment I realise that a beam is shining at my face. A lanky man with a flashlight is being tugged along the towpath by a large young hound. Except for his sandals he's dressed like a runner in a marathon. The floppy puppy's lead is wound several times about his right wrist, and he's poking the flashlight ahead of him with his left hand. "Excuse me," I call, "can you bring that here?"

Perhaps my effort to keep my voice steady makes me sound aggressive, because he retorts "What do you want?"

"Can you shine that over here?"

His pet is more eager to reach me than he is, and he follows at an alarming backwards slant. "Heel," he says to minimal effect as the puppy sets about leaping at me. "What are you asking for?"

"Just over there." Since this fails to shift the flashlight beam, which is drowning beside the towpath now that he's finished scrutinising my face, I say "What's that against the drain?"

He winds more of the lead around his wrist before raising the beam. "Bottles," he says with some contempt for them if not for me.

"Not those. What's the other thing?"

"Keep still," he says fiercely enough to have some venom left over for me, and jabs the flashlight towards the drain. "Just somebody's glove."

"I'm not so sure. I think—"

"Shut it, Sherlock."

Even though the hound has begun yapping I don't immediately realise he's addressing it. As the flashlight beam returns to the towpath I say "Can you keep that over there?"

"I've said what I think," the lanky man objects, and has started to let the puppy drag him onwards when he jerks to a halt. "What are you doing?"

My movement may have been dauntingly abrupt, but I'm not reaching for a weapon. The pale fingers sway back and forth in the water, and I'm almost certain they belong to a large blurred shape that's just distinguishable under the murky surface. I could imagine they're groping in search of some kind of help, far too late, if not trying to give me a sign. I look hastily away from them and show the man my phone. "I'm calling the police."

17

AT THE GRATING

Long before the police arrive I wonder why the man is waiting—after all, he thinks it's just a glove. He has turned the flashlight off and stuffed it in his waistband so that he can use both hands to control the dog. When Sherlock isn't straining to reach me he's lunging at the canal, either in a bid to investigate its contents or just for a swim. The fingers by the drain are as helplessly restless as ever; they might almost be desperate to wave the dog away. "Pipe down," his owner keeps repeating, which only encourages the hound to bark louder still, especially when a whirring object swoops across the roofs and a light appears overhead.

It's a police helicopter. The spotlight beam glides along the canal to fasten on me. When I point almost blindly across the water, the fierce beam veers to the far bank and finds the drain. The fingers seem to waver up to clutch at the light, but they're borrowing life from a series of ripples. The reality is dismaying enough—the sight of the limp fingers at the mercy of the water—although the bright circle in the midst of so much darkness puts me in mind of a lighting effect on a stage. The disc is folded almost exactly in half with the upper semicircle propped against the drain and the surrounding wall. The arc of mossy brick resembles an illuminated headstone awaiting a name, and the rusted bars aren't unlike railings around a grave, but I don't want to pursue the comparison while the light displays the agitated fingers in the water. I could fancy that the dog is yapping at them as the helicopter attempts to drown the sound. The row accumulates inside my head, so that I'm close to turning on Sherlock's owner by the time a cluster of pulsating lights races onto the Oxford Street bridge. They're on the roof of a police car.

A policeman and his brawny short-haired colleague tramp down the steps to stare at the drain and then at me and Sherlock's owner. "Who called this in?" the policewoman shouts above the duet for dog and helicopter.

"Shut it, Sherlock." I'm gratified to see that the policewoman thinks he means her until he bellows "I was talking to the dog."

"Who made the call?"

"He did." He's visibly relieved to displace her attention onto me. "I wouldn't have," he yells. "I don't think there's anything to bother you about."

"Then why are you here?"

"It's all right, Sherlock. The lady doesn't mean us any harm." When this seems to impress neither her nor the dog he roars "He needed my torch."

"You're together."

"Never saw him before in my life." He looks insulted, and I wonder if this might offend her. "He wanted a lend of it," he bawls. "You couldn't see what's there without it."

She peers across the canal and then into my face. Before she speaks it's clear that she's transferring onto me any antagonism he has provoked. "It was you," she says—proclaims, rather.

"I called you if that's what you mean."

What else could she? Her frown may be asking that too. "You said there was somebody in the canal," she shouts.

"I thought so. You wouldn't have wanted me not to call if I wasn't sure, would you?"

Perhaps she thinks she oughtn't to be questioned, like any representative of the police in fiction. Her frown doesn't relent as she retorts "Is your eyesight better than your friend's?"

"He's already said we're strangers. Maybe I'm more alert, more concerned if you like." Louder still I holler "I'm Graham Wilde. I work up there at Waves."

"That's where you've been."

"I was on my way back home."

Throughout the interrogation I've been aware of the constant movements of the fingers at the edge of my vision. They could almost be as restless with impatience as I am. "Please wait here," the policewoman shouts.

"What about us?" yells Sherlock's owner.

She scowls at the dog before deciding "I'll just take your details."

Meanwhile her colleague has been talking to his phone as a crowd gathers on the bridge. A little sooner than she finishes writing in her notebook, Sherlock drags the man in the direction of the crowd. As he stumbles at an enforced run up the steps, the dog starts to bark at someone who's descending. The policeman holds up a hand to detain her, but Christine points at me. Whatever she says persuades him to let her by, and she calls "What are you doing here, Graham?"

"Waiting because I've been told to." Since I'm not sure if she hears this—she still looks puzzled if not worse—I shout louder "Don't start thinking it's another of my secrets."

I'm so close to deafening myself that I only belatedly notice that the clatter of the helicopter has withdrawn across the roofs while a new set of lights sails along the canal. How many people heard my protest? Christine might be speaking on behalf of all of them as she asks "What do you mean?"

"I didn't know what was here till I walked past tonight," I say, adding not just for her benefit "Twice."

"What is, Graham?"

"What does it look like to you?"

She shades her eyes and peers where I'm pointing. The flood-light on the police boat has yet to reach the drain. The police-woman and her colleague are staring at it too. My vision must need to recover from being nearly blinded by the helicopter; the bars and the clutter bumping against them are almost impossible to distinguish. By straining my eyes I manage to isolate the lifelike gestures in the water, and Christine whispers "It isn't a body, is it? Is that what you think?"

"You see it too."

"I don't know what I'm seeing, Graham," she says and gazes into my face.

The boat chugs to the drain, and a policeman swings the flood-light beam towards the water. As the light finds the drain I could imagine that the fingers are struggling to acknowledge the search. "Don't say you're right," Christine says while she grips my arm.

Her sharing my conviction makes the imminent discovery alto-gether too real, and I turn to the policeman. "Do we really have to stay?"

His colleague scowls as if I've slighted her. "You were asked."

"She doesn't, surely."

I'm only trying to protect Christine, but too late I hear how it sounds. "Not your partner," I say with more of a laugh than I'm entirely able to control. "Mine."

This isn't too fortunate either. Who said I had a way with lan-guage? Perhaps I'm thrown by the appearance on the boat of a masked shape with flippers and black reptilian skin. It isn't the frogman's resemblance to a monster from a vintage film that trou-bles me; it's knowing why he's there. Christine grips my arm harder, and I think she's about to retreat until she says "I'll stay with you, Graham."

Her grasp feels like my apprehension rendered palpable. I watch the frogman tip backwards into the water and vanish with no sound that's audible above the chugging of the engine. Almost at once he grows visible again, a vague shape gliding under the surface of the lit section of the canal. He's setting off ripples that darken as they expand towards me, and every one seems more ominous. I can just make out some confused activity around the submerged portion of the drain, and its lack of definition robs me of breath. Then I gasp, not only because Christine's nails have dug into my arm. A head has bobbed above the water by the drain.

It isn't the frogman. I'm put in mind of a sleepy teenager poking her tousled head out of the sheets, sulkily reluctant to be wakened by a parent. Her puffy eyes look swollen shut—and then I realise that the face framed by hair like waterlogged brownish string isn't discoloured just by the glare of the floodlight. Worse, she appears to have left some of her face elsewhere. I turn hastily away to put my arm around Christine's shoulders, urging her to look away as well. "They've found her," I mutter, though I didn't recognise the face. "The Goodchild girl."

18

A SORT OF NEWS

"What took you down by the canal last night?"

"I just wanted a chance to think."

"You weren't looking for Kylie Goodchild."

"I wasn't, no. Well, hang on, let me answer that again. I suppose I've always been looking for her, I mean since I heard she was missing, like anybody who did must have been. I've kept an eye open for her, but I didn't go by the canal to look."

"You weren't expecting to find her."

"Of course I wasn't. How could I be?"

"So when did you know you had?"

"I didn't. That's to say I didn't know. I just thought it was best to call the police so they could investigate."

"And what made you do that? What did you see?"

"Jesus Christ, Trevor." In case this is insufficiently disruptive I add "You're never going to put this on the air."

"I like to get as much as I can and then edit. That's how I work."

"Be a bit more careful with your questions or you'll end up with no interview."

"I don't think Paula would like that."

"I'll have to do without my sweet, will I?"

"Come on, Graham. I appreciate you must be shaken after last night, but we're all professionals here, aren't we? We want to get this out as soon as we can for the sake of the station. I'd have caught you earlier if you'd let us know you'd found her."

We're in the conference room, and the interview feels altogether too reminiscent of my interrogation by the police. I even have a plastic cup of water, because my throat keeps growing dry at the thought of the girl's face rearing up from the canal. At least I'm beyond the reach of the sunlight that slants into the room, but the controlled temperature gives me shivers even if I brace myself. Trevor ignores the latest one and says "Ready to go on?"

Perhaps I'm being unreasonable; I agreed to be recorded, after all. "If you've thought of something else."

"I've nearly finished with you." After barely enough of a pause to leave him room to edit, Trevor says "How did you feel when they found Kylie Goodchild?"

Of all the questions the media ask the bereaved these days, that's the kind I loathe most. I shouldn't take it personally—I'm not involved in her death, after all—but I can't help demanding "How do you think I felt?"

"I wouldn't claim to know. People don't all react the same."

"Sad." When he turns one hand palm upwards as if he's lifting an invisible burden I say "I felt as I imagine anybody would. Sad to see a young girl go like that, losing her life for no reason."

"And finally, do you have any message for her family?"

"Good Christ almighty, Trevor." I'm almost provoked to shout that or worse, but instead I say "I hope the family can remember her as they knew her. I'm sure they will in time."

I can't be sure of anything of the kind, nor even if I should have said it. Before I'm able to make this clear Lofthouse says "Thanks for that, Graham. Let me get on with putting it together."

"Aren't you going to interview Christine as well?"

"She says it was all you," he informs me and marches off with the recorder to evict whoever's working in the news studio.

I'm heading for the water cooler when Paula appears in the doorway of her office. "Before you go public, Graham, I just want to say that as long as someone had to find that poor girl, I'm glad it was someone from Waves."

"Only someone?"

"Not only that at all. It was nobody but you, the increasingly famous Graham Wilde."

There are achievements I'd rather be famous for, not least my novel. I've yet to write down the ideas I had by the canal; I would have felt uncomfortable if Christine had observed me doing so. "Build on it, Graham," Paula says and shuts her door.

I might have expected her to offer me a sweet if not the entire bowl. I drain a plastic cup of water and refill it before heading for Christine's desk. "Apparently," I say not too low for her neighbours to hear, "I'm expected to take advantage of finding Kylie Goodchild."

Christine frowns, though not as much as I was hoping. "Do whatever you feel you should, Graham."

I'm in the studio with my headphones on by the time the news bulletin starts. "Police have confirmed that the body of a girl discovered last night in the Rochdale Canal is that of missing fifteen-year-old Kylie Goodchild from Crumpsall . . ." I'm afraid that Lofthouse or one of his team may have bothered the Goodchilds for a comment, but perhaps they're giving them time to recover if not to compose a sound bite. "The police were called by Graham Wilde, the presenter of Wilde Card on Waves Radio . . ." This is followed by my voice, which seems more removed from me than ever. "I suppose I've always been looking for her, I mean since I heard she was missing. I've kept an eye open for her, but I didn't go by the canal to look. I just thought it was best to call the police so they could investigate. I felt as I imagine anybody would. Sad to see a young girl go like that, losing her life for no reason."

At least Trevor has left out my message to the Goodchilds. Christine is in the control room, widening her eyes at me while she tilts her head. If that expresses sympathy, I don't think I deserve it. "Save it for her parents," I say into the microphone, but she looks puzzled if not disappointed. Sammy Baxter tells us to expect an even hotter one, and then it's time for me.

Today is Plant A Plant Day. For no remotely useful reason I'm conscious that the words mean Children And Children in Welsh. My first caller says just one plant won't help the climate, and remains unconvinced when I point out that it's supposed to be a plant for every person in the country if not the world. Another listener suggests that the idea is a conspiracy of florists, and the next contributor insists that it's the latest plot to make us all feel guilty for everything that goes wrong with the world. She's followed by a woman who argues that if we don't know if vegetation can change the world, we should have faith and plant it just in case. Once I've agreed she says "Everyone who's listening should plant a flower for Kylie Goodchild."

"I shouldn't think there would be any harm in that."

"And let me just express my condolences to you and her family."

"Honestly, you shouldn't do that to me."

"You had to find her, poor thing."

Surely the description is meant for Kylie, not for me. Now every caller seems to feel obliged to offer some commiseration, even if they name the Goodchilds before me. I'm relieved when the one o'clock news interrupts the parade of sympathisers, even if I have to listen to my displaced voice again. "Sad to see a young girl go like that," it repeats, "losing her life for no reason. I hope the family can remember her as they knew her. I'm sure they will in time."

It feels as though my voice has declared its independence—as though part of me has escaped my control. Christine doesn't look nearly as disconcerted as I think she ought to be. Trevor's gone up on the roof for a cigarette, and he hasn't reappeared by the time

Sammy Baxter tells everybody to take lots of water with the weather. "First we have Marcus from Fallowfield," I announce. "Marcus, you want to talk about how we use language."

"Just how you do. Half the time you don't say what you think."

"I'm here to play devil's advocate."

"The devil's got enough support these days. You'd do a damn sight better staying clear of him." Marcus hasn't quite left his Lancashire accent behind, and now it's catching up. "You're told what to say, are you?" he objects.

"Not by the devil or anyone else, Marcus."

"You never thought of that girl's family till after you were told."

"How do you know what I thought?" This sounds too much like an admission, and I don't spare any time to breathe before adding "You aren't going to tell us you're psychic."

"I've no need," Marcus says as Christine blinks at me through the glass. "We all heard how you decided to say something to them on the news after everybody kept reminding you about them."

"That wasn't me." I have to struggle not to let my anger carry off my words. "I mean, it wasn't my decision. I'd already recorded the message but we didn't put it out at twelve o'clock."

"Didn't you like how you sounded?"

"I didn't think I ought to intrude." When Marcus lets his silence lie I'm compelled to add "When you say how I sounded . . ."

"Folk can make up their own minds like you say you want," he says and rings off.

More than one listener comes to my defence, protesting that Marcus shouldn't have attacked me, at least not so soon after I found Kylie Goodchild. While I feel undeserving of their sympathy, I don't want to offend them. I do my best to bring us back to Plant A Plant Day, which prompts a caller to suggest planting a garden in memory of her. By the time the news crowds me off the air there's talk of opening one in Crumpsall. As Rick Till blunders into the studio, bumping the door open with an elbow while he fumbles with his tie and smooths his hair, I stalk through the control room and over to Lofthouse's desk. "What was the trick with my interview, Trevor? Did you decide I hadn't said enough?"

"Paula did. She wanted you to be more sympathetic."

I'm heading for her office when the phone rings on my desk. "Somebody's here for you, Graham," Megan at Reception says.

Shilpa is in Delhi for a wedding, and either her replacement hasn't learned to ask the names of visitors or doesn't think it's worth the exertion. Megan is examining her face in a compact mirror—I've heard her say the tan she's gained from lying in the sun can't compete with the studio product. A large man is standing with his back to her, facing the blind eyes of the zeros above the lifts, but turns as I leave the newsroom. He's Kylie Goodchild's father.

The features on his broad head look even more inadequate, as if they've been shrunken by grief—not so much the flattened nose as the small mouth and the eyes set still closer together. A trace of a scratch near his right temple reminds me how he dragged his nails across it when Jasper claimed to see Kylie under something unspecified, certainly not the canal. I do my best to put Jasper out of my mind as I say "Mr Goodchild."

"Robbie." Even pronouncing his own name appears to take an effort, and he pauses in order to be able to say "Margaret wants me to say we appreciate everything you did."

"I don't know if I did enough."

"Can't be helped now." His mouth looks close to dwindling as he adds "Nobody else did what you done."

I'm increasingly unsure why I'm being thanked. "Did you hear what I said on the radio today?"

"No offence, but I don't listen to you."

I'm ashamed of presuming that either of Kylie's parents would just now, if at all. "I was hoping all your memories are good ones."

If possible this sounds even more fatuous than the wish I

expressed on the air, and I can't blame him for wanting to change the subject. "Can I ask you summat?" he says.

"Anything," I say and regret it at once.

"How did you find her?"

For an awful moment I fancy he's enquiring about her state. I do my best to fend off any details of the memory by saying "I didn't know I had."

"Summat must have made you call the law."

"I just thought something might be wrong and I didn't want to let it lie."

Perhaps he doesn't care for my turn of phrase; I don't think much of it myself. Megan has added quite a contribution to the silence by the time I ask "Can you say when the funeral will be?"

"When they've finished whatever they're doing to her," he mumbles, raising his crooked fingers towards his face. I'm afraid he means to claw at it until he turns on Megan. "Are we embarrassing you, love?"

The last word sounds far from affectionate. "You are a bit," says Megan.

"Then I'd better fuck off where they're used to me." He stares at her with his hand still raised, as if he's challenging her to respond. When she returns to looking in her mirror—she might be searching for an outraged blush under the tan—he swings around and deals the button between the lifts not much less than a punch. As the numbers start to add up he glances at me. "Are you coming to it?" he says.

He can only mean the funeral. It sounds more like a demand or even a dare than an invitation, but I say "If you and your wife want me there, of course I will."

"She'll want it all right."

I can't tell whether he's conveying her view or declaring that she'll do as she's told. His gaze finds me again as the lift shuts. "See you at the crem," he says.

If that seems almost frivolous, it must be his way of controlling his emotions. As the numbers head for zero I tell Megan "He's just lost his young daughter."

"That's no excuse," she retorts, and I can't help thinking how unreasonable girls sometimes are. Of course it isn't only them, but until I retreat into the newsroom, professionally adjusting my expression on the way, I'm shaken by a rage I barely understand.

19

INTENTIONS

I've hardly stepped out of the lift when Megan says "Paula wants to know as soon as you're in."

This sounds a good deal too reproving for my taste, an impression her look aggravates. Is she paying me back for yesterday's disapproval? As she reaches for the phone I say "You can leave her to me."

In the newsroom several people rather more than glance at me, but their expressions aren't telling me anything. I stop at Christine's desk to murmur "I've just got to go and see miss," and knock on Paula's door as soon as I've collected a plastic cup of water from the cooler. I'm about to knock a second time when Paula shouts "Advance."

Perhaps she's too busy to use any more words, because she doesn't spare me much of a glance from her perch behind the desk. "Don't stand on ceremony, Graham," she says and stares at the computer, "unless you're anxious to be somewhere else."

The flabby leather seat feels more uncertain of its shape than ever. As it takes my weight it releases a sound like an imperfectly held breath. Paula's round plump face sinks to remain level with my antics while her hair keeps as still as a helmet. As I labour to sit forward it occurs to me to say "There is somewhere I should be sometime soon."

"Should I be surprised?"

"You might be. I've been asked to go to Kylie Goodchild's funeral."

"You'll be representing Waves there, will you?"

"By all means if you like. I'll let you know as soon as I know when it is."

"You must be feeling in demand, Graham."

"I wouldn't put it like that. If I feel anything it's guilty."

"Now why should that be?"

"It's not as if I ever knew the girl," I say despite an odd suspicion that Paula had something else in mind. "I hardly even met her."

"You must have made more of an impression than you like to think."

There are surely better ways to phrase it, but I've said enough about Kylie for a while. "Anyway, you wanted me."

"Our new owners will be here next week."

"I hope it isn't the day of the funeral."

"You'll have to decide what you're doing, won't you?" Paula stares at me as if she expects to learn my decision at once, and then says "I hear you've been hiding what you are from us."

"What in particular? I mean, what's anyone saying I am?"

"I believe you're writing a novel. Is that for publication?"

"I hope so when I've got it how I want it." When she revives her stare I say "Are you asking whether you can tell the Frugo people about it? I don't see why you shouldn't if you like."

If she does, there's no clue in her expression. I shift on the chair, which amplifies my movements, making them sound absurdly nervous. "Is there anything else you'd care to have me tell them?" Paula says.

"Such as . . ." When this sinks into her gaze without a trace I have to say "Such as what, sorry?"

"About your intentions for the future."

So Christine hasn't only told her about my novel. I do my best to choke off my rage before saying "I've had some interest elsewhere, if that's what you mean." Her silence and her gaze drive me to add "I was going to mention it. I never seemed to find the proper time."

"Sooner would have been proper. May I ask what they're offering?"

"It looks like the chance to interview people the way I interviewed Frank Jasper."

"Can you use the same trick?"

My rage is close to surfacing again. "I didn't use any on him."

"Maybe you could learn from him." Before I can attack this Paula says "I wasn't asking what they'll let you do. What are they saying they'll pay?"

"It isn't settled yet, but I wouldn't expect to take a drop."

"And is there anything that's made you unhappy at Waves?"

"We don't know about the new regime yet, do we? We don't know how we may get along with them."

"We should be seeing we do exactly that. I'd advise making up your mind."

"You know I'll deal with them like a professional. That's what I am."

Paula's gaze is growing weary, or she wants me to think it is. "I'm saying you need to decide who you're going to work for."

"Can I have until we're visited? To be honest, I don't know myself yet."

"If you really have to leave me in the dark that long. Meanwhile don't forget you're still on the air."

It seems I haven't earned a sweet today. I struggle out of the infirm chair and am nearly at the door when Paula says "Oh, and Graham . . ."

I open it and turn to her. "I don't think you should trade so much on finding Kylie Goodchild," she says. "It didn't mean much to our friends from out of town."

I almost slam the door and stalk to her desk to demand what she's accusing me of. The twelve o'clock news has begun, and so I shut the door with a gentleness that feels like a secret threat and march to the water cooler before making for the studio. As Sammy Baxter reports that the police are awaiting the results of Kylie Goodchild's autopsy, Christine blinks at my face. "Oh dear, was it trouble?"

"Someone wanted her to know I've had another offer."

My stare might be why Christine retorts "I hope you don't think it was me."

"Who else would have had a reason?"

"What reason do you think I'd have?"

"You might want to keep me here," I say and dodge into the studio as the newsreader prophesises suntans all round. I don my headphones while Christine watches me with an expression I can't interpret. It's Join In The Joke Day, and I feel as if the joke's on me. I'm bracing myself to deal with puns and gags and whatever else the listeners may throw at me—and then I deal the console a thump that makes Christine's face waver. I've thought who else could know about Hannah Leatherhead's proposal.

20

HANNAH LEATHERHEAD AGAIN

"What's it going to be, Mr Wubbleyou?"

"Nothing just now, thanks."

"No need for the face. I don't mind if my regulars just drop in sometimes for a natter. I was nearly feeling I couldn't talk to you."

"Where did you get that idea?"

"Your lady friend wouldn't let me."

"Which one's that?"

"How many have you got on the go? Hang on, don't say. I'm no champion at keeping secrets. The girl that puts you on the air, she wouldn't let me tell you a joke."

"I'd have had you on my show, would I? Who knows what reception you'd have got."

"I'll tell you it now and see what you reckon. Why don't Muslims like to draw Mohammed?"

"I've no idea, and right now—"

"Because they're not Jews."

"I don't get it, and to be frank—"

"They're not so keen on making a prophet. Get it now?"

I give Benny a grimace I don't want him to confuse with a grin, even a pained one. No wonder Christine kept him off the air, though she could have let him on as her revenge for my accusation. When I apologised for the mistake she seemed less appeased than I'd hoped. That's another reason I'm enraged, a condition Benny either doesn't notice or feels it's his job to ignore. "A customer told me that one for nothing," he says. "Go on, tell me I was robbed."

"It was a crime all right."

"Hey, you made one. Thought you were leaving it to the rest of us," he chortles, though I didn't mean it as a joke. "I expect you've got bigger things on your mind. How's the writing?"

I clench my fists, but out of sight. "You don't miss much, do you, Benny? What else did you hear?"

"When you were with the other girl? Seems like you're in demand."

"We were having a business discussion, and you told someone about it, didn't you?"

Benny straightens up, stiffening his neck while his shadow that the footlights cast on the wall behind the bar mimes his umbrage too. "Are you having another joke?"

"Come on, Benny, I'm not accusing you of anything." I am, but I'm more concerned to establish the truth. "You just said you're no good at keeping secrets," I say as I manage to relax my fists, which have begun to ache. "Maybe you were boasting about the kind of customer you have."

"I don't do that."

"Benny, if it wasn't you—"

"It was one of the rest of them that heard. If I could, don't you reckon they did?"

I strain to remember who else was there, but nobody comes to mind. "If I was wrong I'm sorry, but somebody's been talking about me."

"They will when you do what you do."

His expression leaves me undecided whether that's a compliment or some other species of remark. I take it he's still hurt by my accusation. "Have one on me, Benny," I say no less awkwardly than I fumble out a fiver to leave crumpled on the bar.

The fierce sunlight falls on me with a roar as if it was lying in wait, a sound it borrows from the traffic. The heat and the uproar seem to crowd every thought out of my skull except one: I need to speak to Hannah Leatherhead. I'm finding her number on my mobile when a not especially slim young woman emerges from the concrete bunker of the BBC across the road. I shade my eyes and squeeze them thin before I'm sure. "Hannah," I shout.

She doesn't seem to hear me. As she turns along the side street occupied by one length of the bunker I dart into the traffic. A driver treads on his brakes, but the car doesn't stop enough to let me cross. I retreat to the gutter as Hannah glances around at the hysterical screech of brakes. She sees me and gestures, but a truck obscures the movement of her hand. She must have been telling me to stay where I am, because when she becomes visible once more she's making her way along the pavement opposite me. Once the traffic halts she ventures across the road.

Her long white muslin dress hints at the outlines of her lingerie. It makes her look oddly vulnerable, and so does her apologetic smile. "I was going to call you," she murmurs.

"Well, now you don't need to. Where shall we go?"

"Do you fancy a stroll by the canal?"

"I don't much."

She's already heading in that direction, and my response appears to throw her. "Excuse me, I didn't realise . . ." She's glancing around her, and all at once she's less distracted. "Of course, we'll go in here," she says and dodges into the Dressing Room.

Is it too late to call her away? As I hurry after her, Benny shouts "Same as last time? It's on Mr Wubbleyou. He's set you up."

"In that case," Hannah says to both of us with some bemusement, "thanks."

At least we're the only customers just now. I usher Hannah to a corner booth from which I can keep an eye on the entire room, and then I touch my lips with a finger. Once Benny has brought glasses of New Zealand white—"Newsie's Wee for both," he confines himself to announcing—I clink mine against Hannah's. "So you've made the news," she murmurs.

"Honestly, I wish people wouldn't keep mentioning that. I really didn't do much at all."

"I shouldn't think it will do your image any harm."

"If it helps us I suppose I shouldn't complain." As Hannah parts her lips I say under my breath "I'd better tell you our last meeting isn't secret any more."

"How did that happen?" Before I can answer she says "Who knows about it?"

"The station manager at Waves." Without quite glancing at Benny I mutter "I think it was someone in here."

"Would you rather talk somewhere else?"

"Not unless you would," I say but keep my voice low.

"Well, Graham." Hannah takes a sip of wine and then another. "I spoke to our people," she says, "when I came back."

I take hold of my glass in preparation for a celebratory clink. "What's their verdict?"

"I want you to know it's the longest discussion of the kind I've ever been involved in." She gives me a moment to savour whatever substance this contains, and then she says "We came to the conclusion that it isn't the right time."

"The right time." The echo doesn't sound much like my voice, and I can't judge how loud it may be. "When is, then?" I whisper, which makes me feel like a secretive child.

"Unfortunately none of us could foresee one."

For a crazed moment I'm tempted to retort that they should have consulted Frank Jasper. I feel as if the bulbs that frame the mirror above the booth have focused all their glare on me, turning the rest of the room into a dark barren emptiness. The gulp of wine

I take leaves my throat parched. "Maybe I can give the situation another look," Hannah murmurs like a nurse attempting to comfort a terminal case, "in let's say a couple of years."

"Years." The echo seems more detached from me than ever. "Can I ask what their problem was with me?"

"It wasn't just theirs, Graham."

"What's yours?"

I'm no longer bothering to lower my voice, and I glimpse Benny leaning across the bar to take the order he assumes I'm about to give him. I grimace and just as fiercely gesture at him, only to discover that he has his back to me; he's replenishing the bottles that hang their heads down. Hannah waits for me to look at her and says "We couldn't very well not take into account all that business with Frank Jasper."

"You said you were impressed with how I handled him."

"The first time."

"Not just then. You told me more than once."

"After I came back as well, that's right. I'm sorry, Graham. I hadn't realised you'd had him on your show again."

"So I did. What's wrong with that?"

"The consensus was you didn't deal with him with the skill we were looking for, and there have to be questions in some people's minds."

"Which?" As Hannah meets this with a look that hopes to be silently sad I protest "Maybe if you'd heard what actually happened—"

"I listened to a playback."

In a moment my rage overtakes my confusion. "Wait a minute," I say in a whisper that makes my teeth ache. "You want me to think you hadn't heard it last time we met."

"That's the truth, Graham."

"But you talked about it."

"I couldn't have. What are you thinking I said?"

"You started talking about the photo I signed for Kylie Goodchild, and then you said there was no need. You certainly didn't give me the idea there was any kind of problem. It was after that you went into all the details about our programme."

"Graham . . ." Hannah's sounding like a nurse again, and her expression goes with it. "I meant the photographs in here," she murmurs. "I just thought you might be unhappy there isn't one of you."

I can't bear her concerned gaze or her explanation. I stare past her at Jasper performing his pantomime between the seven dwarfs and the clown. He belongs in a circus with them, but I could imagine they're all watching me in a parody of sympathy—at any rate, that's how he looks. The dozens of dressing-room bulbs glare in my eyes like lights in an interrogation cell, and I turn away to find Hannah keeping up her concern, which provokes me to ask "Shouldn't helping find Kylie Goodchild make a difference?"

"Maybe it will when it's all anyone remembers." Hannah maintains her caring look while she drains her glass and stands up. "Will you excuse me now?" she barely asks. "Forgive me for running, but I was on my way somewhere."

A roaring blaze of light worthy of a furnace spills into the pub, and then I'm alone with the barman. "If there's anything to celebrate, Mr Wubbleyou," he calls, "this one's on me."

I throw my head back to swallow the last mouthful of wine, but there isn't that much in the glass. Will more help me to feel better? It can hardly make me worse. "I'll take you up on that, Benny," I say, only to wonder how many of his jokes may accompany the drink. They aren't likely to improve my mood, but then I'm struck by a relatively welcome thought: I still have a secret to keep. I needn't tell Paula that Hannah has taken back the proposal.

21

ON HIGH

Since Christine dislikes being told how to drive, especially by a computer, no navigation is built into her car. On the map Middleton appears to consist largely of roundabouts, and it's perhaps twenty minutes away from the centre of Manchester. As we drive north the streets grow narrower and more dilapidated. Beyond villages that the city has reduced to parts of itself, distant hills are parched brown as old carpets. Along the Blackley road obstinately green trees shut out the rest of the world, and then we're in Middleton, where bouquets decorate the railings that divide a carriageway. They might be portents of the graveyard, but none of the signs by the roundabouts refers to the crematorium. At last we find a passerby who knows where it is, and we follow an even narrower street to the smallest roundabout of all.

It's Saturday, and so we're both off work. I suppose Christine has no less of a reason to attend the funeral than I have; she was with me when the police found Kylie Goodchild. The message Megan took for me simply gave the place and time. As the churchyard comes in sight a hearse bereft of its coffin turns out of the gateway, followed by an assortment of cars, and I catch myself hoping we've missed the funeral and any awkwardness it may involve. In fact we're so early that Christine's is the only car in sight when she parks it beside the chapel.

The small pale sandstone building is dominated by an outsize chimney like an omen of cremation. A rudimentary tower—little more than a stone bracket—holds a solitary silent bell. Two rows of bare unadorned pews are awaiting a congregation. In a separate room a calligraphic book of remembrance is open at today's date. The right-hand page is blank but occupied by a pair of white gloves, and I wonder if Kylie Goodchild was the kind of girl to wear gloves to a funeral. Knowing so little about her, why am I here at all?

Grey squirrels are scurrying among the graves beneath the trees, where black headstones resemble negatives of their neighbours. I sit with Christine on a bench near a wire basket piled with dead bouquets. I don't know whether she wants to embrace the peace or simply has nothing to say for the moment. Myself, I don't seem able to benefit from the stillness; too many thoughts are dodging about inside my head like the squirrels the colour of stones on the grass. I haven't told Christine I met Hannah Leatherhead again; I don't want to risk letting the news spread until well after I've met our new bosses. To some extent I'm relieved to see another hearse and its procession of cars arriving at the churchyard.

The hearse halts at the chapel, and an undertaker's man lets the Goodchilds out of a limousine. Wayne is with them, and they're all in black and white; he's even donned a suit, though it doesn't look like his own. They stand by the door of the chapel while drivers park near Christine's car as slowly as a funereal ritual. Kylie's mother looks oddly fearful, possibly afraid of emotions that may catch up with her at any moment, while her husband looks as determined as Wayne to stay gruff. None of their faces wavers as the other mourners, quite a few of whom must be Kylie's schoolmates, converge on the family. I'm waiting for everyone else to go into the chapel, and then I see Frank Jasper.

He's very much in black—suit, shoes, socks, polo-neck. He murmurs to Kylie's parents and her boyfriend as he takes his place beside them. He looks as if he's surveying the turnout for the funeral. His gaze comes to rest on me, and he mutters a few words to Kylie's father. "Don't do anything, Graham," Christine says at once.

"I wasn't about to." Her assumption infuriates me even more than Jasper's behaviour. I stare at him as expressionlessly as I can manage, and then I watch three teenage girls dab at their eyes while they giggle at the antics of a squirrel. When I glance back at Jasper he's heading for our bench.

I'd clench my fists if Christine wouldn't see. I make to stand up, but she holds on to my arm. Jasper doesn't speak until he's almost within reach. He dabs his forehead with a handkerchief, and I'd be happy to imagine he's sweating with nervousness, but it's the heat that even the trees can't fend off. As he pockets the handkerchief he murmurs "Have you been put in the picture?"

He hasn't finished speaking when his gaze shifts from me to Christine, so that I could think the question is meant just for her. That's one reason I demand "Is that your job now?"

Keeping my voice low to avoid being overheard has reminded me of trying to be secretive in Benny's bar. The memory inflames my rage, and Jasper doesn't help by saying "I guess nobody here wants to upset Robbie and Margaret."

Even his adopted accent infuriates me, since it's part of his act. "Who's going to do that?"

"Anyone who asks them for the latest on their daughter."

"Why do you think I'd do anything of the kind?"

Perhaps fury is confusing me—perhaps he didn't mean I would. Christine strokes my arm and says "So what is the latest, Mr Jasper?"

"I need you to keep this to yourselves just now."

"It's okay, Frankie. It's all right, Frank." I've rephrased it to placate him and obtain the information, but I can't resist adding "We aren't on the air and I'm not recording you this time."

"We're good at keeping secrets," Christine adds.

He seems bemused by the hint of a rebuke, but of course that's aimed at me. My remark may have antagonised him as well. He lets us see that he's making some kind of allowance before he murmurs "It looks like it wasn't the canal."

"What wasn't, Mr Jasper?"

Perhaps Christine thinks the fake name is the best way to coax the details out of him, but I'm about to quiz him more vigorously when he says "How Kylie died."

"What are you saying it was then, Frank?"

"It seems like she was dead before she hit the water."

Though I asked the question he's still eyeing Christine, who clasps my arm as she says "Do they know what happened?"

"I'm hearing she may have been knocked down. Just a single blow, it could have been. They'd have given her no chance to call for help."

Is it possible he's claiming to have heard this from the afterlife? Apparently this doesn't occur to Christine. "Who could have done something like that?"

"It wouldn't have taken too much strength. She looks like a delicate girl. Maybe he lost control for a moment. That's all it would need."

Before I can enquire how the police know it was a man, Jasper glances at the chapel. "You'll pardon me if I leave you to it. They're going in," he says and turns back to add "Remember I'm trusting you."

Christine takes a firmer hold on my arm as though to prevent me from lurching after him to grab him. Even if my rage is virtually indistinguishable from the heat that's settled on my scalp, I was only making to stand up; I do know where I am. "I'm a hundred per cent more trustworthy than Mr Frankie Pattercake," I mutter.

"Are you sure you're all right to go on with this?"

"As all right as anyone is at a funeral," I say and bring her to her feet as if I'm fishing her up.

The last of the mourners are filing into the chapel, above which the vapour trails of an airliner doubly underline the emptiness that's heaven. Wayne and Kylie's father are standing by the hearse, and Wayne stares at me until I reach the chapel, where a pastor hands Christine and me a pamphlet each. Despite the stone walls, the heat feels as if it presages a furnace. Many of the small latticed windows are frosted, but however much they blind us to the world outside they can't shut out the sun. Among the reasons I head for the back row is that it's furthest from the rays that are advancing through the chapel.

Music is hovering under the rafters—"Amazing Grace" performed by a young choir. According to the pamphlet they're from Kylie's school. The white letters on the pale blue cardboard cover say **Kylie Goodchild: Celebrating Her Life.** Some of the mourners seated on the straight-backed pews are using their copies to fan themselves, and I'm tempted to follow their example until Christine touches my arm. She's showing me a poem in her copy, and I turn to it in mine.

Life by Kylie Goodchild

Life's everybody who's alive and everything that is.
I'm a part of it and so are you, and we shouldn't think we're
any better than the rest.
Find out how you're like other people and how they're like you,
and then we'll all be more alive.
We're all the same before we're born, and babies never fight, so
why can't we just remember how it was and be glad
everyone's alive?

Apparently she wrote it when the English teacher asked the class to write an essay on the subject, but we're told he's glad she wrote it and stood up for doing so. I rub my right eye with the back of my hand, because a sweaty trickle is on the way to blinding me. The next page bears a tribute by her class—*Kylie, you're living in eternity. God owns our dear classmate. He's incarnate love divine*—and I've just worked out the secret of the words when the coffin noses its way into the chapel.

I stumble to my feet, but Wayne seems to think I wasn't swift enough. While he doesn't turn his head, his eyes appear to redden as he glares sidelong at me, perhaps from the strain it takes. He's at the rear of the wicker casket with Kylie's father on the other side and two of the undertaker's men supporting the front end. I can't help wondering if Patterson offered a shoulder and hoping he was rebuffed. At least he hasn't managed to talk his way into the front row, even if he's directly behind Margaret Goodchild; I could imagine he's poised to breathe some kind of message in her ear. The casket passes the empty rows in front of us and then brings rank after rank of mourners to their feet until it's deposited beside the pulpit. Wayne and Kylie's father mop their foreheads as they join her mother in the front row, and then the pastor climbs the steps to the pulpit. "We are here to celebrate the life of Kylie Goodchild . . ."

This scatters sniffs throughout the chapel, and they multiply as the pastor continues. "She was devoted to her parents, and they were devoted to her . . ." I take this to mean she was an only child. "From an early age she was an individual with an imagination bigger than she was . . ." I'm already certain that the pastor never met her, any more than the priest at my grandfather's funeral had met him. "Everything mattered to her, and she took care of her favourite toys just as much as her friends . . ." I can't quite grasp this, perhaps because I'm remembering my grandfather's funeral, my father looking as if some aspect of the situation is my fault, my mother giving the impression that she would like to apologise to me at a more opportune time. "She excelled at reading and writing, but she wasn't one to boast about her achievements. In some ways she was a private person, but never an unfriendly one. You had the chance to be her friend no matter where you came from, and many people here today are glad they took that chance . . ."

How different is all this from Jasper's trickery? Some of it isn't much less generalised, but at least the people who provided the information know they did. The pastor must have used it up, because she's saying "Let us not dwell on the shortness of life but try to live it for others as well as ourselves. Kylie did, and that's why she will live on in the hearts of all who were blessed with knowing her. Now her father would like to say a few words to us."

His wife and then Wayne rise to their feet out of respect, except that they're making way for his bulk. He seems to have some difficulty with the steps up to the pulpit, unless he's taking time over his words or steeling himself to speak. He grips the rail at the front of the pulpit and leans over it, then straightens up and hides his fists behind his back. By the time he opens his mouth I can't help being put in mind of a man in a witness box.

"Her mother thought she was a gift from heaven," he says but doesn't look at his wife. "I'm a liar, we both did. She's the only one we'll ever have. At least whoever blessed us gave us fifteen years of her. We had our arguments, but she was a teenager, so you've got to expect that." He takes a breath so fierce that it echoes beneath the rafters and says "That's all she'll ever be now."

The effort to contain his emotions is clenching his face, which helps to set off another chorus of muffled sniffs. When he lifts a hand I'm nervous of seeing him claw at his forehead. He digs the hand into his trouser pocket instead, producing a handkerchief with which he dabs at the upper half of his face. "That's all I can do, padre," he mutters.

Once he's back in the pew Margaret Goodchild remains standing until the pastor glances at her, which makes her hastily resume her seat. "Would anyone else care to speak?" the pastor says.

For some moments there's no response other than a sob I can't locate, and then Wayne lurches into the aisle. He takes a step towards the pulpit before shaking his head violently and retreating into the pew, mumbling "I can't." As Kylie's mother reaches out to comfort him, Jasper leans over her shoulder. "If it's all right with you," she says to the pastor, "Mr Jasper would like to speak."

"Anyone's welcome so long as there's time. I expect that's what your daughter would have wanted, aren't you?"

It's plain the pastor has no idea who and especially what he is. If anyone can speak, can't I? They ask for objections at weddings— why shouldn't one be raised at a funeral? I'm leaning forward when Christine looks at me and shakes her head. I didn't realise I was so predictable, and the notion shuts me up while Jasper sidles into the aisle and ascends the steps to gaze down at us all.

Perhaps even he feels he's presuming too much. He turns his eyes towards the coffin and clasps his hands loosely together, but despite parting his lips with a small dry sound that reminds me of the action of a switch, he doesn't speak. "Say whatever's in your heart," the pastor urges him.

Jasper lifts his gaze to the Goodchilds, which Kylie's mother seems to take as a sign. "Can you see her, Mr Jasper?" she pleads.

All at once I know what he resembles most: an uncle at a children's party, pretending to be reluctant to perform a trick until his audience persuades him. He stretches out his hands to the Goodchilds, widening his eyes as if to make room for extra sympathy in them. "She's behind you, Margaret," he says.

His tone is almost reverential enough for a sermon, but it sounds like a pantomime to me. Kylie's mother twists her head around to blink at the place he vacated, and her yearning or at least the way he's playing on it almost brings me to my feet with rage. I clench my teeth while she turns to face Jasper. "How is she?"

"She wants you to know she's at peace."

Her mother's question was barely audible, and I have to strain my ears at the next one. "Can she say what happened to her?"

There's an uneasy movement somewhere in the chapel. It may be the pastor who's shifting her feet; she looks as if she's having some doubts about Jasper. He gazes at the emptiness behind the Goodchilds, but his eyes appear to want us to believe he's seeing further. "There was somebody," he says with so little expression that his voice might be attempting not to sound like his. "There was a man."

I've given up wanting to intervene. The Goodchilds invited him, and they're getting what they asked for; the pastor is as well. "Who was he?" Kylie's mother begs.

"The last person she saw." Having explained this, Jasper reverts to the toneless voice that I'm enraged to suspect he intends to imply he's quoting the dead girl. "He's always arguing."

I should think that's true of many people, even here, and Mrs Goodchild has reservations of her own. "What's that to do with Kylie?"

"He didn't like where she went. He wanted to stop her seeing him." Jasper seems uncertain which voice he's supposed to be using. "Wait, I'm getting something else," he says, perhaps to the pastor, who has turned to him. "Something he does."

The pastor glances at her watch and makes to speak. Before she can, Jasper says "He goes on the radio."

He isn't looking at anyone; his eyes seem to be trying to appear sightless in the ordinary sense. It's Wayne who hauls himself around on the pew, so violently that a creak of wood resounds through the chapel. He looks ready to speak if not worse, but the reddened glare he fixes on me is eloquent enough. I'd stand up to be prepared for him—my rage at Jasper's performance needs to be acted upon—if Christine weren't clutching my arm. Kylie's mother takes Wayne's arm in both hands, and he glowers a warning at me before facing the coffin. Even this infuriates me—the way Christine and Mrs Goodchild are treating us as though we're similar—and I pull my arm free of the soft frustrating grasp.

The pastor clears her throat, apparently only to make sure the psychic stunt is finished. "Thank you," she says as Jasper descends from the pulpit, having rediscovered how to see like the rest of us. Once he's back in the seat where Kylie was supposed to be the pastor says "Let's be silent for a minute while we remember Kylie Goodchild."

All I can bring to mind is the bruised bedraggled head rising from the murky water, eyes squeezed shut as if they couldn't bear the floodlight. My rage with Jasper is a good deal more immediate, and I sense fury elsewhere in the chapel. Far too eventually the pastor says a short vague prayer that puts a stop to all the muffled sniffs and earns a murmur of amens. Curtains glide shut in front of the coffin to signify the show's over, and Wayne leads the Goodchilds into the aisle. The congregation is meant to leave in the order of the rows, starting at the front, but I don't want any confrontation in the chapel. I hurry outside and have taken just a few steps in the pitiless sunlight when I hear Wayne at my back. "You'd better fucking run, but you won't get far."

I swing around so fast that the gravel of the drive grinds underfoot, and a fragment clatters towards him. He's stalking at me with his big fists raised, but halts just out of reach. Behind him Kylie's parents and the pastor have emerged from the chapel. "I'm not running anywhere," I tell Wayne. "I didn't think this would be appropriate in there, that's all."

"Wish you was down by the fucking canal again, do you, boy?"

"Just what do you mean by that?" I demand before realising he has our previous encounter in mind. "Here is fine."

"Fucking right it is. They can all hear what you've got to say."

Christine hurries to stand by me as I murmur "Try and stop the language. Remember where you are."

"I know where I fucking am. At my fucking girlfriend's funeral, and she wouldn't mind." His eyes seem to grow redder still as he snarls "And it sounds like I'm talking to the cunt who put her where she is."

Jasper is loitering beside the Goodchilds, and the sight of him helps me to focus my anger—even to control it, I hope. "Is that what you'd say, Frank? Is that what you want everyone to believe?"

"Pardon me?"

"Kylie's boyfriend thinks you were pointing the finger at me."

"I didn't name anyone." For once Jasper looks wary; perhaps he thinks he could be sued. "I can only say what I hear."

"You'll have to do better than that. Aren't you responsible for what comes out of your mouth?"

Before he can respond Wayne protests "He knew all about you the other fucking time."

The pastor holds up her hands, but I can't wait to deal with Wayne's remark. "If we're talking about that photograph again—"

"Not your photo. You're too fucking fond of talking about that." Wayne clenches his fists as if he's imitating me and says "When he said about your dad hanging you off the balcony."

"Graham," Christine murmurs, but whatever she's trying to achieve, I haven't time for it. "And how did you know about that, Frank?" I enquire. "Shall I tell them or will you?"

He shakes his head while looking blank and glances sidelong at the Goodchilds. In the midst of their grief Kylie's father seems even more bewildered than his wife, but Wayne and the faker have gone too far this time. "I'm sorry to be bringing this up now," I tell Kylie's parents. "Last chance, Frank."

Margaret Goodchild gives him a pleading look. "What does he mean, Mr Jasper?"

He's only starting to shake his head when I find I've had unbearably more than enough. "He knew about me because we were at the same school. That's how I know about him."

Wayne's inflamed gaze twitches and then fastens more fiercely on me. "So why didn't you say on the radio? How come you're only fucking saying now?"

"It's true," Christine says, although as if she hopes Kylie's parents may not hear. "I knew about it. Graham told me."

"You've got to say that. You're his bitch."

The pastor clears her throat and brings her hands together quite hard. She might be announcing a forceful prayer or calling unruly children to order. "If you'd care to make your way now," she says, "we have another party waiting."

A hearse and its procession are indeed approaching up the drive with a prolonged discreet rattle of gravel. Wayne glares at them as if they have no right to be here and then turns his hatred back to me. "You wait," he mumbles. "This isn't fucking over."

As he tramps over to the Goodchilds, all the mourners who were watching the confrontation start towards me. I could imagine they've become a mob if I didn't realise that they're heading for the car park. "Come on, Graham," Christine murmurs urgently and takes my arm. We wait in her car for the hearse and the other vehicles to leave, and at last she starts the engine. I don't know why she's making sure the others are out of sight—there's no need to be scared of Wayne—but I wish the delay had let me think. I'm certain something happened at the funeral, unless it was afterwards, that it's vital to remember.

22

SEARCHING THE AIR

"Was there any actual violence?"

"None of that. As I said, we were at the funeral."

"Was anybody threatened?"

"He told Graham it wasn't over, and the way he said it was certainly meant to be threatening."

"Do you remember his exact words?"

"He said, I won't say just what he said, but he said it wasn't effing over. And he told Graham to wait, and he called me a bitch for no reason at all."

"She's asking us to be precise, Chris. Actually, he called her my bitch, and I think that means—"

"I know perfectly well what it means, Graham, and that's not the point. If he was that much out of control at his own girlfriend's funeral I wouldn't like to think how he might behave when there aren't so many people around."

The policewoman looks as if she's suppressing a frown, an impression I've had ever since we met her out here at Reception. She's keen-eyed and efficient but slightly built, which may suggest how trivial the police consider my call to have been. I wouldn't have called if Christine hadn't insisted. "He behaves just the same," I tell the policewoman. "I can handle him."

"You've had other dealings with him."

"He was with Kylie Goodchild's parents and their psychic when Graham had them on his show, and he made a scene then." Christine gives me a doubtful look as she says "Go on, Graham."

"He showed up the other day, before I found his girlfriend." Too late I realise that I didn't tell Christine. "He said he'd put me in the hospital," I hear my voice admitting, "but that's just one of those things people say."

"To you," the policewoman says, "do you mean?"

"To anyone. Haven't they ever to you and your colleagues?"

She raises her eyebrows a fraction, which might be an acknowledgment or a hint that she's offended. "Did you give him any reason?"

"He seemed to have got it into his head that I was hiding some kind of secret about his girlfriend. I wouldn't have expected him to have that much imagination."

As Christine keeps an observation to herself the policewoman says "Whereabouts did all this take place?"

"Just by the canal. He seemed to be at home down there."

"Do you want to put in a complaint?"

When Christine shows signs of answering I head it off. "I honestly don't think it's called for. Maybe you could keep an eye on him."

"We may want to speak to him."

"I expect you'll have done that before." When she betrays no response I try saying "Do you know, I don't think I've ever heard his last name or where he comes from."

This brings me no information either, and she's turning to the lifts when Christine says "Was Kylie Goodchild murdered?"

"Who gave you that idea?" After more of a pause than I can see the point of, the policewoman says "Her boyfriend?"

"Not him this time," I tell her. "Frank Jasper, the character who'd like us all to think he's psychic."

"How would he know?"

I'm not sure which of us Christine is asking. It's the policewoman who says "From the girl's parents?"

"So it's true, then."

The policewoman's face stiffens, growing so blank that I'm afraid she feels worse than tricked. She doesn't speak until she's at the lifts, and then she says "Please keep whatever you think you know to yourselves till it's official."

As a lift shuts away her gaze, which is so relentless that she might almost be trying to leave some trace of it behind, I make for the newsroom. Give 'Em Rhythm, the Sunday independent music show, is playing a track by Babies With Rabies, but I barely hear it—I'm impatient to return to my search. Last night I jerked awake so violently, having realised what I overlooked at the funeral, that Christine moaned in her sleep as if someone had dealt her a blow. How could Wayne have known what Jasper said about my childhood? He must have heard it on Wilde Card. He isn't the type to keep his thoughts to himself, and if I can identify which calls he made I'm convinced I'll learn something that I need to know. I hurry into the studio and restart the playback.

Too many of the callers hold views sufficiently brutish for Wayne, but they sound a good deal older. Quite a few of the voices resemble his, but they're too intelligent or at least more articulate. The voice I've heard far too often during all these hours at the console is my own, however swiftly I skip past it to the next caller. I've sampled every call for several months—I'm just a few days short of the end of last week—and they've left me feeling trapped in an interminable pointless argument, as if all my displaced voice can do is quarrel. The thought fills me with a dull frustrated rage, and the prospect of a future spent in squabbling on the air makes it worse. Perhaps I can suggest an interview show to the Frugo people next week, and there's still my novel if I can recapture the inspiration I had the night Kylie Goodchild turned up. I haven't played back the most recent of my broadcasts when I find an excuse to leave the console. Waves is broadcasting a track by Voodoo Dumplings now. I gulp a cup of water from the cooler and am filling one for Christine when somebody knocks on the door of the newsroom.

It's a security guard, and he's pointing at me. "I'll get it, Trevor," I call as Lofthouse makes to leave his desk. "What can I do for you, Vince?"

Though the guard's broad mottled face looks conspiratorial, not least because his small eyes appear to be using his thick eyebrows for cover, he doesn't bother to drop his voice. "Have you got rid of her?"

"I didn't know he wanted to," Christine protests, having left the control room.

"Not you, love. I'm asking has the law gone."

"I don't see her, do you?" This sounds unnecessarily like hoping the policewoman is out of the way, and I add rather more forcefully "Why?"

Vince's eyes shift as if he might be searching for somewhere more private, but he blocks the doorway instead. "Just so's you know I didn't see anything worth telling the other night," he says, "in case you was wondering."

I'm by no means sure I want to ask "What night? What did you think you saw?"

"Before they found the girl. Well, you did." With another sideways flicker of his eyes Vince says "You was down by the canal and looked like you was giving somebody a thump."

"It couldn't have been me. I only fight with words."

"I didn't say a fight. More like just a punch that'd have knocked even me in the water."

"You can't be saying that was me."

"I'd have to if they asked. That's why I'm telling you I never saw you hit anybody that I saw."

"I still don't know what you're—" I interrupt myself with some kind of laugh. "Wait there," I say with an attempt at mirth. "Was this it?"

Christine cries out and stumbles backwards, almost colliding with a desk. I hadn't realised she'd ventured so close, and the fist I throw out with all my strength only just misses her head. "Careful," I say to at least one of us. "Was it like that, Vince?"

"Pretty like, except she wasn't there."

"Nobody was apart from me. I'd just had an idea for a novel I'm writing and I was excited, that's all. Didn't you hear me shouting yes?"

"I thought you sounded like you was shouting at someone."

"Just me, and I wasn't angry either. You don't need to keep any of this quiet. Tell anyone you have to tell."

His expression is on the way to changing as he makes for the lifts. I'm heading for the studio when Lofthouse says "I didn't realise you were into telling stories, Graham."

I take time to draw quite a breath. "Which story do you think you heard?"

"I can't say, can I? We'll have to wait for you to go public."

My eyes begin to sting as I stare at him. "What are you trying to get at, Trevor?"

"Your secret self." When I give no sign of understanding he says "Didn't you say you were writing a novel?"

My mistake or whatever it was enrages me further, which makes me blurt "Did you listen to me talking to the police as well?"

"I didn't have to listen very hard. You weren't what I'd call discreet."

"You did get a bit noisy, Graham."

I'm furious enough without Christine's contribution. "Maybe you heard a story you can use, Trevor. The girl they sent as good as admitted they're looking for a killer. There's an exclusive for you."

"That isn't how we work here, Graham. We couldn't be as sure of it as you seem to be."

I'm uncertain what he's rebuking me about, which only aggravates my rage. A Shakespearian rap by 2 2 Solid Flesh starts up as I tramp after Christine into the control room, where the door shuts with a thud like a gloved punch. I've nothing to say to her just now—I don't want to discuss searching the playbacks, though I can see she's more doubtful than ever. I shut us in the studio and clamp the headphones to my skull before she can speak.

Wayne isn't there. I am—I've listened to hundreds of fragments of my estranged voice by the time the latest Wilde Card comes to an end—but I can't hear him among the callers, however aggressive some of them are. When I remove the headphones I feel as if a dull weight has been left on my cranium and inside it too. "I don't get it," I mutter.

"I'm not sure I do either." Christine lays down her headphones and swivels her chair to face me. "What exactly were you looking for?"

"I told you. Kylie's boyfriend, if he even deserves to be called that with his attitude to women. As long as he thinks he knows so much about me it'll do no harm to find out about him."

"I still don't understand why you were so sure he'd be there. I did say I thought he'd never rung up." She seems to want to head off any argument by adding "You still haven't told me why you think he listens to you."

"He knew what Frankie said about my father, and I can't imagine anyone less likely to go and see him at the theatre."

"Perhaps he wouldn't do that, but couldn't Frank Jasper have told him afterwards?"

I feel as if the burden inside my skull has grown more solid. Have I really wasted all these hours? What should I have been doing instead to lessen my frustrated rage? Shoving my chair away from the console doesn't help. "Let's go home," I say in case something in my apartment or hers may improve my state—but as I follow her into the newsroom, where Trevor is sitting all by himself like a guard or a watchman, I almost turn back. For an instant I'm convinced that I've been conducting the wrong search, that I need to identify some other feature of the playbacks. The idea vanishes before I can grasp it, and I trudge after Christine past the stack of copies of my face.

23

A CHATTERING SHOW

It's We're All Coloured Day, and I'm ready for all comers. I just wish the Frugo people were here now instead of tomorrow. If Paula wants controversy she can have some of the honest kind. I hope Bob from Blackley puts in an appearance; it's time we heard from him again. As I don my headphones Sammy Baxter reports that the police are treating Kylie Goodchild's death as suspicious and asking anyone who may have seen her on the night of the twelfth of May to contact them. The news ends by predicting the kind of heat people used to go abroad to find, and I remember hearing from a listener who insisted our climate had changed since, if not because, the country had joined Europe. I thought of suggesting that the weight of all the immigrants had tilted the world on its axis, and now I wish I had. For the moment it's my job to announce Jessie from Gorton, who declares that there's no such thing as a white person and then makes albinos an exception. I suggest they mightn't want to be singled out, and she agrees with this along with too much else to let me argue. No doubt we're irritating some of the audience, and perhaps Steve from Collyhurst is provoked. "You're on the same subject, are you, Steve?"

"What she was talking about before, I said."

"It's your choice of topic. What would you like to say?"

"They ought to talk to the feller that ran off."

"Who should?"

"Want us to think you don't know? The police."

"Are we talking about some kind of racist attack?"

"Why's it going to be one of those?" Steve emits a noise somewhere between a snigger and a spit, which seems to thicken his Lancashire accent. "I'm not on about today. I'm on about Kylie."

I pause until Christine frowns at me. I'm working out that Steve meant Sammy Baxter rather than Jessie from Gorton, that's all. "Who are you saying ran away?" I ask him.

"Don't you know?"

"Would I ask if I did, Steve?"

"You'd do that all right, but you can't pretend this time."

I feel as if the headphones have gained weight and grown clammy on my skull. "Who is this?"

"It's who you said. I don't mess with my name or where I'm from."

That applies to Jasper, not to me, and I almost waste time saying so. Instead I urge Steve "Try and make yourself clear."

"Everybody saw you run off at Kylie's funeral."

I lower my gaze to my fists on the console to avoid seeing Christine's worried face. "You were there, were you?"

"Everyone that cared about her was." With another version of his sound, this one more unambiguously a spit, Steve adds "And you."

"Forgive me, why would I have gone if I didn't care?"

"You cared all right. Cared what somebody might say about you."

"That's absolutely not the case. If you're talking about Frankie from Hulme—"

"I'm talking about Frank Jasper that's helping Kylie's family and the police. Why'd you run away from him?"

"You've an odd idea of running. I stayed and had it out with your friend Wayne. Something tells me he's your friend."

"Graham," Christine says in my ear.

I almost wrench the headphones off, I'm so enraged by her interrupting my Jasperish trick. "I'm handling this," I cut off the call long enough to tell her. "Sorry, Steve, what did you just say?"

"I said why'd you think Frank Jasper was talking about you?"

"Do you really want to know?" The moment I give him to respond only lets my rage gather. "I think he was trying to get his own back because I told everyone who he used to be."

"Graham . . ."

I shake my head fiercely at Christine as Steve says "He put that on his web site."

"Only after I'd given him away. It's a trick like everything about him."

"You're only saying that since he told us all about you at the funeral."

"He didn't tell anyone about me if you noticed. He's too sly for that. He knows if he'd named me he'd have been the one in court when there wasn't any proof."

"Who says there's not?"

"Since you ask, the police. They've spoken to me and I've no reason to suppose they aren't happy, satisfied, I mean." While I can't judge whether this placates Steve, it silences him. "I know you must be concerned about Kylie," I tell him, "but you're going to have to look elsewhere for whoever was responsible."

He has no reply to this either, and so I thank him for his call. "Now I think Eunice from Miles Platting wants to return to the subject of the day."

"Why was he saying you ran away from a funeral, sweetheart?"

"I didn't." My rage was fading, but now it's back. "Somebody who calls himself Frank Jasper and plays a psychic on the stage—"

"We all know who he is, pet. You had him as a guest."

"Well then, him. They let him speak at the funeral and he gave some people the impression I know more about Kylie Goodchild than I do."

"What are you supposed to know, honey?"

"I don't." Her syrupy epithets feel like toothache, but I need to be clear. "Not a thing," I say. "That's the truth, believe me. You didn't actually call about that, did you?"

"They're trying to tell us we're all coloured, dear."

"That's because we are."

"Only some are more coloured than others, darling. That's all I want to say," she declares and rings off.

I'd opened my mouth for an argument, and it feels idiotic until I clap it shut. I'm less frustrated by the time I finish disagreeing with Wanda from Ancoats, who insists we soon won't be allowed to listen to "Good Golly Miss Molly" or call anyone a boy or say snigger or spick and span or Day-Glo. I end up suggesting we'll be forbidden to say a horse has been spayed or refer to a packing case, and as for the astronomer who dared to mention a black dwarf . . . I feel as if I'm understudying Benny at the bar, though I hope to sound even sillier. I'm ready for another confrontation as I say "George from Micklehurst, you're going to tell us something else we won't be able to say."

"They can't call them convicts now, can they? They've got to call them custodial service users." Before I can argue he says "Anyway, I didn't ring up about that. Strikes me you could be like your friend who put on the show at the funeral."

"He's anything but a friend, believe me." I feel as if the headphones are forcing my head down towards my clenched fists. "What are you saying we have in common?"

"It's like you said, maybe you're as psychic as he is."

I said that in another context, and that's as much as I recall. "How would that be?"

"Something must have led you to that poor girl."

"Trust me, nothing did. I just happened to be there."

"We'll have to make up our own minds about that."

"That's how I like it," I say and do my best to mean it, but I'm happy to end the call. "Levi from Newton Heath, you want to talk about differences, do you?"

"You don't want anybody talking about Kylie Goodchild."

I can't tell whether this is meant as a question or a complaint, and so I say "The phone-in isn't meant to be about me."

"We're let then, are we?"

"I thought I'd made that clear. Are you a friend of hers?"

"Was."

"Of course, forgive me. I wasn't meaning to sound like Frankie Jasper." With an unspoken vow not to mention Patterson again I say "I didn't see you at the funeral."

"You'd know me, would you?"

"Sounds as if I should. I'm guessing Eunice who called before would say you're more coloured than some."

This is almost devious enough for Jasper, and I'm ashamed of it at once. I feel Christine's gaze adding to the burden of my head-phones until Levi says "Kylie was cool with it."

"I imagine she would be." In case this isn't unambiguously positive I add "Anyone could see that from her poem."

"Know some stuff about her after all, do you?" Before I can re-spond he says "Remembered what you said to her yet?"

"Not a word and believe me, I've tried. It couldn't have been too important." I hope nobody thinks that's my view of her, and I work on being clearer. "Whatever made her come back, it couldn't have been anything I said or did, or I'd remember."

Levi lets me have a silence, and I'm assuming he's satisfied until he says "Come back where?"

Too late I realise this hasn't been made public, but I don't see how to avoid saying "It seems she was round here the night she died."

"Who says?"

"If you want to know all about it, ask the police. And," I'm far too belatedly prompted to say, "while you're at it, talk to her class-mates."

Christine might be frowning on his behalf as he demands "Who says they were there?"

"They were here the only time I met her. They must have seen nothing went on between us, and I'm sure they'll have told the police."

I'm waiting for him to respond when I realise the line is dead. Christine ducks so close to her microphone that it obscures her expression. "Are you sure you're all right with this, Graham?"

"Why wouldn't I be? It's what I'm about," I assure her. "It's the real me." That's quite enough for the listeners not to hear, and I release the switch. "Now here's Manny from Cheetham Hill. Tell us why you've called in, Manny."

"You left out jews."

"Sorry." I'm not prepared for this, since the screen gives today as his subject. "Do you want to put them in?"

"D'you care?"

"Well, of course I—"

"D'you think and jew mind and jew cause and jew date. Watch out or they'll be banning all of those next, and it won't be jew to us."

So he's joking, and Jewishly to boot. "Better not even think of giving the devil his jew," I contribute.

"That's a cracker," Manny says, although I seem to sense resentment, perhaps because he didn't come up with that one himself. "We've had a long time to get used to it. Some of this new lot, they're going to have to. Nobody's got any right to tell the rest of us what to say."

"But you wouldn't want anybody to be made into a scapegoat, would you?"

"It's been sounding like some people want to make you into one. I'll tell you what you ought to do to shut them up."

"I'm not sure I want to do that. I mean, I don't. I wouldn't have a show without all you callers." Nevertheless I add "What?"

"Take a test on the air."

"A test," I repeat, which seems to leave even more meaning behind.

"A lie test. That'd shake up anyone that needs shaking."

"I suppose it might." I'm uncertain who he has in mind and bemused by his suggestion too. "Well, Manny," I have to say, "I see
the news bearing down on me, so—"

"Don't take it so serious. It's only a show."

This simply reminds me I've most of an hour's worth of calls still
to take on the far side of the one o'clock news. Before I can speak
again Manny has gone, and I leave the Wilde Card jingle playing
while I hurry to the water cooler. I gulp a cupful and refill the cup
and hurry back to the control room. "Keep them coming," I tell
Christine, since she clearly has a question. "Just try and make sure
who they are and what they want before you put them on."

24

THE HESITANT RESEARCHER

"Mary Chrystal speaking."

"Forgive me for calling you between funerals. I was wondering if you could tell me—I'm sorry, I don't know how you like to be addressed."

"No need to keep apologising. Call me Mary, of course. All my friends do."

"Well, thank you, Mary. Is it right you were officiating at the funeral before Sheila Cartwright's on Saturday?"

"Wasn't that Kylie Goodchild? Then yes, I was."

"I was wondering what you could tell me about the young man who seemed so upset."

"What would you like to know?"

"Why he was, if you've any idea."

"He was poor Kylie's boyfriend."

"Are you saying that's all? I realise it should be enough."

"Do you mean the argument he had outside the chapel afterwards?"

"I did see that."

"Mrs Goodchild called me about it later. Apparently Wayne felt the gentleman he spoke to shouldn't have been there."

"Why was that, do you know?"

"He, that's the gentleman, he's the host of a radio programme Kylie must have liked. Perhaps Wayne thought he was there for the publicity and not because he cared about her. I'm not saying that was the truth."

"Wayne, you said."

"Wayne Stanley. I had him down to speak about Kylie but when it came to it he couldn't. Sadly that's often the case."

"I wonder how I could get in touch with him."

"May I ask why, Mr . . . ?"

"Of course you can. The name, my name's Childer, by the way. I'd like to give him something that might help the situation."

"That's kind of you, Mr Childer. May I know what it is?"

"Just something personal. Would you happen to know where I can find him?"

"If you'd like to leave it here for me I could pass it on to him."

"I don't want to put you to any more trouble."

"You've put me to none at all yet, and that wouldn't be any either."

"Well, thank you," I murmur and end the call. I've asked her enough, and she has given me some of the information I need. Besides, keeping my voice low to disguise it has been quite a task, if not as much of one as carrying off the second half of today's Wilde Card, where I kept thinking callers might be cronies of Wayne's, whatever name they gave and wherever they said they were from. If they were using mobiles they could have called from anywhere, and I couldn't trust them to address the subject they said they'd called about until they finished speaking. In fact nobody referred to Kylie Goodchild, but I still felt as if she might bob up unannounced. When the show was done at last Christine told me she'd kept nobody off the air, which only left me suspecting she had.

I'm in her apartment, sitting on the pale plump firm sofa that barely admits to its pattern of delicate silvery leaves. Shelves are built into all four corners of the room, and whichever way I face I'm aware of books with names that end with question marks. The memorial brochure from the funeral identified Mary Chrystal, though I had to phone the chapel to discover which service she'd conducted next. I wish it listed the people who'd undertaken to speak, but at least it reminds me of the name of Kylie's school. It's St George's Comprehensive, and Christine's laptop gives me the phone number. "St George," says a secretary's brusque voice.

She sounds more like the dragon. She's certainly not inviting jokes, perhaps having been greeted with too many of them. I'm about to speak when she says "Tell me you're calling about the machine."

"Which machine is that?"

"The wretched computer."

"You're having problems with it."

"We never have anything else. Pen and paper's worked perfectly well ever since I've been here but no, we have to change it or we won't be up to date."

"You have all my sympathies. I'm sorry, though, I'm not the chap you're waiting for. I'm from attendance."

"Are you? You don't sound familiar."

"I won't, that's right. The person I expect you usually hear from is on holiday, and some of the details I need are locked up on, wouldn't you believe it, their computer. I'm guessing you'll know what that's like."

"It's just typical of those things." All the same, she pauses in order to think. "Won't he have a password? What's wrong with using that?"

"Unfortunately he didn't leave it with anyone, though I'm sure he's got nothing more to hide than I have."

"You'll know where he is, won't you? Can't you ring and ask?"

"Believe me, it's been tried, but he's either switched his mobile off or there's no signal where he is."

"Those things are more trouble than computers. Every child has one and they won't be told not to bring them into school. It's about time they stopped inventing things and gave the world a rest."

"Perhaps there ought to be a law."

"That'd be going a bit far." I'm afraid I may have until the secretary says "So why were you ringing up?"

"I'm about to make a home visit and I'd like to get some information I'm missing."

"Which of our pupils is it?"

"Wayne Stanley. I think we may have had to deal with him before."

"Which year is he in?"

"Do you know, I haven't even got that information. I don't especially need it, of course."

"Don't you?"

I'm hoping I didn't hear any suspicion in her voice. "It'll be either year ten or eleven, I'm certain."

"It's year ten," the secretary says like a rebuke to at least one of us and perhaps to her records as well. "What else are you asking for?"

I didn't need that information, and I'm worried in case it has used up my chance to ascertain something crucial. "Could you remind me of his father's name?"

"Remind?"

"It's possible I may have heard it, but I can't recall it for the moment."

"I should think you would if you had." Her silence makes me desperate to concoct another prompt until she says "The man responsible goes by the name of Eldridge Stanley."

"You're right, that's certainly one to remember. They live there in Middleton, don't they?" I have to take her lack of response as a yes and ask "Could you give me the address?"

"Haven't you got any of this anywhere? I know my records are in a mess just now, but really I'd have thought yours—"

"I'm not thinking, am I? I should know you won't be able to find it just now on your computer." A worse mistake is trying to obtain too much information from a single source; it enrages me to find I'm less deft than Frank Jasper. "I won't get in your way any more while you're waiting to hear about it," I tell her, not too hastily, I hope. "We're bound to have the address somewhere."

I manage to stop short of claiming I've just found it after all, though I hope it won't be long before I do. Less than a minute on the laptop shows me an Eldridge Stanley—the only one. He lives in Burgess Road in Harpurhey, which isn't far from Middleton, and the listing gives his phone number. Once I've worked out how to speak to him or Wayne or some unknown person who may answer, I make the call. I've grown infuriatingly tense with waiting for the ringtone to be interrupted by the time I cut it off.

At least now I know nobody's home, which may be helpful in itself. A search for the road produces an address just two doors away from Eldridge Stanley's—Nazir's News, Food and Video. Feeling confident now, I phone at once. I've begun to fear the shop is closed if not defunct when a voice protests "Hello, please."

He sounds weary, perhaps resentful of having been roused, and it seems best to ask "Is that Nazir's?"

"Yes, please."

If this is an invitation it's more dutiful than heartfelt. "I'm sorry to trouble you," I tell him. "I was wondering if you could help with one of your neighbours."

"Who is that, please?"

"Stanley from next door but one, if you know him."

His voice sharpens—it almost sounds awake. "Which Stanley, please?"

"The young one."

Before this has a chance to net me any information I hear the ringing slam of a cash register, and a less obviously Asian voice demands "Who is it, dad? Is it some of their mob?"

"Ali." Having warned his son in some way, the older man says "It is someone about Wayne."

"Is it one of his gang? Are the swines calling up now?"

"I do not think. He does not sound like them."

"Then let's hope it's the police. Here, let me talk to him." A confused noise suggests a struggle, and I assume a hand is attempting to muffle the mouthpiece while the father says "Take care." The noise ends, and Ali demands "Who—"

"Mr Nazir, I understand you and your family have been having some trouble with Wayne and his friends."

"Us and a lot of others. Who is this? Are you the police?"

"Just someone else like you, I'm afraid. I've been having problems with him as well."

"So what are you going to do about it?"

"I believe I can get him dealt with as he deserves if I collect enough evidence. Do you mind if I ask what you've had to put up with?"

"I don't mind in the slightest bit. It's about time someone asked. You'll have met the killer, will you?"

"Ali, have a care."

"He's not afraid to talk about the Stanleys, and it's a bloody sight past time we weren't either."

What have I just learned, and can it be true? "Killer," I repeat.

"That's what they call that brute of an animal."

I'm still not certain, but I have to risk sounding so. "You mean the dog."

"The one they say isn't illegal, but it should be."

"Like a few other things about Wayne."

"You won't hear me differing with that."

I need him to be more specific, and I'm enraged to catch myself wondering how Jasper would handle him. "It isn't just the dog that's been giving you a problem, is it?"

"He wouldn't be so big without it. They think they own the street."

"What are you saying it lets him do?"

Ali either doesn't like the question or is determined to stay with his theme. "It uses the street for a toilet. You should see the pavement outside here. I think it has been trained to go there."

"Have you approached anybody about it?"

"I would but my father thinks they would make life worse for us."

"You were saying what Wayne thinks he can get away with because of the dog."

"Not just him. Mr Stanley thinks the pavement is his personal car park, and there's woe betide anyone who says they haven't room to pass. You tell me how he affords a car like that with the job he does."

"Which job is that?"

"Scrap." With even more contempt Ali says "I call it rubbish."

"Ali, be more careful."

I'm willing him to be less so as I say "You think his home life has made Wayne what he is."

"Like the father like the son, do you mean? Or—"

Presumably this isn't true of the Nazirs, or so Ali wants to think, even if his English isn't quite as accurate as he seems to believe. "In their case I'd say it was."

"Wayne is responsible for what he does."

"We all are, but don't you think his family is too?"

"When they see what he does, most truly." Ali's grasp of the language appears to be deserting him as he grows more impassioned. "And when they do not do the single thing to stop him."

"What haven't they stopped?"

"Drinking with his friends in the street till all the hours and smoking what they smoke."

"The police must be interested in some of that, surely."

"If anybody dared calling them we would all be blamed."

"There's already been violence, has there?"

"Violence, I say so. I will talk."

His last words must be aimed at his father, who says "How do you know who you're speaking to? Suppose it is a trick?"

"He sounds a good man. You heard him." Closer to my ear Ali says "Yes, violence. There was a boy with the similar dog and Wayne set Killer on it."

"What happened?"

"The other dog was killed and Wayne's gang told the police it made the attack. A boy who will do that will do worse."

"And he has, hasn't—"

It isn't the ping of a bell that cuts me off, nor even realising that someone has entered Nazir's; it's hearing Ali's father speak at not much less than the top of his voice. "Mr Stanley," he says, by no means only as a greeting.

"We won't talk any more," I tell Ali and end the call at once.

I'm gazing at the blank screen of the laptop and wondering how much I've learned when I hear Christine's key in the lock. I switch off the computer and hurry past the prints of imaginary destinations to meet her. "How's your research going?" she says as she shuts us in. "Will it help your novel?"

"I'm sure it's going to be a help," I say, hugging her to hide my face.

25

THE NEW OWNERS

It's Raise Your Voice Day, and I'm more than ready to raise mine. The Frugo people are at Waves, and I mean to give them their money's worth. The day is supposed to encourage people who don't ordinarily speak up to make themselves heard, and I suspect some of my listeners may ring up to complain they're being silenced. If Paula and the bosses want controversy I don't expect to have to manufacture it. I just hope nobody brings up Kylie Goodchild.

The guard at his desk greets me with a wink. "I haven't told nobody anything."

"Honestly, Vince, all you need to tell is the truth."

He looks disappointed by my response. "Nobody asked."

On the top floor Megan glances up with a hint of a smile or at least a straight-lipped pledge of one. "Are the headsmen here yet?" I need to know.

I wouldn't have thought her lips could grow straighter, but they manage. "Who are you talking about?"

"The chaps with the axes. Our executioners." I should have realised by now that she lacks a sense of humour, or at any rate my kind, and so I say "The Frugo folk."

"They're with Paula. One of them's a woman."

She must resent my not having considered the possibility; she's acting as if I denied her a voice. "I hope they'll be listening to me."

"Why should you think they'll be doing that?"

"I imagine they'll be listening to every one of us. Even you, Megan."

I mean this more as a warning than an insult, but I don't much care how it sounds. Most of my colleagues are at their desks in the newsroom, intent on looking not just busy but essential. Presumably that's why those who glance at me return immediately to their work. I fill a plastic cup from the cooler and hurry into the control room, where the twelve o'clock news is just beginning overhead with no mention of Kylie Goodchild. I've borrowed Rick Till's routine and arrived with little time to spare, boosting my adrenaline, I hope. I wave at Christine and dash past her to chase Lofthouse out of the studio. "You're in the wrong place, Trevor."

He carries on donning the headphones but lifts the right earpiece. "I'm afraid you are, Graham."

Before I can argue Christine follows me into the studio. "You didn't give me a chance to say. Paula wants Trevor to take the phone-in."

"You're my understudy, are you, Trevor?"

"Just for today." He lets the earpiece down and adds "As far as I know."

"Why didn't anybody tell me sooner?"

"I was with the visitors when Paula arranged it," Christine says.

Trevor gazes at me as if I have no right to be there, and I tramp after Christine into the control room. "Were they interviewing you?" I murmur. "How did it go?"

"They haven't fired me yet." Before I can establish how much of a joke this is meant to be Christine says "They want you now."

"They sent you with the message, did they?"

"They said as soon as you came in."

I shouldn't appear to be blaming her—she looks anxious enough. I drain my cup on the way to the cooler, where I refill it and then knock on Paula's door. The sound seems oddly hollow, not least since it brings no response. I'm raising my fist to knock harder when somebody whispers "Conference room, Graham."

The voice is so stifled that I can't identify the speaker or even their gender. It puts me in mind of a nervous child in a school-room, trying surreptitiously to help a classmate with the answer to a question. The impression infuriates me, and I rap on the door of the conference room with quite a helping of my strength. I'm ex-pecting Paula's standard summons, but a man says "Yes, come in."

Three people are seated at the near end of the long table, well out of the rays of the sun. Paula has her back to the door and glances around at me. She's flanked by a man and an equally young woman, both of whom have the scrubbed bright-eyed look of evangelists; they remind me of the pairs who go from door to door. Their ex-pensive lightweight pale grey suits could almost be a uniform. "Graham Wilde?" the woman says, reaching a hand across a docu-ment folder that lies beside an open laptop. "I'm Meryl."

"Dominic," her colleague says and holds out a hand the instant she lets go of mine.

His handshake is no less firm and terse than hers—like hers, as smooth and cool as his precisely shaved face looks. He has a laptop and a folder too, lined up so nearly opposite hers that they might almost be playing at reflections. As Paula joins the visitors in ob-serving me, not so brightly in her case, Meryl says "Sit wherever you're comfortable, Graham."

Both laptops are tuned to Waves. Lofthouse's muffled voice feels multiplied, as if a pair of invisible but not entirely insubstantial headphones is clamped to my skull. I'm heading for a seat when the first caller says "Have you taken Graham off?"

"I don't think anyone would want to do that," Lofthouse says with a mumble of a laugh.

"Imitate him, I expect Trevor's saying," Paula wants the visitors to understand.

"We get that," Dominic says. "It's not too local."

"Not that local is necessarily bad," Meryl puts in.

I sit on her side of the table, leaving an empty seat between us. She switches off Wilde Card, but half the muted voice that's replaced mine lingers in the air until her colleague shuts down his laptop. I don't know what expression my face betrays, but Dominic says "Don't you think he's suited to the job?"

Of course this is a test, no doubt of loyalty, but it could be a trap as well. "He's perfectly good at his own. I just wish you'd heard me doing this one."

"We have," says Meryl.

"I'm glad." Nevertheless I'm anxious to learn "What did you play for them, Paula?"

She lifts her head, but her face stays as stiff as her hair. "We've been monitoring your output for some time," Dominic says.

Though he can't mean just mine, I feel I should say "Then I'm gladder."

Meryl rises to her feet at once, and I wonder what I've done until I realise she's turning her chair towards me. "Tell us why," she says.

"You'll have heard what I've been doing for you."

"What would you say that was?" says Dominic.

"For one thing, increasing the audience."

It's Meryl's turn again. "How do you feel you've done that?"

"I'm sure there are people listening who weren't before."

"Yes," Dominic says, "but how are you doing it? That was the question."

"We agreed I should take it as far as I could, didn't we, Paula?"

Before Paula has finished parting her lips Meryl says "What were you taking where, Graham?"

"Challenging people. Shaking their beliefs up," I say and keep my eyes on Paula. "You thought I should be a bit sharper with them."

"I believe I said you should be honest, Graham."

"What did you have in mind?" Dominic enquires without looking away from me.

"I wasn't suggesting he wasn't," Paula says, "or anyone else at Waves. I was encouraging him to make it central to his presentation on the air."

Her conference language must be designed to impress the visitors, but something seems not to have done so. After a pause as brief as her handshake and Dominic's, Meryl says "You feel it's your mission to challenge everyone's beliefs, Graham."

"I wouldn't go quite that far. I'd say—"

"We all need a mission in our lives."

It's plain how strongly she feels about this—she's taken Dominic's turn to speak—but he contributes "We like all the members of the Frugo family to have one."

"I didn't say I hadn't. I was going to say I question beliefs I think need it. You'll have heard a few that did."

"Are you leaving out your own?" says Meryl.

"I don't think anyone needs to know what those are. If a caller says, what can I think of, if they say something's black I'll do my best to prove it's white."

I've an odd sense of having chosen an unfortunate example until Paula breaks the silence. "No, Meryl's asking if you ever question yours."

I can't help hoping the visitors feel she has assumed too much, but when they only gaze at me I say "I'd like to think so."

"We felt you weren't too comfortable," Dominic says, "with alternative beliefs."

I'm close to giving him the kind of argument that I suspect Lofthouse isn't having on the phone-in. "Alternative to what?"

"Dominic's thinking of the psychic you've kept involving in your show," Meryl says. "What was his name again?"

"Frankie Patterson."

"Frank Jasper," Paula says with a blink at me that might denote reproach.

"We ought to remember," Dominic says. "We've heard the name often enough."

"What does he mean to you, Graham?" says Meryl.

"Not much at all. Not nearly as much as he thinks he does, as he thinks he means to anyone, I mean."

Paula in particular appears to be waiting for me to finish, but it's Dominic who says "You've been making quite a lot of him."

"Not half as much as he makes of himself."

"Some people," Meryl says, "could think he's the star of your show."

"Well, I'm sure you don't. I shouldn't fancy even you do, Paula."

Dominic turns to her as Meryl says "Why even Paula?"

"I'm waiting to hear that myself," Paula lets everyone know.

"You asked me to invite him in the first place, if you remember. You thought he was what we needed. I don't know if you two both heard that."

As the visitors meet this with matching neutral looks I realise that although they may have listened to that edition of Wilde Card, Paula's instructions won't have been recorded. I gaze at her until she says "He could have brought an alternative element to your show."

Surely the Frugo duo must see that she's just trying to sound like Dominic if not Meryl as well. "What do you think he brought, Graham?" Dominic says. "After all, it's your name on the show."

"Exploitation of the gullible. A few cheap stage tricks. Pretending he's someone and something he's not." I don't say any of this aloud; it's obvious that the trick is to sound positive, and so I tell the three of them "Publicity for us."

"There are different kinds, Graham," Meryl says.

"True enough, but as you say, everything we do is advertising."

"I don't remember saying that."

"Nor do I," says Dominic.

"Actually, it was your line, Paula."

"Let's try and concentrate on your Mr Jasper," Meryl says. "The way you presented him on the air was up to you."

I don't know how many rebukes I've just been given, but I can do without all of them. My rage at being harassed by or rather about Jasper yet again is rising closer to the surface. "He had something to do with it too."

"Not when he wasn't there," Dominic says.

"Though you did have him on your programme twice," Meryl points out.

"Forgive me for saying, Paula, but you brought him in that time."

"It wouldn't have been Paula," Dominic says, "who put him on the air."

"You told me to, didn't you, Paula? Once he was in the studio you wanted him to have the mike."

"I'm afraid you're mistaken, Graham. I was trying to remind you that you were live."

I recall her nodding through the window at the microphone. If she didn't mean what I assumed, why didn't she make it clear then? I manage to control my rage by saying "Anyway, you were happy afterwards with how I'd handled the situation."

Before Paula can voice the response that I see in her eyes Meryl says "Did you take the decision to cut him off, Graham?"

"I had to clear the studio," Paula says at once.

"You did rather seem to be losing control, Graham."

"I don't think I did at all under the circumstances. I'd any number of people crowding into the studio when as Paula says it was live. I don't know if she's told you she had to call security to get rid of one of them."

"You don't think you're losing it now," Dominic says.

"I don't. I never do. If I didn't have it I couldn't carry on here."

"No need to take it the wrong way," Meryl says. "There's nothing wrong with caring about your job."

However she means this, surely they must realise it applies to Paula too. Paula is a good deal more defensive than I am, and worse than that as well—not far from an outright liar. Even if I can't risk saying this I can put some of it into my eyes, and I'm meeting her stiff gaze when Dominic asks me "How would you describe Wilde Card in a sound bite?"

"Letting people have their say but making them think about it."

"That's quite a big but," Meryl says, "do you think?"

I'm on the edge of a joke no better than the worst of Benny's when Dominic comments "A bit cumbersome for an ad."

"Not a phone-in," Meryl says, "not a drone-in."

As I deduce she's enthusing about the slogan Paula says "You weren't too fond of that one, Graham, were you?"

"I came up with it, though."

"We'd hope you'd think that's part of your commitment, Graham." Before I can tell Meryl I wasn't complaining she adds "Did you have thoughts about changing your show?"

Is she referring to Hannah Leatherhead's proposal? If so they can't realise it's no longer in the game, but I won't be the first to bring it into the open. Instead I say "I wouldn't mind doing more interviews."

"Have you had much experience with those?" says Dominic.

"The only way to get that is to do it, don't you think?" When he turns up his left hand on the table but leaves the other one palm down, a gesture that suggests some kind of trick, I say "You heard the interview I did."

"You've Mr Jasper in mind again, have you?" Meryl says. "You do seem rather concerned with him."

"I'd say he was obsessed with me."

"Nobody said you were obsessed, Graham." Dominic gives me a moment to sift this for meaning and says "We've been hearing quite a lot about him."

"What sort of thing?" I feel I also need to ask "From whom?"

"On your show, he means," says Meryl.

I mustn't assume they're colluding in the kind of verbal ma-
noeuvre Patterson might use, but I have to struggle to suppress my
rage. "Maybe you didn't hear enough."

"What would you like us to hear?" Dominic prompts.

"Not you. Everyone, not just you, I mean. I wish I'd said on the
air who he was and how I knew before he fiddled it onto his web
site."

"Instead of pretending to have some of his talents, you mean."

"I hope I'll never be so desperate, supposing he has any." In a moment I realise what Dominic has in mind. "You're saying I should
have told the listeners how I read his past. You thought I shouldn't,
didn't you, Paula? You wanted me to keep them in the dark."

A minute frown pinches the skin between Meryl's eyes. As I
wonder if she'll say I'm obsessed with Paula too she enquires
"Didn't you want your listeners to think that was how you were led
to the girl who drowned?"

"Why in God's name and anyone else's you'd like to throw in
would I have wanted that? I was being ironic about, I'm sorry to
bring him up one more time, Frankie Jasper again. Maybe I should
stop if it isn't obvious."

"It wasn't publicity for your show," says Dominic.

"That's right, it wasn't." I'm instantly unsure that he was asking
a question; could it have been a rebuke? "And attending Kylie
Goodchild's funeral wasn't meant that way either," I protest. "Her
father wanted me there."

Meryl nods but frowns faintly as well. "You said your shows
weren't meant to be about you."

Did I tell her that? No, she heard me tell a listener. "I'd say they
aren't, yes."

"But another time," Dominic says, "you told someone there
should be a Presenter Awareness Day."

"That was a joke." I don't know how much of my rage escapes as I add "Obviously I'm no good at those."

"You just need to be aware what impression you're presenting," Meryl says.

The renewed silence has to be designed to make me speak. "Which do you think I am?"

"Rather on the defensive yesterday, we thought," says Dominic.

"Just like Paula's been today, you mean." I keep this to myself, instead saying "You heard what I had to deal with. How would you have handled it?"

"Perhaps some of it shouldn't have been broadcast," Meryl says.

I'm not about to blame Christine, and I won't give Paula the chance. "If that's anybody's fault it's mine. What do you think I oughtn't to let through in future?"

"Some of the content was bordering on racist," Dominic says. "That's got no business being part of Frugo's image."

"What, the chap who made the Jewish jokes? He was Jewish himself. They're allowed if anybody is, surely."

"They're talking about some of your comments," Paula says.

I take hold of the plastic cup, only to find I've drained it. "Can we hear what I'm meant to have said?"

"We already have." Meryl lets me glimpse sympathy as she says "It won't help to go over what you meant. We've established it's the impression that counts."

"I'd rather have the truth."

"Would you?" Dominic says, and I have the notion that he and Meryl are refraining from sharing a glance. "I should think your listeners might too. We know one would."

I let go of the cup before it splinters and hide my fists under the table so as to clench them. My mouth isn't far from sharing the contraction as I demand "Which one?"

"Your Jewish caller."

So Dominic didn't have Jasper in mind after all, and I lay my open hands on the table. "Because he thought whatever people say about us can't really harm us, you mean."

"No," Meryl says as if she thinks I've made a not especially appropriate joke, "because he thought you should take a lie detector test."

"It certainly oughtn't to do any harm," says Paula.

"Especially not to your ratings," Dominic says.

I can't hide my hands again so soon, and I manage not to dig my nails into the table. "If we're talking about impressions mine are that those tests are for criminals and liars, and I'm sure many of our listeners would think so too."

I can't judge what kind of silence I've provoked until Meryl says "We both took one."

"It's standard practice in Frugo recruitment," says Dominic.

"Does that mean everybody here will have to take one?"

Perhaps I shouldn't have been looking so directly at Paula, who retorts "Will you, Graham?"

"What sort of thing are we talking about?"

"Demonstrating your innocence once and for all," Meryl says.

"On the air," Dominic says, "of course."

I don't know why that should be taken for granted. Before I can say at least this much Paula says "There's a good deal riding on it, Graham."

"Well, if it's for Waves . . ." I give them time to appreciate my loyalty, but I still have to say "I'll do it. I've nothing to hide."

"We'll arrange it," Meryl says.

"Let's make it as soon as possible," Paula says and stands up at once.

I could imagine she's eager to see the arrangements made immediately until she adds "Shall we break for lunch now? You've a lot still to deal with."

Since she isn't looking at anybody in particular, I'm not sure if any of this is addressed to me. As I push myself away from the table I'm disconcerted by my sweaty handprints, which glisten until I rub them out with my sleeve. At least nobody else appears to have noticed them; in fact, Paula and the visitors seem happy to ignore me now that I've agreed to put on their choice of a show. Paula opens the door and turns to me. "Here's the news," she says, and I might assume she's about to give me some or referring to me if she didn't add "You'd better take over the phone-in. We don't want anybody wondering about you, Graham."

26

SITTING THE TEST

"It's Bite Your Tongue Day, but I won't be doing that. I haven't taken any sedatives or sprayed deodorant on my fingers, and there aren't any tacks in my shoes. You've checked that, haven't you, Jeremy? Introduce yourself to the listeners before I go on."

"I'm Jeremy Kessler, and I'm a polygraph examiner."

"The things I was mentioning are ways people try and cheat the test, but they aren't going to fool the experts, are they?"

"Nobody's ever succeeded with me."

"Jeremy comes with the job now we're owned by Frugo. Anyone who wants to join their team has to pass your test first, isn't that right, Jeremy?"

"There are more of us than me but yes, I think it's right that your employer's entitled to look into your character."

"Watch out, people. Pretty soon we'll have no secrets where we work or anywhere else." Perhaps I might have left this unsaid, to judge by Christine's look through the studio window. "Nothing personal, Jeremy," I try saying. "It's my choice that we're both here."

He gives such an unhurried nod I could fancy his large squarish head is descending into a doze. His eyelids are heavy enough, though this might be one way he puts his subjects at their ease—too much of it unless they're careful. All his movements appear studied, and his head looks weighed down by a mass of greyish hair, samples of which lurk beneath the surface of his jowls and jutting chin. "Just for today," I tell the listeners, "Wilde Card isn't taking any calls, so all of you out there will have to bite your tongues until tomorrow. For one day only it's all about me. I'm wired up to a polygraph, and it feels like nothing so much as being in hospital . . ."

In fact I know very little about that—I've always been the healthy type—but I certainly feel like a patient in some kind of ward. Two rubber tubes are wrapped around my midriff to catch variations in my breath. I'm wearing a puffed-up cuff on my upper left arm to monitor my blood pressure, and two of my right fingertips are fitted with detector plates to measure any sweat. All these devices are wired to Kessler's laptop, which sits on the console with the back of its screen towards me. Describing all this makes me feel oddly fragmented, as if both my voice and my sensations have become detached from me, even though I'm not wearing headphones. It's some relief to ask Kessler "Do you want to explain anything?"

"We've taken an hour to agree on the test questions." Even his voice is deliberate, and just a shade more amiable than neutral. "And we've got to know each other, would you say, Graham?"

"So long as you know me that's fine, but I don't mind saying it's mutual."

One thing I'm sure he doesn't know. While the laptop is hiding its face from me, the screen is dimly reflected low down on the window beyond the corner of the console. I can make out vague stripes on the indistinct rectangle, and they aren't entirely static. "Are you going to tell everyone about the test?" I prompt Kessler.

"I'll be asking some control questions and the ones you've chosen to answer."

"Just in case anybody isn't clear, you mean the ones we chose together." When he gives another ponderous nod I say "And how is all this going to work?"

"The control questions let me measure your reactions to compare them with the rest."

"Which you'll be asking because—" I don't need him to explain. "In case," I say, "there are any rumours that need killing off."

"What kind of rumours, Graham?"

The blurred reflection of the top line jerks. I take it for the anger graph, though it puts me in mind of a disturbance in water. He knows the answer perfectly well, but perhaps he thinks the listeners should. "About Kylie Goodchild," I inform anyone who should know. "Shall we get started? I'd like you to give us the results before we're off the air."

"My name is Jeremy Kessler and I'm conducting a polygraph examination of Graham Wilde. Have we been on the air all the time, Graham?"

"We still are." When he raises his head less than an inch, as if the task requires some effort, I say "Sorry, was that my first mistake, my only one? Were you asking a control question?"

"That's correct, Graham."

"Just let me tell the listeners I'm only allowed to answer yes or no. Go ahead, Jeremy, ask me again."

"Has everything we've said been broadcast?"

"Yes."

All three indistinct lines give a discreet flutter, which I assume makes it clear that I'm speaking the truth, or are they hinting at my reservations? I wish Kessler hadn't changed the wording of the question. "That's to say," I'm driven to add, "everything we've said since we came on the air. Do you mind if I just explain something else?"

"No."

He might almost be demonstrating how to answer questions; his response is weighty enough for a rebuke. "We decided you'd run the test in here because it's where I'm used to," I tell the unseen audience. "And we didn't want to record it beforehand in case anybody thought it had been edited."

I'm not implying either of us would tamper with the results. It was Paula's idea to broadcast the test live, no doubt also to attract a bigger audience. "All right," I say as Kessler gives me a slow blink, "ask me whatever you've got to ask."

His gaze sinks to the monitor. "Do you have a girlfriend, Graham?"

"Yes."

I'm allowed to say so, aren't I? I send Christine a wry hopeful smile, which she seems to find unnecessary. I've just glimpsed the blurred lines flexing themselves when Kessler says "Have you kept any secrets from her?"

"Yes."

I give Christine another smile that tries to communicate a good deal—an apology, a reassurance that she knows exactly what I mean and that she's learned all my secrets by now. Is this too much for the polygraph to sort out? The indistinct lines seem troubled, and when I glance back at Christine her face is as good as blank. "Did you ever see Kylie Goodchild," Kessler says, "after her school class visited this radio station?"

"No."

I hold Christine's gaze until it softens or at least grows better than resigned. The lines jerk at the edge of my vision, but they do every time I tell the truth. "Do you remember anything you said to her?" says Kessler.

"Still not a word." I'd like to say that, and I hope the sense of it is conveyed by my solitary syllable. "No."

"Do you work at this radio station?"

"Yes."

The dim lines stir—I'd describe the movement as an electronic shrug. I'm suppressing my resentment at the thought of Hannah Leatherhead when Kessler says "Did you ever see Kylie Goodchild after her school class visited this radio station?"

"No." I have to look away from him at once, to see what Christine makes of the repetition. She's waiting to give me a frown that's puzzled if not worse, and I feel as if I've kept another secret from her. "I'd better explain," I tell Kessler. "It's your standard method, isn't it? You always ask the test questions more than once."

"We repeat them when it's necessary."

Do I sense resentment? Perhaps he dislikes revealing the tricks of his trade, in which case I could easily be reminded of Frank Jasper. I hope nobody thinks I keep interrupting the test for any reason of my own, and so I say "Well, go ahead."

"Is your name Graham Wilde?"

"No."

Kessler rests his gaze on the monitor before scrutinising me with no gain in his expression. "Sorry," I say and try adding a laugh, which seems to tug at the tubes around my midriff. "Even you need an explanation this time, don't you? It isn't my whole name."

"You might have told me when we were getting acquainted."

"I might if I'd thought you'd bring it up, but I don't mind admitting the rest of it's my secret. Well, it isn't any more. It's Herbert, Graham Herbert Wilde, and maybe you can understand why I buried it."

Does Kessler think I'm being too talkative again? This is my show, after all—still my show. His silence prompts me to ask "Did you want to say anything?"

"It's a family name."

"That's right, my father's. I'd rather not go further into it, if you don't mind."

With as little expression as his face betrays, Kessler says, "My family."

"Good God, I'm sorry. Not that you've got it in your family, I mean." I hope the laugh that overtakes me sounds remorseful; it's hard to judge while my reaction feels fettered by the rubber tubes. "Please don't be offended," I say. "Ask me why I have a problem with it if you like."

"That isn't the style of question I ask."

"Sorry again. I don't suppose you've conducted a session like this in your entire career." When his face doesn't change it provokes me to add "I do have to entertain the listeners, you know. That's part of why we're here."

He has to be concealing some emotion, but I could fancy he's as devoid of them as the computer. I can feel my anger rising to fill the vacuum. How might it affect the polygraph? I mustn't clench my fists; my hands are outstretched on the fake leather arms of the chair. One of the reflected lines is performing a series of impatient jerks, which I attempt to soothe by saying "At least you can tell I'm not trying to hide anything. I can't keep my mouth shut, you may think. I can't unless you speak."

"Are you ready to continue?"

"Yes."

I don't know if I've driven him to put the question or even if it's meant to monitor my response, and the doubt may be why the lines give quite a jig. Perhaps he's establishing that we've returned to the test, because he says "Did we agree in advance what I was going to ask you?"

"Yes."

This isn't strictly true. We didn't discuss the control questions—this one, for instance. I could feel his method is as devious as Jasper's. The idea enrages me, and I wish I'd clenched my fists as soon as he attached the plates to my fingertips; presumably that way it wouldn't have skewed any of the readings on the monitor. I can't tell if it's my anger or the ambiguity of the question that troubles the indistinct lines, and I'm close to protesting when Kessler says "Did you know where Kylie Goodchild was before you found her and called the police?"

"No."

The blurred lines twitch. They do at any of my answers, but I've started to wish they weren't visible. Suppose my concern with the graphs affects them? Would trying to ignore them do so as well? I'm nowhere near deciding by the time Kessler says "Have you ever told a lie?"

"Yes." I let him open his mouth again before I add "But not today."

For some reason the graphs are unhappy with at least the second part of my answer. If I am, why shouldn't they be? They've no business contradicting me, and I struggle not to close my fists. Kessler pauses for an inexpressive moment and says "Do you know for certain how Kylie Goodchild met her death?"

The cuff seems to take a firmer grip on my upper arm while the tubes tighten around my midriff. I composed the question for the benefit of Wayne and anyone who shares whatever suspicions he was trying to express. I hope Christine understands this, though she seems to be attempting to outdo Kessler's blank look. "No," I declare while I hold her gaze.

The ill-defined lines at the edge of my vision do their best to divert my attention. I can't help feeling they represent how my voice has become separate from me. They subside as Christine risks a subdued though encouraging smile, and Kessler says "Do you ever wish you were somewhere else?"

I'd suspect him of wry humour if it weren't for the situation. Perhaps he has some, though there's none in his eyes when I look. "Yes," I tell him and hold up the hand that isn't wired, isolating the answer before I add "But not now, in case anyone's wondering."

Kessler matches my pause and says "Do you know for certain how Kylie Goodchild met her death?"

The rubber cuff feels as though it's holding me for interrogation, but I don't mind giving him the answer. "No," I say and only just refrain from sending Christine a wink.

"Were you ever in a fight when you were a child?"

How is this relevant? It isn't, of course. It's simply a control question Kessler might ask any of his subjects; it's not unlike a Jasper trick. Mustn't being attacked by my father count? I don't want anyone to think I've a reason to procrastinate, and so I answer "Yes."

"Did you know where Kylie Goodchild was before you found her and called the police?"

"No."

I raise my eyebrows to invite the next question, if indeed the test isn't over. I'm about to ask whether that's the case when Kessler says "Do you know for certain how Kylie Goodchild met her death?"

It's the most important question. I don't mind answering it a third time if it helps to establish the truth. As I open my mouth I glimpse a convulsive movement from the corner of my eye. Surely it can't be the scribbling that describes my voice or the emotions I'm supposed to feel. No, Christine is waving at me, and points at the spread fingers of her right hand before twirling a finger in the air. Somehow we're five minutes away from the news. "No," I say and nod at Christine. "Please don't anybody think I'm asking for a break, but we're going to have to take one."

"Graham's saying his producer has given us the sign." Kessler rests his heavy uncommunicative gaze on my face and says "Do you want the results of your test now?"

For a distracted instant I mistake it for another control question. "Yes," I say, of course. I mean it more than any other answer I've given him, and the graphs leap eagerly as well.

27

RATING THE ANSWERS

Kessler didn't mean immediately. By the time Wilde Card is overtaken by the news he's still tabulating his results. I don't want anyone to think I'm anxious to leave the test behind, and so I stay tethered to the polygraph and tell the listeners I am. When Trevor Lofthouse gazes at me on his way to the next studio I have the absurd but not entirely welcome notion that he's about to include me in the news, but the first report isn't even about Kylie Goodchild. Gangs that used to stay on their home turf are venturing into the city centre now; one lot took every bottle of Frugalky cocktails off the shelves of a Frugo Corner store in broad daylight and kicked the security guard senseless when he tried to make them pay up. As I wonder if this item leads the news because it concerns our employers, Christine gestures at me to put my headphones on. "You kept that going well," she says, adding a tentative smile.

"You think I've still got it, whatever it is I've got."

"I didn't know if it was a good idea to do this live, but now I'm sure it was."

Kessler has lifted his head, though not far. "Why's that?" I'm keen to learn.

"Because you made it into a show," Christine says. "You kept the listeners guessing."

"I'd rather they knew I've nothing to hide." Kessler's head sinks with the weight of an untypical frown as I say "I was asking why you didn't think it was a good idea."

"I wasn't sure if you'd be able to stay in control."

"Trust me, I'm a professional."

"Do you feel like being more of one?"

"I feel fine." The blurred graph doesn't seem to contradict me, but I don't want her to think I'm incapable of a straightforward answer. "Yes," I say and wait.

"Only Megan has been getting calls from listeners who wanted to talk to you while you were wired up."

"Why not? I'll take anybody on. I'd better ask the man in charge, though." As Lofthouse tells us how much heat the air conditioning will have to fend off I say to Kessler "Some of our listeners want to call in while you've got me on the polygraph."

He gazes at the monitor until I have to break the silence with an ad for Moptimum, Frugo's new all-purpose household cleaner. "You know that isn't how it works," he says. "I agree just a few questions with the subject beforehand."

"If the test's over, why am I still hooked up?"

"Because of the unusual circumstances," Kessler says without raising his head or his eyes, "I was asked to keep you monitored till I've finished with you."

Presumably he means because we're live. The ad comes to an end with the disconcerting sound of a mirthful vacuum cleaner, and I bring us back on the air. "I'm afraid we're going to have to disappoint anyone who wants a word with me today. Jeremy's the only one allowed to question me, and you're done, aren't you, Jeremy?"

"That's correct, yes."

"So are we going to hear the results?"

"That's the procedure."

He's beginning to put me in mind of a machine—an extension of the computer. He gazes at the screen for so long that I wonder if he has forgotten we're on the air. I'm about to fill in with a comment when he says "I asked you whether you remembered anything you said to Kylie Goodchild."

"You did."

He brings his gaze to bear on me, if only to make clear that he didn't expect me to speak. "The results were positive. In my judgment you were telling the truth."

"Absolutely right. I'll vouch for your machine."

This earns me the same heavy look, but I need to enliven the show if he means to evaluate my answers one by one. Perhaps he understands that some variety is called for, because he says "The rest of the results . . ."

Has he found that he isn't at home on the air? I'm sure I sense discomfort. I let the suspense build for a few moments, but we can't have too much silence. "Go on," I urge him. "Give us the rest."

"For the remainder of the questions," he says and gazes at me without blinking, "the results were inconclusive."

I'm aware of a flurry of movement somewhere at the limit of my vision. Christine hasn't risen to her feet; she's peering at me across the console, looking as bewildered as I feel. I must have glimpsed the jagged response of the graphs. My voice in the headphones sounds dislocated if not unfamiliar. "What do you mean?"

"Did you ever see Kylie Goodchild after her school class visited this radio station? Did you know where she was before you found her and called the police? Do you know for certain how she met her death?"

"No. No." I don't know how often I've given this answer, but I can't repeat it too frequently, since it's the truth. I glare at the blurred jerking lines as I say even more angrily "No."

Kessler gazes at me almost long enough to make me need to

speak again. "I was reminding you exactly what questions you answered."

"And I was asking you what does it mean, the results were inconclusive."

"Not positive or negative enough to be susceptible to a definite
interpretation."

"In other words you're saying you can't read them."

"No, I'm saying I can't find you were telling the truth."

"And you can't say I was lying either, which I most certainly was
not. Maybe you didn't ask me the questions often enough. Do you
want to let them have another chance?" Even if this sounds like an
attack on his expertise, I'm more concerned with the impression
he's giving of me. "All right," I say as his gaze remains wearily blank,
"you did just ask them again. Did it make a difference?"

Kessler shakes his head, which seems almost to rob him of the
energy to say "No."

"Well then, let's see if we can work out what must have gone
wrong. Yes, wait a minute." I'm addressing Christine too, since she
has taken hold of her microphone. "Maybe the questions were," I tell
Kessler. "I'm not just blaming you, I came up with some of the wording, but they aren't as precise as they might have been, are they?"

As if he's heard the objection before he says "What do you think
was imprecise?"

"For a start, asking whether I saw Kylie Goodchild after her class
were here. Sadly, I saw her when the police found her." When Kessler only gazes at me I say "Same thing for the next question. I did
know where she was before I found her. I knew she'd been here."

He seems reluctant to offer me so much as an expression, and so
I glance at Christine. I haven't had time to read her face when she
ducks towards the microphone. She parts her lips but turns to see
what has distracted my attention. Paula's door has flown open, and
she's striding across the newsroom.

She doesn't stop until she reaches the control room. Her words to Christine don't look by any means as muted as the window makes them. She gestures at my microphone, and as she shoves the studio door wide I play in the first item that comes to hand—the Moptimum advert again. "I want to involve the listeners," she tells Kessler.

"I should think they are involved."

It's the closest to a joke I've heard him venture. Perhaps he doesn't even mean it as one, though Paula seems to think he does. Rather more sharply she says "I've just had several of them insist on speaking to me. They think they should have the opportunity to talk to Graham while you have him rigged up, and I can't see why anybody should have a problem."

"I can't take responsibility for the results."

"No," Paula says, "I'm responsible."

I'm amused to see Kessler rebuked, and I say "I've already said I'll take on all comers."

"Just remember you're still representing Waves and Frugo. Give Mr Kessler some phones." As Paula leaves the studio she says "I've told Christine to put anybody through that wants to talk."

The Moptimum cleaner utters its vacuous laugh, and then my voice fills the headphones. "We're changing format by special request. Anyone with a question can ring in after all. I'm still attached to your machine, aren't I, Jeremy?"

"That's what your manager wanted."

While I wouldn't have minded taking the credit for continuing the test, it's time someone else held Paula responsible for a change. She's just outside the control room, watching me and Christine if not Kessler. When a name and a location appear on my monitor I wish I'd thought to ask Christine to display the question too. "Mavis from Wilmslow," I say. "What do you have for us, Mavis?"

"Are you wishing you hadn't taken your test?"

"Not really, no. Sorry, Jeremy, do you still want me to say just yes or no? I'd better explain that Jeremy isn't completely happy with carrying on."

"It will be closer to the real thing if you only give the standard answers."

"Did you catch that, Mavis? Could you ask me again?"

"Do you wish you'd never taken the test?"

"No." As the indistinct lines subside I say "I'm guessing Paula would like you to tell us the result, Jeremy."

Beyond the windows Paula's expression grows as artificially stiff as her hair. I could think she dislikes being read, in which case she shouldn't have inflicted Jasper and now Kessler on me. "Inconclusive," says Kessler.

It sounds less like an observation than a protest at the routine he's being forced to perform. As Paula heads for her office Mavis says "I should think anyone would feel that way."

"Well, thank you, Mavis," I say, since she seems to be offering some form of encouragement. "Now here's Benny from the city centre. What's your question, Benny?"

"Everything comes if you wait long enough. I've got on your show at last, Mr Wubbleyou."

Before he spoke I was afraid I'd recognised him—afraid of the kind of contribution he may plan to make. "Benny is the barman at the Dressing Room. He's famous for his jokes, but none of those on here today, Benny, agreed?"

"I'll bite my tongue." Even this sounds too much like the threat of a quip until he says "Don't you reckon tests like this are just a bit of a laugh?"

"No." I wait for the graphs to finish wriggling, and then I say "Not this one. Not for me."

"How's that answer shaping up, Mr Keester, is it?"

"Kessler." Either he has no time for jokes or doesn't realise it was one. Just as tonelessly he says "Inconclusive."

"He's a man of few words, isn't he, Mr Wubbleyou? Sounds like his catch phrase. None too keen on committing hisself, do you reckon?"

"I'm sure Jeremy's doing his best."

"I expect you've got to say that, eh? See you in the bar next time you need your usual. Just don't go giving away any of your secrets in there. Never know who may be flapping their lugs."

I could have done without most if not all of this. Once he rings off I say to Kessler "Don't let Benny bother you. He just likes to have a laugh with people. He doesn't mean any harm."

"You don't need to mean it to do it."

"I've never known him to do any either."

Kessler's gaze remains so inexpressive that it suggests I've missed some point, but I haven't time to wonder. Is Christine screening out callers who spoke to Paula about me? I can't see why Mavis or Benny would have insisted. "Here's Leona from my old home of Hulme," I say and feel as if the headphones are extracting my voice. "Remember I have to answer either yes or no."

"Is there anything you haven't told the police?"

"Yes." I'm tempted to leave it at that, trusting nobody to misunderstand, but perhaps there are listeners who might deliberately do so. "I wouldn't know where to begin," I say. "We'd be here all summer."

"You know good and well what I mean. Is there anything you haven't told them about Kylie Goodchild they should know?"

"No."

It sounds like an echo, but the graphs leap to my defence; the blurred lines jerk, at any rate. When gazing at Kessler fails to prompt him I say "Jeremy?"

In the pause before he speaks I'm convinced he's about to deliver a verdict other than "Inconclusive."

"You're sure of that," I say, though it sounds like a bad joke.

"It's all I can say under the circumstances."

"You're saying he can't prove he told the truth," Leona interjects. "Or otherwise."

I would have said that, though with a good deal more conviction, if Kessler hadn't been speedy for once. "So are you satisfied, Leona?"

"Not with either of you."

I could imagine Kessler's eyes are hiding rage, or am I finding my own anger in them? I can't hear mine as I say "Now we have Patrick from Chorlton. What can I tell you, Patrick?"

"Do you think you deserve to be tested like this?"

As far as I can see the answer's yes, and that's the one I give him. The graphs are readier with a response than Kessler, but when I raise my eyebrows high enough to make me blink he says "Inconclusive."

I've finally grasped that it's all he is prepared to say—that he won't commit himself while he thinks the conditions aren't ideal— but I'm not about to seem reluctant to answer any questions. No, I don't know why Kylie Goodchild was interested in me. No, I don't believe I know more about her than Frank Jasper. No, I don't think being owned by Frugo will reduce the quality of Waves. Yes, Kylie's parents had the right to employ Jasper, though I'm glad the caller didn't ask if I think they were right to do so. I feel as if I'm trapped in a parody of Wilde Card; in fact, I feel like a fairground exhibit at whom all comers can lob questions in a bid to win, though I can't imagine what the prize would be. At least the two o'clock news will release me soon, and meanwhile here's Lester from Middleton. "You look like our final caller, Lester, so make it a good one."

"Can I talk to the feller?"

"No," I say—humorously, I hope—since Kessler has shaken his head. "Now you can't tell us that was inconclusive, Jeremy."

"I'm not here to take calls."

"Was that all you wanted, Lester?"

"The machine's still on, is it?"

"Yes."

I'm about to ask whether that was his question—it would certainly provide a parodic end to the last two hours—when Lester
demands "Can't the feller say if that's the truth?"

When Kessler barely even shakes his head I say "I'm sorry, he's
not prepared. I promise you I'm still attached, so take your shot."

"Tell the feller to watch the machine." Presumably he doesn't
mean me to repeat this, because he says "Here's all we want to
know. Did you kill Kylie?"

My vision seems to shudder. Perhaps it's just a movement at its
edge; Christine has jerked her head up, or the blurred lines have
grown as spiky as my rage. Only Kessler seems monolithically un-
affected. When I glance at Christine she looks apologetic, not to
mention troubled. "It's all right," I mouth so fiercely that it tugs a
scowl low on my forehead, and then I say "Do I know you?"

"I knew you'd never answer that," Lester says in a tone like an
embittered smirk.

"I certainly will, you've my word on that, but we've got time to
talk. Is your name really Lester?"

"Fucking right it is. It's not me that doesn't tell the truth."

I'm suddenly afraid that Paula will insist on taking him off the
air before I can answer his question. "Please don't say things like
that, use words like that, I mean. I apologise if I mistook you for
somebody else." I'm still not entirely convinced he isn't Wayne, but
I mustn't waste any more time on it. "Now please go ahead," I say,
"and ask me your question again."

He's silent while the studio clock ticks off several seconds. I
stare at Paula's door, but it doesn't open. Kessler has fixed his gaze
on the polygraph monitor, and Christine is visibly trying not to
look worried for me. I'm about to prompt Lester afresh when he
says "Did you kill Kylie?"

"No." When the blurred lines jab at the air I repeat "No."

"That's what they call a double one at school, isn't it?" I have the grotesque fancy that Lester means to discuss grammar with me until he adds "Let the feller say what the machine said."

"Yes, tell everyone, Jeremy. Please just tell them exactly what you see for once."

I succeed in leaving the last two words unspoken, and I hope he doesn't sense them. I know Christine is gazing hard at me, but I don't want to meet her eyes until I've heard from Kessler. He stares at the monitor and then lifts his stare to me. It contains no more emotion than his voice does. "Inconclusive," he says as if the word weighs almost too much to utter.

28

CREATING A SCENE

Before Kessler has finished stripping me of wires and tubes Rick Till rushes into the studio. He might be desperate to help or simply urging me to leave. He peers at us both and rakes his scalp with a comb as though trying to enliven his brain. Eventually he asks me or Kessler "How did it go?"

"I'll say it for you, shall I, Jeremy?" When Kessler carries on removing the pads from my fingertips—it seems to me that he's taking more care with the equipment than he expended on me—I intone "Inconclusive."

"Oh." Till pockets the comb and rubs the ridges of his forehead so hard it's audible. "I don't suppose that's bad, is it?"

"I'd say it wasn't anything, or maybe that's what it is." Now that I'm off the air I scarcely know what I'm saying; I feel released from having to watch my words and not far from hysterical. As soon as Kessler unshackles my arm with a ripping of Velcro I lurch to my feet and hurry into the control room. I'm anxious to speak to Christine—to ask "What's the news?"

She frowns and does her best to add a reassuring smile. "I don't know if there's any yet."

"Not about me." In fact that's precisely my concern, and as Lofthouse warns us to expect more heat I say "What was Trevor reporting?"

"The same as last time."

If he'd referred to me she would surely tell me. Perhaps my last two hours are already growing insignificant, or will do once whoever heard the show finds another target for their views. Christine's about to start producing Rick Till Five, but I can't wait to ask "What did you think of all that?"

She glances past me and gives a sharp nod. Kessler is struggling to let himself and his apparatus out of the studio, and I hasten to get rid of him. "Thank you," he says in a tone he might address to somebody he's never previously seen.

"No, thank you."

I suspect my irony is lost on him, and I turn back to Christine, who says "I thought you were up to it, Graham. We'll talk about it later, shall we?"

If that's a promise, it's a dismissal too. I would leave her a token squeeze if it mightn't look awkward or even contrived. I step into the newsroom, where Kessler isn't to be seen; perhaps he has hurried away so as not to be questioned himself. I'm making to follow him when Paula appears from her room.

I assume I'm about to be summoned, but she doesn't look directly at me. Fixing her gaze on a space more or less above my head, she calls "Can I have everyone's attention, please?"

A chorus of squeaking could almost suggest she has uncovered a nest of mice. It's the sound of the pivots of some of the chairs as my colleagues turn to face her. Trevor has just left the news studio, and strides quickly to sit down. I stay where Paula caught me in the act of heading for the exit, and feel singled out even before she says "I don't know how many of you have been listening to Graham."

I don't know either, since I'm confronted mainly by the backs of heads. I could imagine Kessler's inexpressiveness has overtaken most of the staff. Paula's gaze roves around the room—she reminds me of a teacher preparing to launch a question or demand an answer—and I suspect nobody wants to admit having heard me in case she asks their opinion. At last she says "As far as we're concerned he did all he could for us."

Not just the silence prompts me to speak. "You're saying you've heard from Dominic or Meryl."

"I haven't yet. I'm speaking for Waves." She obviously resents the implication that she has to be fed any words. "I'm saying every workplace needs to be built on loyalty," she explains, if that's an explanation. "I believe we're entitled to expect it here."

Trevor clears his throat. "Graham's an example, do you mean?"

"I'll tell you exactly what I mean," Paula says and stares at me as though I asked. "Until we hear from upstairs I'd rather not have any speculations about how Graham's show went, not in here and particularly not outside this room. I'm including you, Graham."

"That's kind of you." The words leave my mouth as if my voice is declaring its independence. The thought was so sarcastic that I didn't mean to utter it, and I'm driven to add "What did you make of the show?"

"You did what was asked of you. I wouldn't have expected any different."

"Yes, but what—"

"As I said, speculation won't do us any good, and it might even harm the station. We need to present a united front. As far as we're concerned for now you undertook the test and answered all the questions you were asked without attempting to avoid them. If anyone's approached for any kind of statement, please refer the matter directly to me."

Paula sends her gaze on a tour of the desks before shutting herself in her room. I sense resentment of the strictures she's placed on everyone, but it's feeble compared with my rage, which is entangled with confusion—I can't decide whether she said too little or too much or both. Chairs are squeaking again, and I have the impression that my workmates are trying to find items of interest on their desks rather than look at me or even speak while I'm in the newsroom. This enrages me further, and I make for the lifts as if I'm anxious to outdistance what I might otherwise say. "Off home," I tell Megan.

Without glancing up from the switchboard she says "I should be."

The desk on the ground floor is deserted, and so I've no idea what Vince or his colleagues may think of me now. I know someone who ought to be ready with an opinion, and I'm sweating with the fast walk in the heavy sunlight by the time I reach the Dressing Room. Some of the heat fades from my scalp as the door sends a shadow on my trail. Two men are tapping at laptops in a booth, and Benny's behind the bar, but I mostly see Jasper's face. *For everyone I've read and everyone I have to* . . . Rather than yank the framed poster off the wall and stamp on the glass I head for the bar. "Got a joke for me, Benny?" I never thought I'd ask.

He looks up from polishing a wineglass but doesn't offer me a grin. "Can't think of one just now, Mr Wilde."

"It could be something you couldn't say on the air."

The footlights etch a frown deeper in his forehead. "Can't say what that'd be."

"Have I offended you, Benny?" I'm driven to wonder. "Was it something on my show?"

"I'd never say that, Mr Wilde."

I've begun to feel he's learned ambiguity if not slyness from Frank Jasper. "Are you trying to tell me something? Am I being stupid?"

"I wouldn't ever say that either."

"What would you say, then? Don't tell me coming on my show has pinched your sense of humour."

He deals the glass a final wipe and stands it behind the bar. He doesn't look at me again until he has picked up another, and his frown and its shadows are back. "Do you need a drink, Mr Wilde?"

"I don't need one, no. If I ever did I'd give it up. I just wanted to ask you what you made of my show you were on."

"I can't really talk about it right now."

Far too belatedly I wonder if his frown—indeed, his whole demeanour—could be meant as a warning. I jerk my head to indicate the men in the booth and murmur "Should I be able to guess who that is?"

He just about nods, which is all I need, though it isn't enough of an answer. Whoever they are, what business was it of theirs if Hannah Leatherhead approached me? No doubt they'll pass on anything Benny and I say about today's show, and the notion aggravates my rage. "Fair enough, Benny," I say without bothering to keep my voice down. "We'll talk about it next time."

I stare at the men on my way to the door. They're wearing suits but have both removed their jackets and laid them in the corners of the booth. Perhaps that's in the interests of efficiency, but together with their crouched postures and burly physiques it makes them look ready for a fight. I'm not, despite clenching my fists, but I haven't passed the booth when the man who's clacking faster at a keyboard glances up at me. Though he isn't sufficiently interested to stop typing, I'm sure I glimpse some kind of condemnation in his eyes. He shakes his balding head and turns his attention back to the monitor, and even if this didn't remind me of Kessler it would be far too much. In two strides I'm at the booth. "Friend of Paula's, are you?"

His curly-topped companion looks up, saying "Who?"

Benny steps out from behind the bar. "Mr—"

"It's all right, Benny, you won't need to throw me out. I just want a word with your customers here." All this is at least equally addressed to the men in the booth. "Don't you know anyone called Paula?" I ask them.

"Doesn't everybody?" says the balding man.

"Not the one I'm thinking of." I'm infuriated by their visible amusement and by the notion that I'm asking questions like Jasper's. "The one you like to keep informed," I say and show my teeth.

"What's that about?" the curly fellow says.

"About people's jobs, the way I hear it. You're pretty concerned with where some of us work."

"As a matter of fact," says the man crowned with bare skin, "we are."

"That's your idea of fun, is it?" I'm even more infuriated by having heard a threat as well. "Does it make you feel powerful, interfering in people's lives? Christ, at least Frank Jasper does it in public. He's another character who likes to eavesdrop."

"Mr Wilde." Benny has crossed the floor as fast as I did. "They're from the brewery," he says, apparently unsure what tone to use when he's nowhere near making a joke. "They're visiting their pubs to see how they're being run."

"My God, I've been the one cracking jokes and I never knew," I declare with the kind of laugh I usually reserve for his. "Or maybe I'm one myself, would you say, Benny?"

"I wouldn't like to, Mr Wilde."

"That's Benny for you, the soul of discretion. Whatever else I've said, I take it back." Since this only appears to bemuse his employers, I try saying "I should tell you Benny and I are old friends. I'm often in for a drink and a bit of a giggle."

My reflection above the booth makes my performance seem as separated from me as my voice sounds, but I oughtn't to stop yet. "Forgive me for getting you wrong. The light must have blinded me," I say the instant I think it and wave at the bulbs around the mirror. "Anyway, I gave you some free publicity. Let's hope that brings the drinkers in."

I shouldn't have drawn attention to their absence, but I'm distracted by Jasper's poster; I could almost imagine he's spying on my efforts. "How did you do that?" says the curly individual.

"On my show. On Waves." When they both look almost

insultingly blank I say "Our leading radio station here in Manchester. I present the lunchtime show. Wilde Card. I'm Graham Wilde."

The first man's scalp gleams as he turns his head to glance along the walls. "We don't see you anywhere."

"I keep meaning to sign you one, Benny. Next time, I promise."

"Don't bother."

It's the curly character who says this, though Benny doesn't seem too keen either. Without knowing how much of my rage can be contained I say "Why shouldn't I?"

"We were telling Benny we've got enough locals on show. Just major stars from out of town in future. This place wants a wider appeal. There's too much stuff that doesn't mean a thing an hour's drive up the road."

"I'll be in for my usual soon, Benny." This is a bid to suppress my ire and take it outside. "Just let me say I nearly always come in here for a drink or two," I tell the men in the booth. "Today I need to be somewhere else, that's all."

"Somewhere important," the balding fellow says, "we hope."

"It is to me." A hint of skepticism in his tone provokes me to add "I have to go home and work on a novel."

"Is there anything you don't get up to?" the curly party says.

"Plenty." Of course he wasn't accusing me; he seems even more incredulous than his companion, and I mustn't let them make me lose my temper when it might threaten Benny's job. "In fact, that's all," I say and turn my back on the booth.

I'm met by Frank Jasper—not the faker I'd happily punch in the face, just his image. All the lights around the mirrors seem to flare with fury, and I see myself dodging across the walls as if I'm making an escape. I have to open my fist to close it on the handle of the door. It might give me some satisfaction to twist the handle as though I'm wringing a neck or grabbing an arm to force it up the owner's back or even gouging an eye, but the handle isn't the kind that moves. I have to content myself with hauling the door wide and stepping onto the pavement without a backward glance.

Sunlight grabs me by the scalp as the door shuts with a muffled thump like a punch in someone's gut. The top of my head is already crawling with heat and rage, but the insubstantial pressure of the light is worse. I sprint across the road, cursing a furious screech of brakes, into the shadow of the hotel. All the people I encounter on my way home give me more than a glance or try to avoid looking at me. If I look half as enraged as I feel I'm surprised they don't run for their lives. A train adorned with posters squeals across the bridge near my apartment, and the parade of outsize faces puts me in mind of photographs being drawn through a viewer by someone conducting a search.

Walter Belvedere is with a client if he isn't listening to a newscast. I can't tell what's being said as I unlock my door, which I almost slam in my haste to shut away the mumbling voice. In the main room I sit in the windowless corner and switch on the computer. I've been trying to think like Glad Savage all the way home, and I seem to have at least a chapter in my head. The reporter is expecting a promotion, but at the interview she finds she's being fired for knowing too much about her employers: the editor likes illegally young girls, and his deputy is prone to uncontrollable fits of rage, which is why the woman's partner keeps going back to hospital—Glad knows all this just by looking at the culprits. "You haven't got rid of me," she tells them as she leaves the newspaper.

It takes me hours of furious typing to write the chapter, until I feel close to trapped between the walls by the plastic chatter of the keyboard. At last I'm able to scroll through what I've typed, and then I stare at the screen, which seems to have betrayed me as much as Kessler's monitor did. The chapter feels like a revenge, but I can't tell what kind or on whom. It's too much like a guilty secret, and I don't believe I'd care to make it public. When I hear Christine's key in the lock I delete the entire chapter and switch off the computer.

Christine looks ready to raise my spirits if she can. She's carrying today's *Manchester Clarion*, though she rarely buys a newspaper, since we can read them in the newsroom. "What have you been up to?" she says as she leaves the hall.

"Just hacking away at my novel."

"Oh," she says eagerly, "can I see?"

"Nothing to see, as the police say when they're moving you on."

"How can't there be, Graham? You're really writing one, aren't you?"

"Yes, and that's positive. Even Mr Kessler would have to say so. It just wasn't any good, and so I've put it out of its misery."

I'm surprised to see the newspaper begin to crumple in her hands. "What do you mean?" she pleads.

"I've wiped it out. Killed it off. Destroyed it beyond any hope of resurrection, and believe me, that can be bloody satisfying."

Christine looks too distressed to cross the room to me. "You haven't deleted all your work without letting me tell you what I think. Say you've kept a copy."

"We're only talking about today's chapter, and it was no loss." I'm amused as well as touched by her concern, but I shouldn't laugh except affectionately. "I'm sure you'd have wanted me to get rid of something that stupid," I say, "if you'd known what it was like."

"Don't do that to anything else, will you? At least let me see first."

"I will when there's enough to be worth seeing." When this doesn't appear to placate her I say "Soon."

"I just want to help, Graham. I'm certain you can make it work. Maybe it'll be what you'll do in future."

"I'm not out of my other job," I remind her, and then I'm reminded myself. "Did Paula talk to you?"

Christine seems oddly wary of the question. "Why should she have done that?"

"She was advising everybody not to talk about my show. You were busy with Rick."

Christine looks relieved, though I don't understand why. "She didn't mention it. I expect she thought someone else would." Christine hesitates and steps forward, holding out the newspaper. "She didn't mention this either, and she hasn't been in touch with you, has she?" With some kind of hopefulness Christine adds "Or you'd have told me by now."

"Of course I haven't heard from her." The suggestion makes me obscurely angry, and then my anger finds a focus as my fist clenches on the newspaper. "Is that supposed to be me?" I don't really need to ask, because there can't be any other reason why she has brought the paper. The front-page headline, which looks so black that it might only just have been printed, says **SUSPEND SUSPECT PRESENTER.**

29

THE SWITCH

As the lift doors open Megan glances at me and instantly down at the switchboard. I think she's simply avoiding my eyes, unless she dislikes the sight of me or the idea that I'm still working at Waves, until she picks up the phone. "He's here."

"That's conclusive and no mistake. Who are you warning about me, Megan?"

She gives me a look that's worse than blank and then lowers her bovine head. Perhaps that's just meant to convey indifference, but it feels like contempt and a challenge too, as though she's daring me to respond. I clench my fists, and my skull feels as if a similar process is happening in there. As I take a step towards her I have the impression that I can't quite see what I'm doing, unless it's what I'm about to do. Am I blinded by the rage that has flared up from my guts? I'm nearly at the counter before she deigns to acknowledge me with a blink that hardly even bothers to look bored. I haven't raised my fists above the counter when I lurch aside, past a puny heap of photographs of my face, and head for the newsroom at speed. I don't know what I was thinking of, and I'd rather not. I lift my badge to the plaque on the wall and see Paula striding across the newsroom.

Her face looks grimly resolute, stiff as her hair. So Megan called her, not security at all. I let my badge dangle on its shrinking cord and step back. Paula might almost be on her way to swat an insect, since she's holding a rolled-up newspaper—I've no doubt which. She pulls the door open and brandishes the paper. "Don't run away, Graham," she says as the door shuts behind her. "I take it you've seen this."

She plants the *Clarion* on the counter, where it unfolds jerkily beside the photographs of me. I've already subjected myself to its contents more than once—not just the front-page story that transcribes Kessler's questions and his verdicts on my answers, but the editorial that says I shouldn't be allowed to work at Waves until I've been thoroughly investigated, though the writer stops short of saying by whom. "I'm sure a lot of people have," I retort.

"Have you, Megan?"

"I glanced at it."

She doesn't now, and seems to resent being made to own up. I'm close to demanding how her opinion counts when Paula says "Don't let it bother you, Graham. It won't bother us."

I'm as uncertain whether Megan is included as she appears to be, but it's more important to establish "That's Frugo as well."

"I rather think I can say that, yes."

"You've heard from them."

"I expect to very shortly."

I sense she's vexed by having to say so. If she dislikes being over-heard, why didn't she take me into her office? Before I can propose it she says "I think they'll share my view."

"Do you mind if I ask what that is exactly?"

"Why should I mind?" Paula lifts her chin, and the tips of her cropped hair rise precisely as much. "We're independent radio," she says, "and that means we don't let other media dictate policy to us."

Even if it sounds stupid I need to say "About me, you mean."

"About any managerial decision."

I take this to mean yes. Megan's face has grown as blank as Kessler's, which is a comment in itself. Yesterday I was distracted by the antics of the polygraph, and now she's providing the unspoken judgments I'm unable to ignore. As I struggle not to turn on her Paula says "Megan, Wilde Card will be going on as usual. If anybody calls about that, put them through to me."

As she holds the door open I grab the newspaper, not wanting Megan to have it. "Shall I bin this?"

"Do what you like with it, Graham," Paula says.

I'm tempted to rip it to shreds, but I wouldn't like Megan to see, and so I hold it between a finger and thumb as I follow Paula. Some of my colleagues glance up at me; some even take the time to look encouraging. I flourish the *Clarion* at them and hurry into the control room. "Was Paula talking to you?" Christine wants to know.

"That's why I'm here," I reassure her and hurry to put on my headphones, having dropped the newspaper on the console. Today is Elderly Excellence Day, but I suspect I won't be hearing much about that. "Let them all on," I tell Christine and read the monitor. "Kicking off is Les from Swinton. What do you have for us, Les?"

"Why are you still here?"

On some level I'm delighted with the question. If Paula wants confrontational broadcasting, I'm more than angry enough. "Where would you like me to be?"

"You wouldn't want to hear it. I'm asking why you are."

"Somebody must want me."

"And a lot of us don't, only we don't matter. We just have to put up with everything the likes of you and your friends in high places inflict on the rest of us. It used to be if you were under a cloud you'd do the decent thing and resign without needing to be told."

"I haven't seen a cloud for quite a while, have you?" Since this would sound worse than facetious I say "If enough people want me to I'd have to think about it."

"The paper does."

"That's just a few people at one paper." I grow aware that I've been tearing fragments off the front page and strewing them across the console. As I set about collecting the rubbish to bin it I say "Maybe they ought to get their readers to vote. Thanks for your thoughts, Les."

The next caller thinks the vote should be confined to my listeners, and someone else advises me to sue the newspaper, but Harold from Beswick has a question. "Do you think lie detectors work?"

"I have to say yesterday's didn't for me."

"Then you're a liar, Mr Wilde."

The strip I'm tearing off the newspaper removes the first letter of the last word of the headline. "Will you be telling us why, Harold?"

"Because it said one of your answers was true and now you're saying it didn't work."

"It did for that one, and you heard the examiner wasn't happy with the conditions either. Just think how he sounded when people started phoning in." Harold meets this with a silence I'd like to take for agreement, and I say "Madge from Melling, you're on."

"Can I call you Graham, Graham?"

I nearly give her an answer too reminiscent of Jasper's. "Of course you can."

"I'm going to upset some people, Graham. Nobody except an idiot could trust a lie detector."

"Do you think that's a little harsh? I know—"

"Graham," she says like a maternal rebuke. "It's nothing of the sort, Graham. They should be ashamed of themselves, damaging your reputation with that nonsense. Tests like those, Graham, they're just a performance. They're as fake as your friend who tried to make out he was psychic."

"I wouldn't call him a friend, but—"

"I was being sarky, Graham. Graham, nobody that's not an idiot would want him for a friend."

"Well, again, Madge, perhaps that's a little—"

"Graham. He's the one who should have had a lie test, but I'll bet my pension he'd have turned it down, Graham. Shall I tell you why?"

Surely I've no reason to hesitate. "Go ahead."

"Because he didn't know you were the killer, Graham."

My vision quakes, or there's a nervous movement somewhere at its edge, or both. Paula's door hasn't burst open, but Christine has jerked her head up. I hold her gaze without being able to judge what either of us is thinking as I say "That's because I'm not one, and if anyone—"

"You didn't let me finish, Graham."

I hardly think I'm the one to be accused of interrupting, but I hear my voice say "Then please do."

"Graham. He was there with you in your studio, wasn't he? How far away, Graham?"

My name has begun to feel as though it's adding weight to the clammy headphones. "Close enough to touch," the voice that's my job says, "not that I did."

"Well, there you are, Graham." I'm about to demand where she thinks that is when she says "He didn't mention anything about it when he was supposed to be so psychic, Graham, but he's trying to make out you're a killer now."

"I don't believe he's ever said that."

"Some people should watch what they're saying, Graham, and they ought to be careful what they think as well."

"I'd rather people spoke out on here, but thanks for your support, Madge." She must have meant it that way, and yet I feel in need of a break. I run an ad for Frugarden Centres—"Bring a bit of Eden home"—and then I do my best not to be reminded of Kessler's monitor as I consult the screen. "Now we have Maurice from Failsworth. What would you like to add, Maurice?"

"May I ask you just one question, Mr Wilde?"

"Two if you count that one, or as many as you've got."

"That's what you say now you aren't being tested." Before I can deal with this he says "What do your parents think of everything you've done?"

My fists clench on the newspaper. I can't pretend to know the answer, which makes the question feel even more like a wistful reproach from my mother. She isn't far away—about thirty miles since she put some distance between herself and my father—but I haven't been to see her for weeks or phoned her either. As for my other parent, I haven't seen or spoken to him since my grandfather's funeral. I feel urged to respond, not least by Christine; I'm aware of her despite if not because of avoiding her gaze. "I don't suppose they think I've done too badly," I say and manage to let go of the crumpled paper.

"Don't you know your own parents, Mr Wilde?"

"I really don't think they need to be brought into this. Was there anything—"

"You were ready enough to talk about your family when you were trying to make your guest look foolish."

So we're back to Jasper yet again. "I think he did that without any help from me."

"Some people might think you wanted to discredit him in case he said too much about you."

"Then they'd be wrong, and I hope I'm not the only one who'd wonder why they said it."

"Thank you for proving my point, Mr Wilde."

I become aware of having closed my fists on the edges of the newspaper again. "Which point was that?"

"You'll do all you can to discredit anyone who dares to say anything against you."

"I'm sure our listeners will make their own minds up, Maurice."

As I wait for him to respond, the line goes dead. The newspaper parts jaggedly down the middle, and I mash it together before chucking the unreadable lump into the bin. I rub my blackened hands on my trousers while I attempt to concentrate on the screen. "Now we've got Liz from Blackburn. What's your view, Liz?"

"It's Oswaldtwistle, Graham."

"That's part of Blackburn, isn't it? I know it quite well."

"Do you?" Before I can judge her tone Liz adds "What do you want me to say?"

"It isn't about what I want, Liz. It's your show."

"It's been feeling a bit like that lately." As I make to ask why she says "All right, I'll tell you. I think you and Mr Jasper—"

The pause is all hers, and it gives my rage time to gather. I can't leave the air dead, and so I say "What about Frankie and me?"

"I think you were a bit hard on your father."

Now the silence is mine until I hear myself demand "What gives you the right to say that? Are you claiming you're psychic as well?"

"Oh, Graham." She seems to think this is enough of a response until she says "I was there."

For a moment I assume she means Jasper's stage performance, and then I blurt "Who is this?"

"You're just saying that for your show, aren't you?" When I don't respond she says "It's your mother, Graham."

"I didn't know." That's unlikely to placate her, and I feel driven to add "My producer didn't say."

"She wouldn't know me, would she? We've never met." Just as reprovingly my mother says "I thought you'd have recognised me."

"People don't sound the same when they phone in." I hope this helps, but I still need to learn "What were you trying to say about my father?"

"It wasn't just him who was violent."

"Who was?" I have to ask.

"Not just him." Her defiance falters, and she says "We used to have fights but sometimes it was my fault as well. You always took my side because you were a gentleman, but I did think seeing all that must have affected you."

I can't let this go unquestioned. "How?"

"You did end up with quite a temper. That time your father swung you over the balcony, I know people will find this hard to credit, but I think he was just trying to take you out of the situation. I know you meant to defend me, but you really were doing your best to hurt him. If one of those punches of yours had landed it would have done him a lot of damage, young as you were. And when you were a few years older and I wouldn't let you go out one weekend in case you got into a fight with someone over some silly thing I can't remember now, you split a panel in the front door, you gave it such a thump."

I can't bring any of this to mind. Perhaps my silence prompts her to say "Sorry, Graham, have I said too much?"

A laugh jerks my head up, but I manage to keep the sound to myself. Only Christine sees my face, and she seems unwilling to share my expression, whatever it may be. "Nobody can ever say too much on this show," I declare without knowing how my voice trapped in the headphones sounds, and then I'm ambushed by an idea. "As long as you're casting your mind back, what do you remember about Frankie Patterson?"

"Who's that, Graham?"

"He went to my school. He was always trying to impress everyone with some trick or other. He liked to make them think he could do things nobody else could."

"He must be someone else I've never met."

"But you heard about him. He stuck a knife in his hand when he was playing a trick he'd seen in a film."

"That does sound familiar."

"Of course it does. He was here on my show calling himself Frank Jasper."

"I do listen to you whenever I can. I just didn't think you'd want me ringing in."

"Well, you have and that's fine. Do you recall anything else about him now?"

Perhaps the pause means she's attempting to remember. As I stare almost blindly at the console, willing her to speak, there's a flurry of movement beyond the studio window. Paula has come into the control room, and she's speaking so emphatically that I can read her lips. "Go and get Trevor," she tells Christine and marches into the studio, gesturing at the microphone with such force that she looks as if she's delivering a blow. "Hold on, I'm being signalled," I say and reach for the relevant switch.

My mother's voice is still clamped to my skull. "Before I go, Graham, do you really have to argue quite so much?"

"It's my job."

"So long as it pays you. I just wondered if it's how you stop yourself doing worse." Presumably she intends this as some kind of defence. "I hope we'll see each other soon," she says.

"Don't go anywhere," I say, though I'm not sure how much I mean her. "Here's a message from our sponsor." I start a run of adverts—Fruground Organic Coffee, Your Morning Mouthful, and Frugrime Household Cleaner and Fruguard Insurance besides whatever else is in the bunch—and drop my headphones on the console. "Sorry if any of that was too much," I tell Paula. "I didn't know I was putting my family on the air."

"I'm sorry too. I'm afraid that has to be all."

She glances behind her so quickly that I could fancy she's hoping for reinforcements. Of course she's looking for Lofthouse, who I suspect is up on the roof for a cigarette break. "You mean you're shoving Trevor in again? What did I do that was that bad?"

Paula takes her time over turning back to me, as if she's anxious not to disturb her stiffened coiffure. "They've agreed upstairs," she says, "we should give you time off till the situation is resolved."

"Agreed with whom?" When her face stays as immobile as her hair I protest "I thought you said you were speaking for them."

"They're agreeing with the *Clarion*."

"It's a victory for the little people, is it?" Just too late I realise this sounds like a gibe at her height. While I don't much care, I do her the favour of adding "The local rag against the firm that owns the world, I mean."

"It isn't like that, Graham." Paula hesitates and says "It isn't public yet, but Frugo have acquired the newspaper chain."

"Is there anyone they haven't bought?" Several people in the newsroom look no less appalled than I feel; they're staring in disbelief towards the studio, presumably having guessed that Paula's here to oust me once again. When she stays as mute as the windows make my colleagues, I say "Then I'll just have to see if the BBC's still interested."

Paula shakes her head, which doesn't stir a hair. "Leave yourself a little dignity, Graham."

"Is that what you think you're doing?" Just as furiously I demand "What are you trying to say?"

"We know they've withdrawn their offer."

The stares of the staff in the newsroom might be expressing my reaction. "Who told you that, may I ask?"

"Your friend there did."

Paula has turned to stare into the newsroom, where Christine has reappeared with Trevor. "Christine," I hiss in a voice that makes my teeth ache.

"Not her. Don't go attacking her." Paula faces me and says "Hannah Leatherhead. She was in the Dressing Room when I had lunch with Dominic and Meryl."

"Bitch." I don't care who Paula thinks I mean. Christine has been intercepted by someone at the far end of the newsroom, but now she and Trevor put on speed. As they reach the control room I say "Here's Trevor to the rescue. If he's taking over for a while he'll have to get a personality of his own."

Christine yanks open the studio door and gives Paula a wary look. "Graham," she blurts, "you're live."

Paula stares wide-eyed at me and opens her mouth as though she's miming silence. I don't know whether the headphones knocked the switch on the console out of position; perhaps it lodged against a crumpled fragment of newspaper. I'm barely able to contain my mirth—I've no idea what kind. "Well, there you are, everyone," I say to the microphone. "No secrets on this show."

I blunder out past Trevor, who steps well aside as if he fears I mean to thump or otherwise mistreat him. Many of my colleagues are watching to see what I'll do. My rage sends me to grab the phone on my desk. As soon as I'm through to the police I say "I want to tell you who killed Kylie Goodchild."

30

STATING THE CHARGES

I've found my keys at last—they're lodged beneath the computer monitor like a secret I was trying to keep from myself—when the doorbell gives a single trill. Its abruptness sounds authoritative, as though I can't avoid admitting the caller, not that I want to put off the interview. I hurry down the hall, only for the intercom to say "It's just me without my keys."

I thumb the button to let Christine in. I needn't have borrowed all of her keys this morning; it feels as though I've forced her to come to my flat because she can't get into her own. From her tone she might have been apologising because she isn't the police. I don't know whether I would have preferred to talk to them while she wasn't here—no, why would I? I stare into the flattened eyes of Robert Mitchum's preacher until her footsteps come upstairs, and then I open the door. "Oh, Graham," she says.

Presumably that means more to her than it does to me, and I do my best to find a joke. "Even I'd have to call that inconclusive."

"I didn't know this was supposed to be a test."

"Let's say we've both passed," I say and shut the door.

Nobody speaks again until we're seated in the main room, where the computer and the television put me pointlessly in mind of Kessler's polygraph. "Have you been working on your novel?" Christine hopes aloud.

"No, I've been looking for my keys."

"At least you'll have the time now if that's what you want to do." She seems to wish we were on the couch instead of facing each other across the room. "And maybe you're better out of Waves," she says.

"You aren't."

"I was let off the lecture, though. Paula couldn't blame me when she'd sent me to fetch Trevor. She was ranting at everyone in the newsroom for not warning her you were both on the air. She wanted anybody who'd been listening to you to own up, but do you think they did? I've never seen her lose her temper before. You don't really know what people are like until they lose control." Christine pauses not quite long enough for me to speak, and almost seems to be interrupting herself. "What are you going to tell the police?"

I'm taking a breath when the doorbell rings, an even terser trill than hers was. As I make for the hall a doubt stirs somewhere deep in me; it feels unreasonably like the twitching of a polygraph. I haven't identified whatever is troubling me by the time I have to say "Hello?"

"Graham Wilde."

"Nobody else but." Christine can be a surprise and if necessary a witness as well, because I've recognised the voice. "Come right up," I tell him.

He brings more footsteps upstairs with him. He's Lippy Linley, and he is indeed accompanied by Beaky Rudd. Neither of them seems to want to show me an expression just now. As I lead the way along the hall I find Christine waiting at the end. I could imagine she's keeping an eye on my behaviour, although she says "Would anyone like a drink?"

"We don't need one," Linley says.

Nor do I, and in any case she wouldn't have meant anything alcoholic. "Can we have your name?" says Rudd.

"Christine Ellis. I'm Graham's producer."

"Are you?" Rudd sits on the couch as if to ensure I can't share it with her, and then he says "Still?"

I head off Christine's answer but just some of my rage. "What makes you ask that?"

"Haven't you been taken off?" Linley asks as he settles in an armchair.

"Only till his name is cleared," Christine retorts. "I hope you'll be helping."

"You've been listening to my show, have you?"

"We wouldn't miss it," Rudd assures me.

"We've been fans for weeks," says his partner.

They sound far too much like a comedy team—one that doesn't care whether I appreciate the joke. I mustn't be provoked, and I concentrate on offering Christine the other armchair. When she mimes giving it to me I take it and wait while she sits on the arm. Both policemen frown, perhaps only at the delay, but Christine must assume they don't want her so close to me. She brings a scrawny chair from the kitchen and perches on it, propping her elbows on its back and clasping her hands to support her intent face. "Are you ready to talk now, Mr Wilde?" says Rudd.

"I wanted to be sure before I said anything. I wouldn't be surprised if you've reached the same conclusion as me."

"Try us," Rudd says and lifts his head as if he's readying his long sharp nose for a scent.

"I think Kylie Goodchild's boyfriend killed her. I believe he's already known to you."

Linley parts his outstanding lips with a small sticky sound. "Why do you say that?"

"He's been terrorising his neighbourhood, him and his gang. He has a dog called Killer I'm told isn't far from illegal. He killed another boy's dog with it and that was reported to the police. He uses drugs and mixes them with alcohol, which I'm sure is helping make him how he is. The way I hear it, those aren't his only problems with the law. It might be worth investigating what he gets up to at school."

Rudd is keeping his nose high. "You've been doing quite a lot of that, Mr Wilde."

"I'm a journalist." Now I know what was troubling me—I didn't tell Christine about the enquiries I made. I give her an apologetic look while saying "I wanted to be sure before I made a statement."

Rudd's partner makes his mouthy sound again. "What would you say was your interest in him?"

"Because he's obsessed with me. You'd do better asking why that is."

Linley has left his mouth open. "I was asking why you're accusing him."

"I'm sure I know his motive."

Do I glimpse Rudd's nostrils twitching at this? "So tell us," he says.

"I believe he was jealous of me."

I don't look at Christine, whom I've begun to find as distracting as the reflection of the polygraph. "Why would he have been jealous?" says Rudd.

"Of whatever she felt about me."

"What are you saying that might have been, Mr Wilde?"

"Maybe nothing we'd call much if even anything, but the point is how it seemed to him. You can tell that from his behaviour on my programme for a start."

"Remind us," Linley says.

"The station manager had to call security and have him escorted out of the building."

"Why are you saying he caused a scene?"

"He saw the photo I'd signed for his girlfriend. I'm sure you'll have seen it yourselves. There's nothing on it I wouldn't have written to any member of the public. It just told her to have a good life."

"It's a pity she didn't get it," Rudd remarks, and Linley says "Why should he have reacted badly to that?"

"At the time I thought he'd fallen for the trick. Frankie Jasper tried to make everyone believe the photo had led him to me before he'd seen it, but I'll stake my reputation he already had." For a moment my conviction wavers like a line on a polygraph, and then my rage steadies it. "Anyway, forget him. The way the boyfriend's acted since, I think he'd go for anyone he thought had even a passing acquaintance with her."

Linley has a question, but I haven't finished. "Or maybe it's something else," I want to establish. "Maybe he's doing his best to make people believe I had something to do with her death so they won't look too closely at him. Maybe he thinks accusing me will persuade people he's innocent."

When I hold up my open hands Linley says "How are you saying he's behaved since?"

"He went for Graham at Kylie Goodchild's funeral," Christine says.

"He attacked him, you mean."

"He did verbally. He looked as if he wanted to do worse."

Rudd points his nose at her as a preamble to asking "Did you report the incident?"

"We definitely did. I'd have thought you'd know."

"I may have made less of it than I could have," I interrupt for fear she'll antagonise them. "Another time he waited for me outside the radio station and followed me by the canal."

Linley's lips make such a noise I could imagine he's smacking them. "What were you doing down there?"

"Walking like a lot of people do. More since I've started working on a novel." My fury at his question almost makes me lose control, but I mustn't let Christine suspect I've kept the secret for so long, and I add "I started it this month."

"I'm trying to establish why you chose to go down there with him. Wouldn't it have been advisable to stay somewhere more public?"

"I don't think he's much of a threat to me. I'm not a teenage girl." When the policemen gaze at me I say "I think she came to Waves that night to warn me about him. He must have chased her away unless she meant to hide from him by the canal. He caught up with her, and they're bound to have had an argument, and who knows what she may have said that made him lash out. I'm not saying it was murder. Maybe he just lost control."

"You think this happened," Linley says, "after Kylie Goodchild tried to see you again at your place of work."

His last phrase sounds ironic if not worse, but I mustn't let anger distract me. "There's no doubt of that, is there?"

"Then I have to tell you it couldn't have been her boyfriend."

Linley's face grows blank before I can interpret his expression, and I'm left just with my anger. "Who says so?"

"His stepfather would for one," says Rudd.

"Can you really trust someone like him?"

"That doesn't fit your image, Mr Wilde. On your show you don't want to sound prejudiced."

"And by God I'm not. I'd no idea he's whatever you're saying he is. I meant the neighbours think he's a bad lot as well, and one of the reasons Wayne acts how he does. Just for the record, it was an Asian who said so. Are you honestly taking the word of a criminal?"

Rudd gazes hard and blankly at me before saying "It wasn't just his stepfather."

I wonder if he's requiring me to ask, but Linley takes the cue. "They were with us," he says. "With the police."

"When?" This sounds too close to skepticism, and so I demand "How long?"

"Several hours, Mr Wilde."

"And what was it about?"

"I'm sure you know we're not at liberty to discuss it," says Rudd. "We'd received an anonymous call that may have been from a neighbour."

"Then the witness must have been wrong. Not the one who called you about them, whoever told you what time Kylie was trying to get into Waves. The autopsy couldn't have been too precise about the time of death, could it? She must have been killed after you let Wayne go or before you brought him in."

"You're a bit determined to pin it on him."

"I just want the killer to be dealt with as he should be. Don't you?"

No doubt there are questions it would have been wiser to put to the police. After a pause that gives me time to sense Christine's concern Linley says "Can you tell us why a girl like Kylie Goodchild would even have known about you? Your programme wasn't meant for people of her age."

"It was meant for anyone who liked to listen to it." Instead of growing angrier I try to think aloud. "Maybe her mother did. Maybe Kylie liked it because I disagreed with the likes of Wayne. If as you say his stepfather is a different colour, maybe Wayne objects to that. She wouldn't have, would she? Not with the kind of poem she wrote."

Once he's sure I've finished Linley stands up, and Rudd does. "Thank you, Mr Wilde," Rudd says. "That's all for now."

Perhaps Christine feels overlooked. As they make for the hall she says "Can I ask something? You don't believe in lie detectors, do you?"

They don't quite halt, but Linley turns his head just enough to let us hear him say "Not by themselves."

I see the police to my door while Christine lingers in the main room. As I return along the hall I'm working out my next words.

"No more secrets," I tell her, only to wonder if this could be wrong. I can't grasp the thought that made me, and who's to say it was true? "If there's anything else I don't know it," I declare and hug Christine until she gasps for breath, and do my best not to feel I'm trying to squeeze any doubts out of us both.

31

GROWING ANGRIER

An hour of wandering around town has brought me back to the Palaces. Surely Christine has had time to finish reading what there is of *You're Another*. If I carry straight on I'll have to pass the BBC, while turning right beside the railway would only bring me to Waves. I could make a detour to the Dressing Room, but I've no idea how Benny feels about me, and I don't want to find out just now. As I hesitate outside the theatre, where posters advertise the Bleeding Feet Troupe in *Giselle*, people dressed for the sultry dusk glance at me and in some cases rather more than glance. I never used to expect to be recognised in the street, and now it infuriates me to hope I'm not. I stare at anyone who might be wondering about me, and then I head for home.

The streets near Christine's flat are crowded too. A sound of brittle splintering is muffled by the hubbub outside a bar, where a drinker has crushed a plastic glass in his fist. Cyclists beyond the first-floor window opposite look desperate to pedal into the distance. They're in Christine's gym, and their artificial silence makes them seem unreal, as if they don't exist without their voices. By the time I reach my building I can hear just my own footsteps, which sound bogged down by the muddy dark. As I take out my keys the action seems to trigger the streetlamps like ranks of security lights. I'm making to unlock the street door when a face looks down at me.

It's Walter Belvedere. He stays at his window until I'm out of sight beneath the lintel. Christine is reading my novel because she wants to encourage me to continue, but I suspect she'll try whatever she thinks of it, and the literary agent's judgment is bound to count for more. I'm on the stairs when I hear his door open, and I'm unexpectedly abashed at the thought of approaching him. I don't need to mention the novel just now, and I tramp upstairs with some determination. "Hot one, Walter," I remark.

He's in his doorway, rubbing his shiny brow as if he wants to erase a few more greying hairs and extend his forehead even higher. He has fallen into his habitual stoop that makes him look incapable of holding up his large-boned frame, a posture that goes with his usual expression—eyebrows on the way to being raised, lips slightly parted in anticipation, prominent ears at the ready. As I leave the stairs I notice he isn't alone, and could my comment have seemed to refer to the young woman behind him? "Hot night," I try explaining.

They could misinterpret this too. Perhaps they have, since they seem ready to frown. Walter's companion is a slim girl in a pale grey lightweight suit. Only her round face appears to have resisted whatever diet she has applied to herself, and her eyes are intent on looking resolute. "Here's someone who's been waiting to meet you," Walter says and makes way for her.

"Are you one of Walter's stable?"

My words have let me down again, to judge by how her inconspicuous eyebrows pinch together. "A writer, I mean," I assure her. "I'm one myself."

This isn't how I imagined telling Walter, who seems less than impressed. He has retreated into his hall, which is narrowed by shelves loaded with books, several copies of every one. "I'm Graham Wilde," I say and hold out a hand.

Of course she knows that. Presumably she doesn't take my hand because she finds the introduction redundant, leaving me to say "And you are . . ."

"Alice Francis, Mr Wilde."

"Call me Graham by all means." I know her name, but from where? Perhaps it's on some of the books in Walter's hall—and then, just as she makes to speak, I have it. "That isn't all you've called me, is it?" I say and feel my fingers start to crook away from her. "Thanks to you I'm known as the suspect presenter."

"I'm from the *Clarion*, Mr Wilde."

"Don't talk yourself down. You're front-page stuff," I say and turn my rage on Belvedere. "This is how you treat your neighbours, is it, Walter? Set traps for them. The others ought to know."

"They already do."

He means about me, presumably the tabloid version. As I take a step towards him he takes several back. He's so anxious to shut the door that his elbow blunders into a clump of identical books, which knock against the wall as if they're rehearsing the slam, and then I'm alone with the reporter in the corridor. "Well," I say, "there's another job you've lost me. What do you want to do to me now?"

"I'd like to ask you some questions if it's convenient."

"You're after my side of things, are you?" I don't know when the hand I offered her became a fist, but the other one has followed its example, and they've begun to ache. I'm aware of standing be-tween her and the stairs, because she glances at them, which helps to provoke me to say "It's a bit late."

"If you'd prefer to be interviewed tomorrow—"

As a journalist she ought to be persisting, but perhaps she's daunted by my look and the emptiness around us. "That isn't what I meant," I say and step towards her.

Though I'd think it wise of her to try and dodge around me, she stands her ground. Perhaps she has remembered she's supposed to be a reporter. I'd be happy if she panicked; she ought to if she thinks of the rubbish she wrote about me. Her stubbornness makes my fists quiver and tingle, and I feel as if they're directing me. She glances at them, and I've no idea what effect this may have; I'm close to being unable to think. She raises her eyes to mine, and I'm about to react to her expression—it seems uneasy, but not enough—when Christine says "Come inside, Graham."

I was so intent on Alice Francis that I didn't notice Christine opening my door. She reminds me of a parent summoning a child, which aggravates my rage. "I haven't finished this," I tell her. "The *Clarion's* here."

"Oh," says Christine and blinks at the reporter. "Are you delivering the paper?"

I haven't time to be amused by her untypical slyness. "She's Alice Francis. She put me on the front page."

"What a gentle name." This seems craftier still, and I can't quite judge Christine's mood. "So what brings you here, Alice?" she says.

"She's here to set the record straight, is that right, Alice?"

"It's a pity you didn't before you wrote about Graham," Christine objects. "You work for Frugo too, you know. I wouldn't expect to be attacked in public by anyone I worked with."

Alice Francis glances around, perhaps in case this is being overheard. "We aren't supposed to know about the takeover."

"We don't have any secrets here, do we?" When Christine doesn't respond I try saying "I expect she has to do what her editor tells her."

"You'll know what that's like," Alice Francis retorts. "I don't suppose you'd have taken that test on the air if you hadn't been told to."

This would enrage me more if I didn't sense that Christine is angry too, which lets me unclench my fists as she says "So what are you looking for now?"

"I think I've formed my impression," Alice Francis says.

"Don't be so sure of yourself. Come in and talk to us." When the reporter doesn't move Christine says "I give you my word you'll be safe."

My rage is back, with reinforcements. "There's no need for that."

"It sounds as if you think there might be," the reporter says to Christine.

"Then it sounds wrong." For a moment Christine seems inclined to leave it there, and then she says "I've never seen Graham so much as threaten anyone with violence, no matter what the provocation."

"You're saying you've seen him provoked."

"Yes, by people accusing him of things he'd never do. Believe me, if he was at all violent I wouldn't be with him. I used to be in a relationship like that, and you won't find me anywhere near one again."

"I'm glad if that's so." They appear to have reached a feminine agreement until Alice Francis says "Some people seem to have to repeat a relationship over and over."

"Perhaps you have."

"I'm not here to discuss my life. So you're saying you absolutely trust Mr Wilde."

Christine takes a breath. "I've said so once. Now can we go inside and you can ask us whatever you came to ask."

"I think I've learned all I need to," the reporter says and turns towards the stairs.

"No, you haven't learned enough." As quickly as I'm speaking I step in front of her. "Just look me in the eye and say if I was telling the truth to the polygraph."

"Or else you'll do what, Mr Wilde?"

I can't find an immediate answer, unless clenching my fists is one. Alice Francis stares at them and then at Christine before walking slowly and deliberately around me. I'm turning to keep her in sight when Christine says "Graham."

She sounds more parental than ever. I watch Alice Francis strut downstairs until she's out of sight, and then I confront Christine. "What did you think I was going to do?"

"I couldn't say. It must be one of your secrets."

In a moment the street door slams, and some kind of a grin tugs at my face. "Well, now we've given her just what she wanted."

"I'm glad you're taking some of the responsibility at least. Shall we continue this indoors?"

"Wherever we need to."

As my door shuts behind us with an enthusiastic thud I feel as if I'm chasing Christine along the hall. She goes straight to a chair, and it's plain that she wants me to stay at a distance. I sit opposite and can't help being aware of my computer at her back. "Am I going to hear what you thought of my tale?"

"Which of them is that, Graham?"

"What do you mean?" Swallowing some rage, I say "My novel."

"I don't know what I think about it just now."

"I can thank the bitch from the paper for that as well, can I?"

"Don't blame her for too much, Graham."

"Who would you like me to blame?" Her sad look makes this unmistakable, and so I demand "Am I going to hear about it or are you keeping secrets now?"

"Maybe you shouldn't have let me read your novel."

This is so unexpected that it makes me wary. "What do you think you've found in it?"

"Nothing." Before I can grasp whether that's a criticism she says "What did you tell the police about it?"

I can't help feeling warier, which enrages me. "I don't believe I told them anything. When?"

"You said you'd been thinking about it down by the canal."

"Yes, and I have. Where's the problem?"

"Just this month, you said."

A thought flickers like a warning in my mind, and then it's extinguished. "So I did," I have to risk saying.

"Graham, you started it months ago."

I'd rather not speak, but her gaze doesn't leave me the option. "What makes you say that?"

"The dates are all on the computer."

If I hadn't kept the chapters separate the onscreen properties wouldn't show the individual dates, just the most recent. The blank screen of the monitor reminds me of the polygraph, and that's not my only reason to be furious. "You thought you'd better check up on me, did you?"

"It was there in front of me."

This is hardly an answer, but perhaps I can take it as one if I try fiercely enough. I don't want the argument to estrange us, particularly when I've already lost so much. I've begun to shake, surely not with rage but with the effort to contain it. I'm about to confess that I didn't want Christine to think I'd been hiding my novel from her all that time when she says "You didn't bother to cover your tracks."

My fists have started to ache again. "Unlike what?"

"I don't understand you, Graham."

"I thought you wanted the bitch from the paper to think you knew all about me. When are you saying I did cover them?"

"Oh, Graham." Christine seems about to stop there, but then she blurts "Why are you making it so hard for me to trust you?"

I'm not sure what my hands have been roused to do until they shove me out of my chair. "All right," I say, perhaps the most inappropriate words ever to escape my lips. "Give it up."

Christine isn't shrinking back in her chair; she's simply lifting her head to watch me. When I turn away, flexing my fingers as if I don't know what to do with them, she says "Where are you going, Graham?"

"That's my new secret," I tell her and stalk down the hall to close the door as quietly as I would act at a funeral.

32

NOWHERE TO GO

In fact I've no idea where my rage may take me. As I give the street door a slam that I hope shakes Belvedere's apartment and reverberates painfully through his skull, I think of heading for the *Clarion*. I'd just be acting as the paper would expect me to behave and demonstrating it to witnesses. It's equally pointless to make for Waves—I don't imagine Paula will have stayed so late, and even if she has there's nothing more I want to say to her. That's true of Hannah Leatherhead as well, and so I won't be humiliating myself further at the BBC. I could spill my secrets at the Dressing Room, but on a night as suffocatingly hot as this the place is likely to be crowded, and besides, our last encounter has left me unsure about Benny. I'm best off ranting to myself as necessary, and I ought to be closest to alone by the canal.

Somebody shouts as I reach the nearest bridge. I don't know if the aggressive yell relates to the brittle crunch of an object trampled underfoot. One of the drinkers outside a pub has trodden on a plastic bottle, and there's no need for me to look back. I follow my jerky shadow down the steps to the towpath.

Humidity settles on my skin at once. At least I've no company beside the canal. A few dim ripples spread to meet me as I head

towards Oxford Street. The confused uproar outside the pubs fades
behind me like a radio that's being turned down, having drifted off
the station. Soon the only sounds are my plodding footsteps and
my voice. "That's enough now," it keeps saying. "That's enough."

It seems even more detached than it used to sound in the headphones. I can't be bothered to decide whether I'm speaking aloud,
since there's nobody else to hear. I'm more interested in learning
what it means, though I'm not too concerned about that either. It
falls silent as I duck under the Oxford Street bridge, which is so low
that I feel as if it's forcing my head down to focus my attention on
the section of canal beyond the arch. That's where I found Kylie
Goodchild.

A ripple so gentle it looks surreptitious passes through the water
as I straighten up. I don't see how it can have started at the drain in
the wall, where the sodden litter has grown restless. Wads of newspaper are plastered against the bars like a pathetic substitute for
the bouquets people leave at the scene of a tragedy. A crumpled can
and an empty bottle of another kind of lager sway against the drain
and rear up from the water as if they're proposing a toast, unless
they're suggesting one reason why Kylie was knocked into the canal. How can they be so active? The water pouring through the bars
doesn't seem violent enough. Why am I continuing to loiter now
I'm opposite the drain? It won't show me anything I'm not already
sure of; I know who must have killed Kylie, whatever the police
believe. Am I hoping that the culprit will return to the scene of his
crime so that I can alert the police? I'm not convinced that criminals behave as obligingly as the media would like the rest of us to
think. Perhaps I'm simply lingering out of respect for Kylie's memory, but the sight of all the litter doesn't help me feel respectful; it
adds to my frustrated rage. When a pale limp hand bobs up from
the depths, fumbling at the garbage in an attempt to clear it away
from the bedraggled head—the depths of my mind, not of the
canal, but just now it feels as if there's little difference—I retreat

towards the bridge. I don't know why I went this way beside the canal.

I'm increasingly uncertain why I left Christine at all. If there are issues we need to resolve, I can't on my own. Perhaps I had to leave her alone so that we'll both be ready to talk. Surely that's what I meant was enough: the argument. I raise my head on the far side of the arch and am picking up speed—I don't want to return to my flat only to find she's not there—when I see people blocking the towpath ahead.

Wherever they've just come from, there are four of them. Perhaps they've been leaning against the wall of the office block that looms over the canal. They're all wearing studded denim singlets, but they remind me somehow of shadows on the loose, and when they advance into the light from an upper floor I see they're black. The thought feels like a trace of racism. I'm ashamed of it but secretly amused by my own unpredictability, and glad I never let it slip on the air. I mustn't hesitate in case this looks prejudiced, and as the largest of the youths mutters something I walk not too aggressively nor with too much caution towards them. We're several yards apart when the man who spoke says "What you looking at, boy?"

"I don't know. What am I looking at?" This is always my reaction to the question, but perhaps it's unwise in the circumstances. "Nothing much" seems ill-advised too, and so I say "I wasn't looking."

"Took his fucking time about it, Si," says the youth who's nearest to the water.

I don't know if he means my answer, which sounds infuriatingly feeble now it's out, or the look. "Just finding my way home," I confine myself to saying.

"That's fucking funny, in it, Si?"

"Fucking right, Jay." Si sounds irritated, possibly with him. "What wasn't you looking at?" he demands of me.

I've had enough. I'm not going to feel like a coward, and I can't keep up the performance. "Why don't you tell me," I say, "since it means so much to you."

"We know, in it, Si?"

"Shut it, Jay."

They've all halted on a dark stretch of the towpath. I'm about to do without an answer and walk forward when Si enquires "Was you going to swim home?"

If this is a threat I'll make sure at least one of them ends up in the canal—and then I grasp that they've been wondering why I loitered near the drain. "Don't tell me," I say with a version of mirth, "there's someone in this town who doesn't know who I am."

"We fucking do, and what you're after." Perhaps to head off another rebuke from his leader, Jay says "Evidence."

At once I suspect who they are and why they're here, which provokes me to ask "What do you think I might find?"

"You don't want to fucking know, boy."

"Fucking shut it, Jay," Si says and turns his ire on me. "Looking for some of it now, is you?"

"I couldn't say what I'm looking at." This is too close to the rejoinders I was trying to suppress, which makes me angrier still. "Don't you boys have anything to say for yourselves?" I ask the silent pair, and then I find a better question. "Can I guess one of you is Levi?"

"Don't you fucking call us boy, nigger," says the youth nearest to the silent office block.

I'm not sure whether he has just inadvertently confirmed he called my show after Kylie Goodchild's funeral. Before I can learn whether they're Wayne's gang and in that case where Wayne is, the fourth member says "Let's give the cunt something to look at, Si."

"Stick your fucking eyes on this, boy," Si tells me and reaches inside his singlet to produce a knife.

I find myself trying to think it's as childish a gesture as Jasper's schoolboy trick, but the blade is serrated and close to a foot long.

When Si takes a deliberate pace towards me his cronies copy him, and the blade glints like all their eagerness made visible. "I'm sorry if anyone feels insulted," I say and hold my ground. "I didn't call you anything you hadn't already called me."

Their only response is another step forward. I'd like to think they look as if they're rehearsing a musical routine in the dark. I retreat a pace and then, with furious reluctance, another. "Look, this is pointless."

It sounds like a bad joke about the knife, but saying so won't help. How far do I have to back to Oxford Street? I won't glance around—it would look too much like fear. "You don't want to use that," I say instead. "There'll be witnesses."

Some must be close, even if I can't hear them. They'll be on the far side of the arch. From this side of the bridge the towpath isn't visible from the street, which is walled off by a block of shops. Si glances beyond me and shows his teeth, then takes a stride that leaves his companions behind. He must mean to catch me before I reach the bridge—and then I'm thumped so hard on the back of the head it turns me sick.

I think someone else—Wayne—was skulking behind me until I swing dizzily around to see I've backed into the headstone of the bridge. Si and the others burst out laughing, if with little humour. At least my blunder should placate them, and I duck beneath the arch. I've stumbled a couple of paces when I hear a rush of footsteps, and Si shouts "Get the motherfucker."

The bridge nearly clubs my skull again as I stagger around to look. Jay is racing towards me with a knife at least as long as Si's. His swiftness seems to drag his lips back from his teeth. Though I want to stand and fight him, I can't deal with the knife. I crouch lower than the bridge and dash beneath. I feel as though it and the gang are forcing me to bow to the site of Kylie Goodchild's death— and then I see what I haven't taken into account. The steps to the street aren't immediately beyond the bridge.

They're about fifty yards ahead, leading to a railed-off walkway. The railings are too high for anyone to vault over, and you have to follow the walkway back to the bridge before you can reach the street. I'm sprinting so fast to the far end of the walkway that my head throbs with every pounding step when I hear Jay and the rest of them run out from under the bridge.

At least they can't get onto the walkway. My lungs are aching almost as fiercely as my head by the time I reach the steps. I'm stumbling upwards when I see that Si and another of the gang have followed me while Jay and the fourth member are staying by the bridge. The next moment Jay's crony squats and cups his hands, and Jay uses them to help him vault over the rail.

Before I can retreat the youth who's outdistanced Si runs up the steps behind me. I haven't time to think—I feel as if my clenched fists are swinging me around to punch him in the face. His lips split and squash wetly against my fist, and his chin bruises a knuckle. I would hit him again, but he flounders down a couple of steps until Si thumps his shoulders with an arm to steady him. They're blocking my retreat, and Si lifts his knife as if I've given him another reason to use it. Jay's helper has run to prevent me from jumping down onto the towpath, even if I could without breaking a leg. My only chance is to take Jay on.

As I start along the walkway he jerks up his knife exactly as Si did. I want to think that all he can do is imitate his leader; it makes him seem less of a threat. Si is tramping after me, and his companion looks determined to prove he's at least as dangerous, wiping his bloody grin with the back of one hand while he pulls out a knife with the other. The elongated window of a restaurant overlooks the walkway, and diners are frowning at the spectacle, but that's as much as they seem prepared to do. No, several have produced their mobile phones, and some are speaking into them, though more than one diner is using a phone to take photographs of me and my pursuers. The people who are phoning may be in touch with the police, and perhaps the others mean to record some evidence, but why isn't anyone coming to my aid? One man makes to stand up, but the woman at his table seizes his arm. Another diner doesn't quite leave his seat but thrusts his hands at the window as I come abreast of him, and I think he wants to ward off the sight of me until I realise he's urging me to jump over the railing and make my escape. Other customers are brandishing their phones to reassure me that help is on the way or to warn off my pursuers, but I don't know if Si and his injured crony are even looking; their deliberate footsteps don't falter. They must think Jay's enough to stop me, but he won't, whatever I have to do. The sight of people passing on the street above the steps behind him lends me courage, and so does my rage at the stupidity of the situation. "Everyone's watching you, Jay," I call to him. "You don't want to do anything you wouldn't like people to see."

He grimaces like a child who's been rebuked and lurches forward. I wonder if he's forgetting the knife, which looks close to drooping in his fist. It's just inches from the handrail, and at once I see what to do. At a moment like this you can only follow your instincts. "He can't help you," I say almost before I'm aware of meaning to speak, and nod at his crony on the towpath.

He glances down, which is all I need. I dodge towards the restaurant, where one diner has put down her knife and fork in order to cover her eyes while the woman beside her mouths some incomprehensible advice at me. If I haven't time to dart past Jay I'll knock the weapon out of his hand, over the edge of the walkway. I'm within inches of the gap he's left when he swerves towards me. "Fucking watch this," he shouts and jabs the knife at my face.

I jerk my head back and punch his arm with all my strength. It isn't enough. He grunts, but the knife scarcely wavers. The point of the blade swells into an enormous close-up, and for an instant it's all I can focus on except for his grinning face. He looks triumphant, proud of himself. I haven't even time to gasp before the point goes out of focus, and I feel it penetrate my eyeball.

The shock of the pain is so great that all the skin around my eye winces as though it's desperate to help me blink. In a moment I can't see the blade at all. I seem to feel my eye bulge helplessly, and liquid streams down my cheek. I have a random nightmare thought that it's about to trickle into my mouth. I see the blade as Jay snatches it back, but only with my right eye—the left one is an aching absence where no light can reach, since I've closed its trembling lid in an attempt to keep in whatever's left of it. Jay stares at me in disgust, then shoves me aside so violently that I almost topple over the handrail.

I cling to it with both hands while his running footsteps and the others fade into the distance. I'm supporting myself for fear I may pass out, but I'm trying to hope that if I don't move it may give my injury more of an eventual chance to heal. The world looks flattened and darkened, and the left side of my face is the focus of a dull ache that feels like the threat of far worse. I'm willing it not to develop when I hear someone run down the steps from the bridge. "Keep still," he says so calmly that it has to be his professional tone, "keep it still." His last words come too late. I barely glance towards him with my right eye, but the left one moves in unison, and I feel the eyeball tear against the lid.

33

WITH MOTHER

"And that's the news from Trevvy here on Waves, your tuned-in chum. I'm your pal Derry and I hope we'll all have major fun together for the next two hours. You don't want me in your ear if I can't put a smile on your face . . ." He plays the jingle for the Derek Dennison Show—"Listening to you. The listener's the winner"— and then he's back. "That's the ticket, if you listen you're a winner. Do you know, we forgot to tell you the weather. What's it going to be, Chrissy? Just don't use any of those long words the rest of us won't understand."

"Hot and humid and it could be thundery."

"Hot and human and it could be blundery. A bit like me, were you going to say? I thought you were here to produce me, not reduce me. No joking, folks, she's the best producer I've ever had on Waves."

"The only one."

"Well, now you mention it, don't. Coming up in the next hour we'll be talking about Twin Town Day. That's me and you at home, not Chrissy, she'll be out there slaving over a hot switchboard. Are there any twins listening? Do you fancy telling us what it's like? And if any of you, that's not just twins, if anyone's been to our twin town and you've got any stories about it, we're all ears. What do we think of the whole idea, anyway? What's the point of being twins with a town in another country? What do we get out of it? Stop there, Chrissy."

"I suppose we get—"

"Nobody's asking you that. It's just for our chums at home. I was going to say somebody's missed a trick. We ought to have hooked up with the radio in our twin town for the show."

"Maybe you can next year."

"Why, aren't you planning to be here? Don't go handing in your notice just because you never thought of hooking me up. We'll forgive you this once. And jeeps, don't make that face or you'll have me thinking you don't love me any more." Having repeated the last six words to a tune, he adds "Just be glad we aren't on telly, folks. Only joking, Chrissy. We go together like fish and chips. I do the fishing and she's got a bunch of chips . . ."

By now I've had very much more than enough. Though the voices in the kitchen are only just audible, they feel clamped to my ears, muffled by faulty headphones. I grope on the bedside table and raise my unenthusiastic head from the pillow to fit the elastic above my ears and pull the velvet patch over the hole where my left eye used to be. It drags the eyelid down and weighs on it, but in a few minutes if not hours I may grow unaware of the sensation; perhaps I'll even be less convinced that the burden is pressing a lump of darkness into my skull. I kick off the single sheet and plod across the floor, which seems cramped by the lack of perspective, to shove my fists into the sleeves of my cheap silk dressing-gown. For just an instant I'm rewarded by a chill on my skin at odds with the heat of the day before I venture into the hall.

Dennison is appealing for identical twins now. Presumably at some point he'll allow callers onto the air, but I can't bear to listen to any more of the show that has taken my slot, even if it covers up any sounds I'm unable to avoid making. I was careful to ease my bedroom door open, but I haven't reached the bathroom when I bump into the left-hand wall, which no longer seems as present as it used to be. At once Dennison is cut off in the middle of a syllable, making way for a different voice. "I'm sorry, Graham, did I wake you?"

"It's time I was up," I shout before locking myself in the bathroom. I use the toilet and brush my teeth, and then I have to wash my face. I hang the eye-patch on the back of the door and shut my eyes—the lids, at any rate—while I splash water at myself and fumble for the soap and eventually rub some of my face hard with a towel as a preamble to patting the left side as if I'm afraid to discover the socket is raw. My behaviour enrages me, and I fling away the towel and jerk up my left eyelid.

The wrinkled pinkish hollow still puts me in mind of an enlarged navel. Certainly the idea is no more grotesque than its appearance. Sometimes I'm tempted to finger it, except that doing so might irritate it or worse, and more often—right now, for instance—my fury at the sight or at the events that led to it leaves me fighting not to dig my thumb deep into the hole. I content myself with thrusting my face at the mirror, which only seems to flatten my reflection further; it looks no more substantial than a photograph. I'm glaring at it with the remaining eye when there's a timid knock at the door. "Are you all right in there, Graham?"

"Even better than last time you asked." I succeed in keeping this under my breath and call "I'll be out in a minute."

"Would you like a coffee?"

"I shouldn't think that could do any harm."

Footsteps retreat, so softly they sound unconvinced, as I turn away from the mirror. I feel as if I'm bringing darkness with me, embedded in my head. I cover it with the patch and unbolt the door, which looks too much like a life-size image of itself, close to drifting out of focus. When I reach the end of the incomplete hall, the space fails to open out as it should, and I feel even more trapped in my skull.

My mother looks around with a smile as I enter the kitchen—with the corners of her stiff straight lips hitched up, at any rate. As usual she's standing erect with her head held high like a burden she's carried throughout her life and doesn't mean to put down now. "At least you got some sleep," she wants to think.

It's rather that I don't feel I have much to get up for. I'm still incapable of sleeping through the night—it feels as if I can't doze longer than a few minutes without being jerked awake by the fear of an agonised pain in the hole in my face, or the sensation of a knife puncturing my eye unless it's a blade clearing out the socket, or just my condition, which is eager to be recollected whenever I succeed in forgetting it, even momentarily. All too often I dream that my one eye is under attack, which is guaranteed to make me struggle whimpering back to reality, not that it offers much reassurance. The best answer I can find is "I hope you did."

"You mustn't worry about me."

I do, of course. I have the unhappy impression that every time she's confronted with my state it ages her. I don't know when her cropped red hair began to pale and exhibit hints of grey like a sunset yielding to the night, but aren't there more of those? I can't avoid noticing, because even with her straight-backed stance she's half a head shorter than me, which makes her look reluctant to meet my eye or more likely the absence of one. If she can't sleep while she's caring for me, having insisted, that's another reason to persuade her to go home. I'm about to try afresh when she says "Sorry I woke you up with that."

"You mustn't keep apologising. Nothing's your fault."

"I just wanted to see what they're putting on instead of you. I promise you it's nowhere near as good."

"I did hear."

"He's the opposite of you, isn't he? He's telling people what to say. I don't know how she can—" My mother looks down as if the sight of me has proved too much for her again. "I didn't realise," she says, "she'd actually be on the show."

"She didn't sound too pleased about it either."

"I hope she isn't." My mother risks a glance at my face before not precisely asking "You haven't changed your mind since you came out of hospital."

"About what in particular?"

"You still don't want to see her any more."

"I've changed my mind but no, I don't."

"How do you mean, Graham?"

"When she tried to see me I was partly blaming her. If we hadn't had an argument I wouldn't have been where I was that night. Now I just think it's better for us both to stay apart. She deserves to have someone who isn't like me."

"She won't find anybody better," my mother retorts as though she's borrowing my anger, which has subsided. "If she cared she'd have tried harder to stay in touch."

"It depends what you said to put her off."

"Enough," my mother says with more satisfaction than I quite appreciate. "About as much as I said to your father when he dared to show his face at the hospital."

"Can I ask what?"

"Nothing you wouldn't have said, I hope. That you didn't need anyone else while I'm here, for a start." When I'm silent my mother turns to the agitated percolator. "And I told him—well, there's no need to bring that up again if you didn't hear."

"I didn't, but I'd like to now. I'm not fond of secrets."

"I don't want to distress you any more if you've managed to forget all about it." My mother makes to pass me a mug of coffee but plants it on the table, apparently for fear I can't see well enough to handle it. She brings her mug and milks them both and sits opposite me, frowning at my interrogative look. With some defiance and more reluctance she says "I told him he was to blame."

"For what, sorry?"

"Oh, Graham, how much are you going to make me say? For how you are."

"Angrier than does me any good, you mean."

"No more than you've a right to be." Her brave straightened smile doesn't let her avoid saying "I mean for how you've ended up."

"I don't see how he's involved in that."

"I wish we could just forget him." With enough resentment to have some left for me my mother says "He hit you in the eye when you went to stand up to him once. It was black for a week and we had to tell the school you'd been in a fight with some boy you didn't know. Maybe if your father hadn't done that—"

She gazes at the eye-patch and then has to look away. Do I have a vague memory of the incident? It feels too much like being told a tale by Frank Jasper. "I can't believe it matters after all these years," I tell my mother. "If anyone's to blame it's me."

"You mustn't say that, Graham. You mustn't even think it. It isn't going to help."

"Maybe it's what I need to remember." When her determined smile wavers I say "If I hadn't let my temper run away with me I wouldn't have walked out on Chris that night. And if I hadn't given one of them a thump down by the canal I might have got away without this."

Though I don't touch the site of my missing eye or even point to it, my mother winces as if I've done both. "I wish you'd given them a lot worse," she declares—she might be expressing rage on my behalf, since she hasn't revived mine. "And why can't the police track them down?"

"I'm sure they must be doing their best."

As I struggle to dislodge the thought that Jasper's father may be concerned with the investigation, my mother says "Have you still not been able to remember anything else about those, I won't call them boys?"

"I haven't." For an insipid excuse, which I wouldn't give anyone else, I add "It was dark."

In fact I can recall no distinguishing features of the gang except the names of two of them, which apparently aren't enough. I was left with the impression that the police found this little better than racist, which I don't suppose I alleviated by suggesting the gang could have been Wayne's, since he somehow proved he didn't even know them. Now my mother demands "Why couldn't the police use some of the photos all those people took?"

"I know they tried." As I lift my mug I'm reminded once again how objects seem to swell up whenever I bring them to my face. Once I've taken a sip that seems muffled by the incompleteness of another sense I tell her "Apparently the photos were too blurred to use."

"I thought they had the works to make anything clear these days."

"Not stuff shot by amateurs on mobiles." My mother's protest brings to mind how I cleaned up the recording of Jasper's act, which could be the cause of everything that's happened to me since, but I don't want to think about it, let alone further back. "Anyway, if you'll excuse me," I manage to distract myself by saying, "I'll get dressed."

The other wall of the corridor seems insufficiently present now, at least until my elbow blunders against it. I'm in the bedroom and rubbing the elbow when, beyond the door that I didn't quite shut, I hear my mother talking in a low voice on her mobile. "Jane, I don't think I'll be able to get to the book group or lunch with the girls for a good while, but I'll do my very best to come to Hester's funeral."

As I drag some clothes on, the flattened perspective seems to turn my legs dwarfish. I'm making my way along the shrunken un-developed hall when my mobile clanks with an incoming message.

I read the number that sent it and say "You'd think we conjured her up by talking about her."

My mother hurries out of the kitchen, trying to decide on a smile. "Don't say it's Christine."

"That's what I'm saying. I'll have a word in my room if you don't mind."

This time I make sure to shut the door, and keep my voice down as well. When I've finished speaking I go back to the main room, where my mother appears to be waiting to learn whether she ought to be eager or anxious. "Let me try and put your mind at rest," I say at once. "Don't feel hurt, but I'm going to give it another go."

"Why on earth should I feel hurt, Graham?" Before I'm forced to be more explicit my mother says "I need to wake up, don't I. You mean she won't want to find me here."

"If she's moving back in . . ."

"You needn't say any more. After what I said to her I wouldn't blame her if she never wanted to speak to me again." My mother lifts a hand as well as the corners of her mouth to forestall any argument. "When are you expecting her?"

"She just has to produce the rest of the new show."

"It won't take me long to pack." It doesn't, and my mother is waiting on the street well ahead of two o'clock. As her taxi to the station pulls up she says "Will you keep letting me know how you are? And try and come and see me soon."

"Of course I will. Maybe both of us . . ." I interrupt myself with a kiss on her cheek. As I watch the taxi dwindle along the depthless sunlit street it seems I've achieved all I can. I've succeeded in sending her back to her friends, and there's another reason to be pleased: I'll never have to listen to Waves again.

34

GAGS

Christine's voice is so close it feels like part of me. She's saying a name in my ear—not my name. For a moment I imagine that I'm hearing her through headphones—that she's telling me the next person I need to speak to—and then I grasp where I am. As I turn my head towards hers on the pillow, one of my knuckles catches my left eye, or rather it pokes the lid into the socket. My head jerks back, and I'm altogether too awake.

I'm alone beneath the tangled clammy sheet. Christine's murmur was the last trace of a dream I can't remember. I no more heard her in reality than I did when I pretended to my mother that Christine had been on the phone. No doubt I was unnecessarily afraid that my mother would see through the trick. I couldn't simulate a call to my mobile to make it ring, but I was able to send it a blank message from itself.

The bedside clock is showing almost noon. It blinks its pair of zeros into shape as if to demonstrate that it can boast one more eye than me. It's nearly time for the dreadful Dennison, but I won't be listening; I wouldn't even if Christine were producing someone else. Whatever my dream might appear to suggest, I've finished with her. I don't deserve anyone except myself.

I fumble for the eye-patch but leave it where it is. There's nobody to cover up for. I could feel there's as little reason to leave my bed, but I mustn't let apathy hollow me out. I kick the sheet away and tramp through my less than three-dimensional apartment to the bathroom, where I can't help flinching as the first spikes of water from the shower jab at my face. I towel myself without looking in the mirror any more than I can help, and then I switch on the per-colator before starting up the computer.

By the time the percolator finishes its work I'm still gazing at the last words I typed weeks ago. I take my coffee black and dump sugar into it, none of which is any use; my mind feels as flat as the screen and as empty as the left side of my face. It isn't that the novel reminds me how I betrayed myself to Christine, since I've decided that ended up for the best. It's that the story, such as it is, seems to have been written by someone I no longer recognise and can't recall.

Could I find my way back into the tale by rethinking it? Perhaps Glad Savage's observations might be keener if she only had one eye, but wanting to think so isn't going to convince me. Suppose I can't write or even imagine her because I'm no longer glad to be savage? The hopeless joke is almost bad enough for Benny, a thought that releases me from staring dully at the monitor. The screen isn't go-ing to change without my aid—it isn't a polygraph. I want to make my peace with Benny, and a drink with lunch may even help me relax with the novel.

I dress and put my patch on and take time over shutting my door. If Walter Belvedere's at home, he's keeping quiet about it. I haven't seen him since he helped the reporter ambush me, but I wouldn't mind flashing my eye-socket at him. All the way down-stairs the treads give the impression of having closed up like a concertina. When I venture into the furious sunlight I feel as if with just one eye I'm required to blink twice as much.

To begin with I don't respond when people glance at me. When I start telling them "It's Pirates Without Parrots Day" nobody seems amused. At least passing Christine's flat shouldn't trouble me, and it doesn't until I see her at the window. She must have a different day off now that she's producing Dennison. I dodge out of sight, almost bumping into the wall of her apartment block, before she can see me or I can identify whatever she has in her hand. I don't want her pity or anyone else's, especially not my own.

When Benny looks up he seems uncertain how to shape his face. He's attempting not to look too wary by the time I reach the bar. "Aye aye, Benny," I say but stop short of pointing at my patch. "Seen any parrots in here?"

I'm almost sure I glimpse a wince. "Just food and drink," he says.

"Don't fight it, Benny. Don't hide whatever you think of my jokes, all right? I'm a changed man."

"I can see that."

"Hey, that's nearly a joke," I say, because he appears to regret it. "One in the eye for me, was it? And listen, call me something. Anything you want."

"What would you like, Mr W?"

"I can live with that." He used to have more fun with it, but then I realise he isn't asking about the pronunciation. "I'll have a glass from down under."

He pours the New Zealand white without commenting on it. When he brings my change I wave it away and raise the glass to him. "Here's looking at you, Benny," I say, which doesn't seem to go down as well as the wine. "And I'm sorry if I caused you any trouble last time I was here."

"Don't lose any sleep over it. You've got worse to bother you by the looks."

Is that a joke? I feel as if it's my fault that I can't tell. "Seriously, I didn't harm your image too much, did I? I mean, you aren't going anywhere."

"Nobody else would have me." I'm about to assure him that he couldn't be replaced when he says "When are they putting you back on your show?"

"When I can afford to buy the station. Meanwhile I'll just have to keep my eye out for another job."

This earns a visible wince. "You'd think they could make allowances," Benny mutters. "It's not as if folk can see you on the radio."

"I'm not after any allowances, Benny. Leave them for the disabled." When he looks uncomfortable I say "You don't mind talking to me, do you? It isn't as if you're up to your eyeballs just now."

"If that's what you need, Mr W."

"I'd better have something to eat as well. How about a rib-eye steak with black-eyed peas?"

"Just the basic menu."

"Better than a poke in the eye. I'll have a burger. Make it a big one and that can go for the wine as well."

Benny keys my order at the till and takes the slip into the wings. As he brings me another glass he leans across the bar to murmur "Stay and talk if you like, but you'd better keep your voice down."

I glance around to find the problem. One booth is occupied by young businessmen, and a table is surrounded by girls at lunch. While nobody is looking at me, I have the impression that more than one just was. I duck towards Benny to mutter "Is there somebody we need to keep an eye on?"

Though I wasn't intending to make a joke, Benny's frown suggests I was. "Just the customers."

"Mustn't upset them, must we? Can't expect to see eye to eye with everybody all the time. Don't worry, I won't lose you any. Customers, I mean, not eyes."

I'm speaking lower still, but he hasn't finished frowning. "I hope not, Mr W."

"Trust me, your job's safe with me. I know what it's like to lose one."

I straighten up and swivel on the stool as the volume of street noise is turned up. A middle-aged couple—a woman in a perilously low-cut summer dress and a man in a shirt just as floral, hanging outside capacious shorts—have come into the pub. A flood of sunlight catches the glass on Frank Jasper's poster, which dazzles me like a hint of having no eyes at all. As his face loses its illumination I grope for the bar to swing the stool around, hearing Benny murmur "Are you all right, Mr W?"

"I'm as fine as I'll ever be, Benny. You look after your customers."

While he serves the couple my vision seeps back, though I could fancy it's flatter than ever. Its return makes me all the more aware of the hole where the rest of it should be. The newcomers, at least one of whom smells as flowered as they look, stay at the bar while I sip and then rather more than sip my drink. Benny lingers with them to chat about, I would say, almost less than nothing in particular. I could easily conclude he prefers their company, but he has to acknowledge me when I drain my glass and plant it on the bar and push it in his direction. "Same again?" he can't very well avoid saying.

"As long as that's what I'm known for." I can still see Jasper's face spotlit by the sun and looking convinced it's no more than his due; it feels as if the image has lodged behind my eye-patch, challenging me to scratch it out. When Benny brings my drink I'm provoked to say "So the all-seeing eye's still with us."

"What's that, Mr W?" Benny says, not quite as if he wants to know.

"My old pal Frankie Jasper. I thought the boys from out of town wanted you to get rid of anybody local."

"They've let me keep some of the posters up that were."

"I should have given you my photo while I had the chance, shouldn't I? I expect they must be pretty rare by now. Maybe they're even desirable after everything that's been mixed up with them. Somebody with an eye to the market could make a profit out of them. There must be people who'd pay for that kind of souvenir."

Benny nods his head, apparently regretfully. He has been shaking it too, no doubt in order not to speak, and he can't hide all his relief at the sound of a bell. He vanishes into the kitchen and reappears with my burger in a bun with chips. "All right," I tell him, "that's shut me up for a while."

I've taken a mouthful of burger and speared a chip with my fork when the woman at the bar turns to me, sending a floral scent to invade the taste in my mouth. "Excuse me, I couldn't help overhearing. Are you in the theatre as well?"

"As well as what?" With less in my mouth I add "Don't tell me you're a listener. Don't worry, Benny, I'm not accusing anyone of anything."

"Mr W used to be on the radio," Benny's anxious to explain.

"Is that how you got into the theatre?" the woman's companion asks.

"I'm not in any theatre. I haven't been since I went to see the worst show of my life," I say and take a bite to quiet myself.

"We thought you must be," says the woman.

"Why, because of this?" To make up for my indistinctness I jab the fork at my eye-patch, but only Benny winces. "I'm not in costume," I say more clearly once I can. "I'm not trying to catch anyone's eye."

"Mr W was attacked by a gang," Benny makes haste to say, "and one of them did that to him."

"Caught my eye, do you mean, Benny?" This time all three of them grimace. "There was quite a crowd watching," I feel driven to add. "Some of them seemed to think it was a show, and some just turned a blind eye."

The man looks offended, perhaps not merely by my choice of

words. "That isn't why we thought you might be on the stage, what you have to wear."

"I'm glad to hear I don't look fake. Nobody wants me to take a test, then. Not an eye test, the lie kind." When he and his companion only seem perplexed I say "So what did make you think I was a performer?"

"You said you were friends with one."

"That was a joke. I'm full of those, you may have noticed."

With more respect than I find appropriate the woman says "Did you get to meet people like him because you were on the radio?"

"I didn't need to be on there to meet his sort. Just put your money where your brains should be and you can meet him too."

The woman frowns, but sympathetically. "You sound jealous."

"Jealous of a fake like him? I may not be much, but if I didn't think I was better than him I wouldn't show my face in public."

"You said he was your friend."

"That was the joke." I can't believe the woman sounds reproachful. "He was at my school," I tell her. "He just wanted to impress people and didn't much care how. He isn't even American. He's from up the road."

"Do you resent him for bettering himself?" the man has the cheek to ask.

"He's bettered nothing, not himself or the world around him. He's just played on what he always was. People like him pretend to see ghosts and the future and the rest of it, and it's all a trick. They see less than I can with one eye."

"A psychic lady put our friend in touch with her mother."

I see Benny dreading my reaction, and that's enough to calm me down. "It's all right, Benny, I'm saying nothing."

"Haven't you got an answer to that?" the woman insists on establishing.

"I would have once. I'd have had plenty, but it isn't my job any more. I can't see my way to it now."

"I don't think you know what to think. Maybe you should go and see your friend."

I'm not sure what effect Benny hopes to have by informing everyone "He's back across the road next week."

"He'll be a sight for sore eyes, do you think?" I won't be distracted from talking to the couple. "Are you saying I should be an eye witness? I could have used a few of those when I got this. Or are you hoping he'll open my eyes? I'm afraid that's all my eye. He's not a patch on some of the shows I've been involved with."

They're staring at me as if I'm not just a bad comedian but an offensive one. I hardly need to hear the man say "Do you think everything's a joke?"

"Believe me, you wouldn't like to see the alternative." I take the last mouthful of burger and stand up, staying by the bar until I'm able to speak again. "Thanks for the hospitality, Benny," I say, "and thank you both for showing me what to do." I'm no longer joking, but I've no time to explain. Perhaps I haven't quite run out of rage, not when it still may be of some use. "Let's see what I can see this time," I mutter as I hurry out to buy a ticket at the Palace.

35

A NEW GHOST

I haven't let myself take the long way round. Well before I'm along-side Christine's building I can see her apartment is dark. Women are pedalling at various speeds in the window of Corporate Sana, and Christine is winning the race. I don't think she has seen me, and I'm not going to dodge out of sight. In any case she seems intent on the race and her iPod, if that's what she has in her hand. I turn away to hide my face, especially the eye-patch, and hurry to the Palace.

A crowd much larger than the one that watched my departure in the ambulance is converging on the theatre. Across the road is the entrance to the steps I nearly reached. I did climb them eventually with help, while every pace I ventured upwards threatened to disturb the throbbing lump of blindness that was embedded in my head. Now people are trooping past the location as though it's mean-ingless, and anyone who looks in my direction glances past me at the posters for Frank Jasper. That doesn't trouble me, or rather I don't mind that they reawaken my rage. I'll be storing it up for him.

Suppose he's greeting his audience as they enter the theatre? While he didn't last time, I wouldn't put any kind of self-promotion past him. I survey the foyer as best I can with just an eye, but only the theatre staff seem to be dealing with the faithful. As one examines my ticket I have the impression that she's concentrating on it so as to avoid looking at my face. It infuriates me to wonder if anybody thinks I'm here in the hope of being healed, although surely even Jasper wouldn't claim he's able to perform that trick.

Around me the crowd looks more solid than cut-outs, but not much. The lack of depth seems to aggravate the congestion and the evening heat, and a trickle of sweat nearly seeps behind my eye-patch. I'm hoping a seat at the back of the stalls will let me remain unobtrusive while I want to be. In case I need extra concealment I buy a programme as well, even though Jasper's on the cover.

Entering the auditorium doesn't give me much more sense of space, but I'm almost used to that—almost resigned to the loss of everything that would never have been stolen from me if it weren't for Jasper. I sidle along a row of flattened pop-up people and sit on the sinking seat and gaze at the curtains that veil the stage like, I'm enraged to think, the entrance to some kind of shrine. They seem only dimly lit despite the footlights and not nearly distant enough. I'm opening the programme, not least to put Jasper's relentlessly watchful photograph out of my sight, when the woman who last stood up for me murmurs "Are you wanting to see about someone?"

"You could say that."

"Ah." This is more than an acknowledgment, since she multiplies the vowel. "Well," she says, "I hope you hear from them."

Some if not all of her sympathy must be prompted by my state, and I can't pretend I welcome it when it involves Jasper. "I believe I'll get what I'm here for," I tell her and leaf through the glossy programme, turning up picture after picture of Frank Jasper. In one he's looking chummy, in the next he's concerned for anyone who wants to think he is. I do my best to avoid his eyes, both of them, by reading what we're allowed to know about him. "Originally from Manchester, he now makes his home in California but will travel wherever he's needed." I have to mask my snigger with a hand, so hastily that I almost dislodge the eye-patch. "He has been involved with the police"—which brings my hidden grin closer to a snarl—"and has advised them in a number of successful investigations"—which is worded as craftily as the claims he makes onstage. I'm dangerously close to pointing out the trick to the woman who spoke to me, but the dim page is growing darker. I think my anger is reducing the eyesight I still have until I realise the show is about to begin.

The babble of the audience sinks to a mumble and yields to a silence strewn with a few coughs as the curtains part to let out a man in an evening suit. He waits for a shrill hacking bout to subside and pats a small cough of his own before saying "Ladies and gentlemen, we are privileged to have with us tonight the return to Manchester of one of the world's leading psychics. Last time we were lucky enough to be graced with his much sought-after performance he had so many messages he didn't have time to deliver them all. Tonight he hopes to make amends if anyone was disappointed. Ladies and gentlemen, please put your hands together for the man who's always sensitive on your behalf—Frank Jasper."

I have to join in, both as a reason to unclench my fists and so as not to seem different from everyone around me. The applause, though not mine, swells as the curtains glide all the way open to reveal Jasper, who's spotlit from above as though heaven is beaming on him. He's as bronzed as ever, which has to betray a few sessions under a lamp, and dressed in white, even his shoes. At that distance I can't tell whether his collarless shirt bears a slogan. As he advances to the edge of the bare stage he draws the spotlight with him. "Welcome, all my friends," he says. "All of you I've met and all the ones I've still to meet. All the ones I'm seeing now and all of them I will."

He's worse than ever. My nails scrape his slippery face as I grip the programme with both hands so as not to clench my fists too visibly. For once in a theatre I'm glad to be sitting behind someone broad and tall, a woman whose extravagantly wide coiffure adds to her usefulness. I'm able to hide most of my face except for my right eye from Jasper as he says "I guess I can predict a full evening for us. There are a whole lot of people here you can't see. There are people who've come back because they need to speak to us."

I just manage not to grin—to bare my teeth, rather. He's telling the truth for once, and that's conclusive. I've come back to raise my voice, but I mustn't be too quick; I need to wait for whatever moment will let me expose his tricks so thoroughly that no one can be fooled by them in future. I clamp my jaws shut, sending an ache up my left cheek to the eye-sized hole, while Jasper declares "I'm hearing from somebody, only maybe who they're here for won't want to believe they are."

That's devious even for him, and I'd call it offensive as well. As I stare at the smooth cartoon he seems to have become he says "I'm getting they've only recently passed. Whoever knew them thinks they went too soon."

How can his trickery fail to be obvious to everyone? Because they want to be deceived and would never admit it—that's his guarantee of success. I'm dismayed to glimpse movements in the auditorium, people nodding their heads in agreement with Jasper or in the hope that he means them. "I'm hearing C," he says, and when nobody lays claim to it "No, it's more like a T. When they were in this world they liked to help people."

I've begun to wonder how blatant he intends to be. Has he developed such a contempt for his victims that he's no longer bothering with any kind of subtlety? I'm tempted to set my trap at once—to say he's in touch with someone I recognise. I've practiced altering my voice, and I'm sure he won't know me until it's too late. I want to see through more of his performance first, and I succeed in keeping silent while training my eye on the unnaturally lit artificially coloured cartoon of him. As he's answered by a murmur that he either can't locate or finds insufficient Jasper says "Wait, I'm hearing more. They were involved with a lot of people, not just the ones they knew. Was that their job?"

Can anybody really think he's after confirmation rather than a clue? His gaze ranges about the audience and, before I'm ready for it, passes over me. I can't help holding my breath as an aid to sitting absolutely still. By the time his attention drifts back to the front stalls, my jaws and the left side of my face have begun to throb. That gives me more rage to save up, but I manage to relax my jaw a fraction as Jasper says "It's not an unusual name, is it? I'm sure I'm hearing a T or a C if I'm not getting both."

"Tanya Cristobel." I have to grind my teeth so as not to shout this while Jasper sends his eager gaze around the auditorium. When it fails to prompt any response he says "They don't want you to be shy. Maybe they always wanted to help people to express themselves. They couldn't be a teacher."

His tone is just ambiguous enough to let this be taken as a question. It has no more depth than the way he looks to my eye, and I'm struggling not to be provoked to speak when someone near the middle of the theatre says almost inaudibly "They couldn't, no."

"Lady in the green dress. I'm sorry, I don't have your name."

Now she's got her voice out she tries to raise it. "Charmaine."

I wouldn't be surprised if Jasper claimed this was the name he was reaching for, but he says "Didn't they call you Charming Charmaine?"

He'll be ready with a ruse if that proves to be untrue, but Charmaine rewards him with an embarrassed giggle. "She did sometimes."

He's learned the gender of the dead at last. "Okay, I'm hearing she passed before she had a chance to teach."

"She did. She'd passed her exams and everything as well," Charmaine says and, overcome by emotion, turns to her neighbour to mumble a name.

"I guess I'm hearing clearer now. Charity, is that what I've been getting?"

He's profited from far too much of it, and I could also point out that everybody must have heard the name—and then I'm delighted to hear the woman say "She was called Charlotte."

"Sure, that's right. Didn't your friends call you Charlie and Charmaine?"

Charmaine rewards this with a muffled sniff. "Some of them did."

"Let me tell you that's how she still thinks of you both, and she'll be with you whenever you need her. And I wasn't wrong to mention charity, was I? She had a lot."

"She gave whatever she could."

"That's how I'm hearing it, she liked to be involved with them. Do you know what she's saying she would love to see? You setting up some kind of Charlie and Charmaine fund for the cause you think she'd most want to support."

"It ought to be you, Mr Jasper."

"Call me Frank like all my friends do, and I want you to put money right out of your mind while you're here. I didn't travel all this way for your dough."

I can't help wishing he were wired up to a polygraph. The memories this rouses inflame my rage, and so does hearing Jasper say "Somebody else wants to be heard now. They're younger than Charlie, and did they pass this year?"

He's met by an uneasy silence in which any restlessness falls short of a nod. Perhaps his listeners are unsure what they're being asked or afraid to hope too much, but I'm entirely sure of him. He's playing his most cynical trick to fasten on their emotions— pretending he's been contacted by a child. "There's a B with a message for a parent," he says. "Who's that who's here?"

Is this my cue? Can I really use the death of someone's child for my own purposes? That's what Jasper's doing, after all. In that case I could be said to be as bad as he is, and I haven't opened my mouth when he says "I'm just about certain I'm hearing B. Is there a B here who's recently said goodbye to a child?"

I'm waiting for him to decide he heard a different letter, but as he makes to speak again a woman gasps near the front of the auditorium. "It isn't Kylie, is it, Mr Jasper? Bob couldn't come this time."

I drop my programme, not just because my fists have twitched open but as an excuse to crouch out of sight. I'd be ashamed if Kylie's mother realised I was here or why. Remembering all that she's suffered has confronted me with what I planned to do tonight—to rob her and people like her of perhaps the only belief that sustains them. Whatever my view of it, destroying it would be no better than vindictive, and my rage goes out like a fire that has been swamped with water. "It isn't, Margaret," Jasper is saying. "I'd know her. Ladies and gentlemen, this is Margaret Goodchild, Kylie Goodchild's mother."

This earns a burst of applause as well as a sympathetic murmur, and Margaret seems not to know whether to stand up. "Mr Jasper brought our Kylie back to us at her funeral," she says in an uncontrolled voice.

I won't let this provoke me. At least she hasn't mentioned how he implicated me. I rise from my seat in as much of a crouch as I'm able to maintain and set about muttering apologies all the way along the row. Some of the people who let me pass appear to think I'm too moved to stay, while others frown at my behaviour. No doubt I resemble a child who's been called up to the stage at a show, but I feel more like a culprit desperate to escape notice. I don't know if Jasper has recognised me, since the left side of my face is towards the stage. Perhaps my eye-patch renders me unidentifiable. Surely if he knew me he wouldn't dare to say. "Maybe whoever I'm hearing from is telling those they've left behind to be happy," he suggests. "Maybe that's the be, but I'm sure there's a child."

As I lurch into the aisle his words almost goad me into confronting him. I'm forcing myself to head for the lobby when a man says gruffly "Our Davina was stung by a bee once in the pram. We reckoned that was why she ended up so weak."

"Davina," Jasper says as if someone other than the member of the audience has told him. "That's the name, of course it is. Didn't you call her your little princess?"

Somebody—the father, I assume—responds with a sob. "She's here with you," Jasper says, "and she wants you to know—"

I would rather not hear. I hurry to the doors, which thud shut behind me like a lid, cutting off Jasper's routine. Usherettes and other personnel glance or stare at me as I cross the foyer, but I won't react; I just want to be out of the Palace, beyond any risk of causing a scene or worse. Even the hot still night feels like a relief. I wipe my forehead with the back of my hand while I stare at the gap in the wall of the bridge, leading to the steps down to the canal. I'm about to move onwards when the gap seems to jerk into focus, almost regaining perspective. At last I've realised what I heard.

36

AT THE GARAGE

"It's Derry here again, your lunchtime chum. Today's Cancel A Crime Day, so let's be a bit serious. I'm sure all of us mums and dads ought to be concerned with crime, and I expect the rest of you are too, specially all you mature listeners. Let's see how many of us can make a difference for everyone today. Are the lines buzzing yet, Patsy?"

"We've a few callers waiting."

"Slap my wrist and call me wicked. I'll bet the jury would let you off for provocation. You don't like anyone calling you Patsy, do you? And nobody who rings my show today is going to be one. So don't get in a paddy, Patty. Man the switchboard or I should say girl it if you'll let me, and let's be hearing from our pals."

The one point worth disentangling from this rigmarole is that it must be Christine's day off, unless she has found another job. She's one problem I won't have to solve, supposing that she would have tried to hinder what I need to do. The radio is turned up all the way, and I can hear every word without straining my ears, despite the shouts and metal uproar in the workshop and the traffic noise out here on the road. There's nowhere to hide unless I move out of earshot of the workshop—the nearest cover is a phone box at least a hundred yards away—and so I'll have to take the risk.

As I produce my mobile a speeding lorry pants hot oily fumes into my face, reminding me that I can't even move away from the road. The fumes that feel like the noon heat rendered thicker and more stagnant are one reason I wipe my forehead while I wait for my call to be answered. By no means immediately a voice says "The Derek Dennison Deal. Who's calling, please?"

It isn't Patty, who must be overseeing the calls, but of course it isn't Christine either. "Say Graham from the centre," I tell her.

"From the centre of Manchester." As I take her to be typing the details on Dennison's screen she says "From the centre of Manchester."

I have to resist thinking I've found a parrot to go with my patch. "Where else," I confine myself to saying.

"And what point would you like to make, Graham?"

I stare towards the garage, which consists largely of an outsize shed full of cars and parts of cars. However many mechanics are at work in there, they aren't visible from my section of the uneven flagstoned pavement. To my eye the building looks even less substantial than the rest of the perspectiveless road bordered by large old houses split into flats, some with shops on the ground floor. I could imagine the garage as not much more than a cardboard replica, capable of being razed by a well-chosen blow. I'm here to deliver one and, I very much hope, to expose a fake at last. "I'd like to help clear up a crime," I say not too loud.

"Could you speak up a little? I'm not quite getting you."

I turn my back on the garage before saying "To clear up a crime."

"That's good, Graham. Can you tell me a bit more about it?"

"I don't know if I can say it twice." I'm just wary of losing my chance. "I've had to get ready to say it at all," I tell her, which is true enough.

"Can you hold on, please? I'll have to speak to the producer."

There's some mumbling beyond a hand planted over the mouthpiece, and then a voice I recognise takes over. "What's it about, please?"

Patty sounds no more amiable than she did with Dennison. "About a crime," I say, having glanced back at the garage.

"I gathered that. What are you asking to do?"

"To put a few details out on the air. I think they might help to get it solved." Patty's silence prompts me to add "They might help your audience figures as well."

At once I'm afraid I've said too much. Perhaps I've betrayed my identity, or suppose Dennison has antagonised her so badly that she'd rather not boost his ratings? As I search for some other way of persuading her to let me on the air she says "Have you got a radio on?"

"I haven't, no."

"All right, we'll call you back."

I could think she hasn't looked into my intentions thoroughly enough. Perhaps that's her way of taking a crafty revenge on Dennison. I keep my back to the garage while I make another call, which takes so long that I'm afraid of blocking one from Dennison's team. At last I'm able to face the garage, where the radio is broadcasting an appeal to her neighbours by a woman whose house keeps being daubed with excreta and racist graffiti. Above the clatter of a drill in the garage a man shouts "If she doesn't like it she should fuck off where she come from."

As if the shout has set it off, the phone vibrates in my hand like an alarm. I'm fast enough to silence all of its new ringtone—Frank Sinatra singing "I Only Have Eyes For You"—except for the first word of the line. Pressing the mobile against the side of my face I can see with, I murmur "Hello?"

"Is this Graham?"

For a moment I'm sure I've been recognised. "That's my name."

"Leave your radio off, but you're going to hear it on your phone. Derek will be with you when he's finished talking to the lady who's on now."

I swing around to look at the traffic. Suppose the response to my other call arrives too soon? I can see only trucks and ordinary cars, oncoming layers of them, and I keep an eye on the garage as Dennison speaks in my ear. "I hope every one of your neighbours who care will stand by you, Swati, and the police will as well. I know they're listening to us today."

I should have realised they might, but Dennison distracts me by saying "Next in for a chat is Graham from the city centre. How are you today, Graham?"

"Better than some."

"Then we're two of a kind and I'll bet you good money there's more. We should give thanks for our blessings and pray other people have the same."

I need to answer, however disconcerting it is to hear my voice in the garage. It sounds more unnatural than I expected—louder than I am and so disconnected from me that I could easily imagine it's beyond my control. I'm also afraid Dennison may hear it and tell me to turn off the radio, and I plant my other hand over the phone as well before saying "I'd like to give someone some of mine."

"That's big of you, Graham. Well, there's a subject for another day. We should have Count Your, I mean Share Your Blessings Day."

"I'm sure that would be your kind of show."

"So long as the listener's the winner." After a pause that's filled by the clang of a hub-cap on the floor of the garage, Dennison says "Tell me something, Graham. Where do I know you from?"

I clasp my hands harder over the mobile on the wholly irrational notion that it will make me inaudible in the garage. "I've been on the show."

"I'm sure I've never spoken to you, but you sound familiar."

"Does it matter? Anyway, let me—"

"Good Lordy. Well, let's hear it for my ears. My senses haven't let me down yet." All this allows me to hope that he may keep his re-alisation to himself until he says "You're Graham Wilde."

How may this affect my plan? I can't hear any reaction in the garage, and denying who I am won't help; it might even get me taken off the air. "You've spotted me, Derek."

"Call me Derry and I'll call you Gray. What's brought you back to us? I should tell listeners in case they don't know that you used to be in my slot."

If he doesn't mean to be disdainful this must be an unintended innuendo, but I haven't time to deal with either. "I'm calling on today's subject."

"I should use my peepers, shouldn't I? It says here what you're doing." Having paused as though to give the drill in the garage a moment to clatter, he says "Are you a regular listener?"

"I won't pretend I have been."

"Only then you mightn't know—" This pause is so prolonged it isn't far from unprofessional. "Forget it for now," Dennison tells me or himself. "Let's hear your call."

I'm even more aware of my giant voice in the garage. I take a breath that I could imagine is audible above the rapid gunning of a power tool in the workshop and say "You'll have heard what hap-pened to me."

"We all have to move on, Gray, don't we? I did from the Beeb."

"I don't mean losing my job." He sounds a shade defensive, but I mustn't let that divert me. "I mean losing my eye. Go on, tell me that's careless."

"I hope you don't think I ever would."

Now I've antagonised him. My huge voice in the unnaturally flattened shed is making me say things I never planned to say. I'm about to reclaim control when the presenter says "Have they found whoever was responsible?"

"Not yet and maybe never. That's not the crime I want to help with."

"Then give it to us, Gray, but just be sure to remember how we have to work."

He's advising me to stay professional. I haven't time to resent that; I need to keep my rage in focus. "I'm guessing you listened to some of my shows or you wouldn't have recognised me."

"I was listening because—I did hear some."

"Maybe you heard some people thought I gave a psychic reading on the air."

"Didn't you?"

He sounds eager to believe, which is an advantage I didn't predict. "They thought I did it without knowing," I tell him. "I expect they'd say I could have developed it since, maybe to compensate for my eye."

"Is that what you're saying?"

"Let me tell you what I see and you can tell me what you think."

I've come to it at last. He shouldn't interrupt me much if he wants to give his other callers their time on the air. "I believe I can see what happened to the girl who was killed by the canal."

I've barely said this when I hear a shout and a door slamming in the garage, though the man's words are indistinguishable. "You mean Kylie Goodchild," Dennison says in my ear.

His voice in the garage has lost volume. Through a grimy window that's open a few inches in the side of the building I see a bulky figure lurch into an office decorated with a nude girl on a calendar. As I turn away to hide my face I glimpse him at the window. I feel as though he's watching me, even if just sunlight is glaring at my back. I have to keep talking, and I say "That's who I mean. I told the police I thought her boyfriend was responsible, but now I know it wasn't him."

"Don't name any names."

Dennison's other voice and my equally distant one are muffled now, because the man at the window has dragged the sash down. When I risk a sidelong glance I find he's out of sight, presumably at his desk. "I won't be doing that," I assure Dennison. "You won't have to cut me off."

"Go on then, but be careful."

"I thought the man responsible objected to her trying to see me, but it wasn't only that. I don't think it was even mainly me."

I'm frustrated by the suffocated mumble of my dislodged voice. I can't make out a word it says, despite hearing them all in my mobile. More important, if there's any reaction in the office of the garage I won't be able to hear. "I'll tell you this much, Derek," I say and pace towards the building, which appears to squeeze it even flatter. "The man used to call up my show."

"No names, remember."

"No need. He knows who he is." I have to free one hand to dab my wet prickling forehead. "That's why Kylie took to me," I say, "and why she wanted to talk to me the night she died. Because I argued with him on the air about issues they disagreed over."

"Make sure you don't name anyone, but are you saying he still rings in?"

"I'm certain he still listens." I found that out yesterday as I loitered near the garage. "He only called me once after that night," I tell Dennison. "He must have been afraid of being recognised."

"Why would he be? I don't understand."

I'm on the edge of saying, but Dennison would take me off the air, and I have more to broadcast. "Let me tell you what I see and maybe you will."

"We're all waiting, so can I ask you to come to the point?"

"I think they had an argument that night about his problem and she ran off to see me. Or maybe she wasn't coming to see me at first, she couldn't have been sure I'd be there, but then she thought of me once she was downtown." Suppose Dennison cuts me off because he finds this too indefinite? How much more will I have to say to provoke the reaction I'm after? "We know he followed her," I say and take another step towards the side of the garage—in a minute I'll be able to dodge out of sight and stay close to the wall of the building. "I don't know how he explained where he went unless there was nobody else around to see him go."

"Excuse me, Gray, but you sound as if you're guessing."

"It isn't just a guess." I'm beside the house next to the garage, and within yards of darting into the gap between them, though that's wider than it looked. "I see him chasing her away from Waves," I say and hear my own words beyond the office window. "Maybe she was trying to hide by the canal until he went away, but he found her. And then she stood her ground. That's how she was."

"Hold on a moment. Is there a radio on near you?"

I don't know what to do or say except "I haven't got one."

"We're getting an echo but all right, don't stop now. Just keep it as brief as you can."

"I don't know what was said between them. Something was too much." I'm hurrying to the corner of the empty house as I say "I see him lashing out. It only took a moment and one blow. It broke her jaw and knocked her out, and before he knew it she was in the canal. Why didn't he try and rescue her? Maybe—"

A face looms at the window of the office. There's a shout of "It's you, you cunt" and the sash rattles up. In my ear Dennison protests "What was that?"

"I didn't hear. I'm saying maybe he couldn't bear anyone to know he'd—"

"You cunt," Kylie's father yells again, "you fucking cunt," and lurches away from the window.

I'm not about to flee—very much the reverse. I switch my phone to loudspeaker mode and hurry to meet him in front of the open workshop. "That's the man," I say and hear my enlarged voice burst out of the office. "I won't name him, but—"

"I'm sorry, Gray. I won't have that kind of language on my show even if you would on yours."

Dennison says this in my aching ear and much louder in the garage; he might almost be alerting Robbie Goodchild. "Wait, Derek, Derry," I hear myself plead in at least two places at once. "Don't you realise—"

I'm already talking to myself. My voice is no longer at Robbie Goodchild's back. As my fist clenches on the useless phone and sinks away from my face, Dennison booms in the garage "Any children who heard that, just you go and wash your ears out and never talk that kind of privy talk. It's never clever and it isn't funny either."

I'm in front of the garage now, and pathetically relieved to see several men at work in the depthless shed. One is underneath a car on a hydraulic platform, while a second is removing the door of a van, and their colleague has just fitted a wheel on a jeep. None of them is looking directly at Goodchild as he stalks fast across the concrete floor littered with tools and vehicle parts, and surely that means they don't approve of his behaviour. They don't look even when he yells "You'll be sorry, you cunt" and strides at me.

"Think what you're doing. There are witnesses this time." When he doesn't falter I shout "You can't ignore this, any of you. He needs to stop before he goes too far again."

The younger men seem to be busier still. Only the eldest—the man under the platform—stares at me. "Deserve everything you fucking get, pal," he says, and at least one of the others nods.

Perhaps the loss of an eye has blacked out part of my brain, because I've made just about every mistake I could. I'm staying in sight of the mechanics for want of any better scheme when Goodchild swings a hulking fist at the blind side of my face. Up to this moment I managed to delude myself that he wouldn't give way to actual violence. I must be as naïve as any of Frank Jasper's faithful. I step back so fast that it feels like flinching, which inflames my anger. "That's like the one you gave Kylie, is it, Bob? When did you find out Wayne's stepfather was black?"

Something makes him hesitate. Perhaps I've roused a memory he's done his best to stifle, unless I've said more than his employees knew. I'm not sure they can hear me above the ad for Frugrab bargain offers that Dennison is playing, and I raise my voice. "Don't you realise you're showing I told the truth? Was that your drawing of Mohammed in her book? You used to phone in attacking anyone who wasn't white. You even said Blackley shouldn't be pronounced how it is."

"Fucking shouldn't either," the man under the platform shouts, and both his colleagues nod.

I still have to try to appeal to their better selves. There's nobody on foot along the Blackley road, and no sign of the kind of vehicle I'm just about praying to see. At least Goodchild has halted while he scoffs "Took you all this time to work that out, did it? You're no more fucking psychic than I am or any other cunt."

I'm overtaken by an insight, and I blurt it out. "You never believed in Frank Jasper any more than I did. You hired him because you thought he'd be no use. It made you look as if you'd nothing to hide and like you cared as well."

"Don't you fucking say I never cared," Goodchild snarls and lurches forward.

"How did it feel, pretending to respect her boyfriend? How does it feel to have to hide what you did from her mother?"

I need him to betray himself in front of the only witnesses that are left—to say something even they can't ignore. I have to stay out of his reach as he takes another vicious swing at me, but I can't back into the traffic. I retreat along the pavement just far enough to avoid the blow. I'm still in front of Goodchild Motors when I say "How did it feel to have to pretend at Kylie's funeral?"

"Hello to Eunice from Sale," Dennison says several times louder, as though he has to shout over the rattle of a power tool on a hub-cap in the garage. Too late I realise the mechanics may not be hearing me or Goodchild any longer above all the noise. They're certainly determined not to watch him throw another hefty punch at my face. "Fucking leave her out of it," he says through his bared teeth.

I can scarcely believe he said that, but it's no more incredible than the situation I've put myself in. My plan has failed, and I've nothing left except rage. When I back out of reach of yet another swing that looks capable of splintering my jaw, I can't be seen by anybody in the workshop even if they would have come to my aid. I won't let Goodchild glimpse my apprehension or make Kylie's error of allowing him too close. "You know I've seen the truth," I tell him. "I'd have seen it sooner if you hadn't called yourself Bob on the air. Who didn't you want to recognise you?"

"Just you and me, cunt." Goodchild shows me his teeth again, practically grinning. "I'm the last fucking thing you'll see," he says and lashes out at my remaining eye.

The fist looks weighty and yet less substantial than I know it is. I only just back out of range—I feel in danger of fancying it isn't as lethal as he means it to be. He's still coming at me. Perhaps he thinks nobody else can see him now. The passing drivers can, but nobody is even slowing down, and it would be gullible to expect them to intervene—I'd be as deluded as any of Jasper's victims. I take another hasty step backwards, and the uneven pavement catches my heel.

The cracked flagstone has been raised at least an inch. No doubt it's where a truck was parked. I haven't regained my balance when Kylie's father lurches at me, swinging his fist. My other foot catches the edge of the flagstone, and I sprawl on my back.

The impact jolts a fiery pain the length of my spine and thumps all the breath out of me. The mobile, which I'd forgotten I was clutching, flies out of my hand. Goodchild grins at the phone and takes a heavy step towards it before swerving back to me. "Say ta-ra to the one you've got left," he says and stamps on my face.

I almost can't believe I'm seeing the heel of his boot swell into my eye. With so little perspective all the substance seems to have been squeezed out of it, and I barely have time to roll out of its way. Pain flares along my spine while grit and flagstones scrape my cheek, almost dislodging the eye-patch. I shove myself onto my agonised back to find Goodchild waiting for me to show my face. As he tramps at me again I hear a distant siren.

It's a police car, and in a moment I see its glaring lights. Goodchild glances furiously over his shoulder and then comes faster at me. The police are hundreds of yards away, and he has plenty of time to injure me or worse. I plant my hands on the hot prickly stone and lever myself upright—into a sitting position, at any rate. It's as much as I can do before he kicks me in the eye.

I jerk my head away, not fast enough or sufficiently far. The steel toecap misses my eye but slices open my cheek, grinding against the bone. The sight of blood doesn't satisfy Goodchild. It seems to encourage if not to excite him, and he kicks out with more force. I'm just in time to grab the boot with both hands to prevent it from bursting my eye.

He leans all his weight on it, forcing me backwards. My whole body shudders with the effort of fending him off, and then my spine lets me down. My shoulders thump the pavement, and the boot descends towards my face to grind my eye under its heel. I can't tell how few inches it is from me—perhaps I'm no longer misjudging the distance, which is no distance at all. My fingers are trembling with the strain, and the flagstones have scraped my elbows skinless, when the howl of the siren swells in my ears. It sinks to a growl as car doors slam, and Goodchild is hauled away from me. "Get your hands off," he protests and attempts to stop shouting. "I'm not the villain. He was robbing from my business."

When I manage to support myself with my twitching hands and shaky arms I see him in the grip of two burly policemen. He's doing his best to appear reasonable, even cooperative. "Ask his workers if

I was," I say in a voice that feels as if it doesn't belong to me. "I don't think they'll all lie for him."

I could be wrong, but what else can I do? I'm groping for a handkerchief to press against my cheek when the driver of the police car steps onto the pavement. "We heard what happened. I've called an ambulance."

What did they hear? As I struggle to my feet and then hold the handkerchief against my streaming cheek I grow aware of a small voice repeating a word. I can't locate it or identify it until the police driver stoops to retrieve my phone. "I think someone's calling you," he says.

"Hello? Hello? Can somebody answer?" It's the girl on the Dennison Deal switchboard. She's been speaking for just a few seconds, but I have to learn "Did you get all that?"

"The police did. They told us to keep the line open for them after you went off the air."

"The police did." So they've been listening as I asked them to once I'd called the show the first time. I see Goodchild understand, and not just his expression but the whole of him seems to collapse, growing smaller and less substantial. Despite the throbbing of my face I feel almost sorry for him. He looks like a man who can no longer avoid knowing what he's done and what he is, and perhaps that's the worst punishment of all.

37

CHRISTINE

As I step out of my apartment building a train sends a prolonged whine through the overhead track. It sounds like a tool in a workshop, and my fingers stray towards the stitches in my cheek, although the memory hasn't revived any anger. I don't think even meeting Walter Belvedere would now, and I glance up at his window, but if he's home he's staying out of sight. The sun is packing the shadows away under the sides of the street, but it feels less pitiless this morning, more like an omen of renewal. While the office workers are at their desks there are still people at large in the streets. Most of them look at me, and I tell several "The other fellow came off worse."

Kylie's father is in custody, though the media have yet to say so. Presumably they're waiting until he has been charged. I wonder how the *Clarion* will report the story and whether Alice Francis or the editor will take back their comments about me. Just now I'm concerned only that Christine should hear I've been exonerated. Even if it's too late to make a difference between us, I want her to know she mustn't blame herself. I can't help suspecting she does, even though she never had a reason.

She isn't to be seen as I cross the road to the apartments. She wasn't cycling in the window of Corporate Sana, and I hope she wasn't elsewhere in the gym; it ought to be too early for her to have left for work. Even if I still had a set of her keys I'd ring the bell; in any case, my mother exchanged them for Christine's set of mine at the hospital. When Christine visited the ward I said I couldn't see her, but now I feel as though it was a hole in my head that spoke. Perhaps I'll tell her so if I have the chance. The intercom grille comes to life with a click, and I'm opening my mouth when a metallic voice says "Ambler."

"If I were you I'd amble off." I don't have the right to tell the man that, even if his presence has taken me off guard. Why should I have expected Christine to stay on her own? I do my best to feel reasonable for only saying "Graham."

"Yes."

This doesn't sound much like an acknowledgment, still less an invitation. "It's Graham," I attempt to establish.

"You said so. What can I do for you, Mr Graham?"

I gather that he hopes the answer is very little if not nothing at all. "Graham Wilde. Is—"

"That still doesn't signify anything to me."

I can't believe Christine hasn't mentioned me, if only in the context of her work. Or has she a reason to pretend there was nobody before he came along? Has she ended up in another abusive relationship? I seem to feel my temperature flaring, not just with the sunlight. "Graham Wilde of Wilde Card," I say louder. "Graham Wilde of Waves."

"Is that the radio station? I don't patronise it, I'm afraid. If you're conducting some kind of audience survey you're wasting your time with me."

"I'm no more interested in you than you are in me as long as you're taking care of Christine. Can I have a word with her? She doesn't have to see me unless she wants to."

Ambler is silent, and I'm growing furious with the suspicion that he's cut me off when he says "Who?"

"Christine. Christine Ellis. The girl whose flat you're in."

"I know nothing about any such person, I'm afraid."

"What are you trying—" As I grow nearly incoherent with the kind of rage I thought I'd left behind, my gaze drifts to the cardboard strip in the metal frame above the bellpush. I hardly bothered glancing at the printed name, but now I see it says CHARLES AMBLER. "I'm sorry," I babble. "I've been, I've been away. Doesn't Christine live here any more?"

"That's my perception of it, yes."

I can't afford to let him enrage me further. "Can I ask when you moved in?"

"Not long ago."

"Would you happen to know where she went? She must have left a forwarding address."

"I know nothing about it, and now you must excuse me. I've business to attend to," Ambler says and shuts off the intercom.

I stare at the grille, which puts me in mind of a fixed mocking grin with bared teeth. I'm tempted to lean on the bellpush, but suppose Christine forgot to leave her address or disliked him as much as I do—too much to entrust it to him? They'll have it at Waves, and surely Shilpa will take pity on my state. If she won't give me the address I can wait for Christine by the counter where my photos used to be.

There are no posters for Jasper outside the Palace. He's moved on and good riddance, despite the help he inadvertently gave me. As I make for Waves I wonder if the last call Bob from Blackley made to Wilde Card was an attempt to pretend everything was normal, since he'd already killed his daughter. The automatic doors slide apart for me, and the left one appears to vanish. Vince is at the security desk, and his expression has to catch up with his stare. "God almighty," he says. "Did you get your fight at last?"

"I was never looking for one and I'm not now, Vince. Can I go up?"

"Nobody's told me different."

Nevertheless he seems doubtful, and I hurry to the lift before he can change his mind about me. The metal cage looks smaller than it used to and approaching two-dimensional. The possibility that I might be faced with Megan makes it feel even more cramped. I'm reminded how determined Goodchild was to be polite to another receptionist, and how I didn't realise that his wife thought he was making too much of Shilpa because it was so untypical of him. The lift doors open once the floor number has fitted together, and I'm relieved to see Shilpa, whose expression turns sympathetic faster than Vince's did. "Oh," she says, "Graham."

"Don't worry, I'm not quite as bad as I look."

As I wonder if she's taken aback just by my condition or because I've shown up at Waves, she says "What happened to you this time?"

"Nothing worth a news report. It's all right, I'm not blaming anyone."

Perhaps the police are withholding the information until they charge Kylie's father, if they bother releasing it at all. "Were you here to see someone?" Shilpa says more in the tone of her job.

"Now who do you think she might be?"

"I didn't realise. She didn't mention you'd be coming in." Shilpa seems pleased for me, if a little puzzled. "Is it to do with yesterday?" she says.

"How do you mean yesterday?"

"The call you made to Derek's show."

"You're right, it's because of that. I can't really tell you how much of a difference it's made."

Presumably that information hasn't reached her either; perhaps the police have told anyone who knows how the call continued off the air to keep it to themselves. "I'm glad for you, Graham," Shilpa says. "Let me tell her you're here."

She puts on half her headphones and flicks a switch on the board before laying the headset down. "Can you wait? She's engaged."

"On the phone, you mean."

It isn't much of a joke, and Shilpa seems to think it's even less. "Would you like me to get you a drink?"

"It's a bit early for the kind I like."

"I expect so." Apparently to take us past any unwelcome implication she adds "You can have a sweet instead."

When it becomes clear she isn't offering me one I say "Which sweet is that?"

"One of the ones on her desk."

"When did she start going in for those?" I can't help feeling guilty; it must have been since she couldn't see me at the hospital. "So long as she still goes to the gym," I say, trying to make it sound like a joke.

"Graham, you can't have forgotten. She's always kept some in her office."

So I've been making jokes without knowing, and perhaps I'm something of one. "Sorry, have we been talking about Paula? I'm here to see Christine."

Shilpa blinks as her lips part. They remain open while she manages to stop blinking and gazes at me. "Graham, she isn't with us any longer."

"I always knew there was more to her. Where's she working now?"

"No." I can't judge if the word is meant to silence me or to serve as some kind of answer until Shilpa says "She's gone."

I won't believe what someone unlike me—one of Jasper's flock, for instance—might assume Shilpa is trying to convey. "Gone where?"

Her eyes grow full of sympathy, close to overflowing with it. With a visible effort she contains it and says "She was coming to see you, Graham. She had something she wanted you to hear."

It seems safest just to ask "What?"

"She didn't tell anyone, but Trevor thought she'd copied part of one of your shows. Some argument you had with a caller she'd recognised from somewhere else."

It must have been Goodchild. She realised who he was before I did; perhaps all the playbacks I searched through caught up with her. I hear my voice complaining or confessing "She never came to me."

"She only got as far as the Palace. She was crossing the road."

I'm hoping at least not to have to ask, but Shilpa falls silent. "What happened?" I blurt.

"You know you have to watch out when you're crossing there. People said she was in a lot of hurry and didn't look. They said she couldn't have known—" Shilpa's determination falters, and she glances past me at the lifts as if hoping to be rescued. With a further effort she says "It was very quick."

I'm not far from demanding why I wasn't told, but I'm too aware of not having listened to Waves for weeks or read a newspaper. Before I can find words Shilpa says "The bus ran over whatever she was bringing."

I don't care about that, but perhaps Shilpa is using it to bring her emotions under control. I don't suppose I help by asking "When?"

"Just a few days after you were attacked by the canal."

At first I'm too confused to speak. "That can't be right. I've seen her since then. She was in her flat and the gym."

Shilpa blinks and runs a swift finger under her eyes. "It must have been someone else, Graham."

I won't argue. I've left that behind, but I know if I took a polygraph test it would find in my favour. Shilpa lets me stay silent for a few seconds and then says "Would you like me to tell anyone you're here?"

"There's nobody who needs to be told."

I thank her, though I'd be unable to sum up why. I'm at the lifts when she says "Graham . . ."

I'm not sure I want to hear. I step into the lift before I turn and hold the door open. "She only did a few shows with Derek," Shilpa says. "I think she was missing you."

"Thanks," I say again, more vaguely still. The shrunken metal cage sinks down the shaft while I do my best not to think of a box being lowered into the earth. Even Kylie Goodchild's funeral seems like an omen now. On the ground floor Vince appears to have run out of words, and I've none. As I step onto the pavement it occurs to me that he must know about Christine. Very possibly he thought I did.

The street looks little more than two-dimensional, not just for my lack of an eye. When I head towards the Palace a wind breathes down my neck. It feels like a reminder of autumn if not of winter. As the wind moves onwards a stray page of newspaper lifts its head on the pavement in front of me. The printed sheet puts me in mind of a poster, but before I can make out the headline the pretence of life subsides, and the page slithers into the traffic. I'm making for the junction when my eye is caught by a word on a poster outside the Palace.

Is it Christine? Surely it can't be Goodchild. No, it's *Good Times*, the title of a production that means nothing to me. People are strolling like sightseers along Oxford Street and Oxford Road, past the Palace and the Palace. Here's where someone poked Graham Wilde's eye out, and here's where they ran over Christine Ellis. I loiter at the crossing, no matter how many people scowl at me whenever the pedestrian lights turn green. I don't know what I'm expecting: to identify where Christine died, or to glimpse her in the crowd? I've done neither and very little else when a car halts at the lights with its radio on loud. It's tuned to the news, and Sammy Baxter says that Robert Goodchild has been charged in connection with his daughter Kylie's death.

It feels like some kind of liberation, and I've only one way to celebrate—one person left to do it with. I cross the road once the lights have made it safe, though I feel disloyal to Christine for waiting. The gust of wind that follows me into the Dressing Room turns over a beer mat like a card trick on the table nearest to the door. Benny's on his own, and looks uncertain whether to welcome my company. "Buggeration, Mr Wubbleyou," he cries, perhaps because he thinks there's only me to hear. "What have you gone and done to yourself now?"

"Nothing I can't live with. Give me the usual, Benny. A drink and a joke. Tell me one about a blind man."

Benny fills a wineglass from a bottle in a refrigerator beyond the footlights and faces me again. "I can't think of any, Mr Wubbleyou."

"A man goes into Frugoptics and asks them what's up with his eyes. When they try to explain he says don't blind me with science." Once Benny has given a tentative laugh, whether out of nervousness or because he isn't certain he's heard the punch line, I say "Want to know the best joke? You're looking at him."

"You shouldn't think like that, Mr Wubbleyou."

"It's true, though. It's conclusive. I should have been able to see it with half an eye." I swing around, nearly spilling the drink, and raise my glass to Jasper's poster. "Here's to a real psychic."

"You've changed your mind about him, then."

"Not about our Frankie. Not while I'm alive," I vow and turn back to the bar. "Me. People kept saying I was psychic but I couldn't see it. I can now."

Benny struggles not to appear wary, but the footlights won't let him. "What can you see, Mr Wubbleyou?"

"What I've lost and never knew I had."

He looks more doubtful than ever, and all at once I hear myself. I sound like one of Jasper's followers, exactly the kind of evangelising proselyte I wouldn't want to be alone with in a bar. I think of telling Benny I'm drinking for two if not three, but it mightn't strike him as humorous. "Don't look so serious, Benny," I tell him. "It's just my story. It'll be my novel."

Perhaps it will. As I take my drink to a booth I see myself dodging from mirror to mirror. Not just the eye-patch and the stitches that resemble stage make-up, but the spotlights as well, give me the look of a performer, even if I can't decide what sort. Is the world ready for a psychic who makes jokes? My spine doesn't ache much now, and I rest it against the wall in a corner of the booth. While I can't predict the future, if Hannah Leatherhead should turn up I might pitch a different kind of show to her. The notion prompts me to lift my glass, and Benny manages to come up with a grin. He must think I'm raising the glass to him, since he can't see anybody at my back. Nevertheless I seem to feel both of them at my shoulders, laying a hand there for less than a breath.

ACKNOWLEDGMENTS

Jenny helped as always, not least by being my first reader. John Llewellyn Probert advised on mutilation. Back in the seventies Julie Davis, one of my editors at Millington, suggested a way of reconceiving *The Face That Must Die* to make it more emotionally involving. Though I didn't take her advice, there's a sense in which *Ghosts Know* develops the theme she thought I should have made central to the earlier novel. An episode of *Derren Brown Investigates* gave me useful insights into the methods of stage psychics, and the Merseyside Skeptics web site (www.merseysideskeptics.org .uk) helped too. Once again Gert Jan Bekenkamp sustained me with food and wine and music. While Graham Wilde isn't based on Roger Phillips, his show often echoes Roger's phone-in on Radio Merseyside, the station where I reviewed films for nearly forty years until the BBC saved themselves the price of a pizza.

Speaking of food as I so often do, and having as usual invented the odd eatery for the purposes of the tale, let me list a few favourite Manchester restaurants: East Z East and the Spicy Hut (Indian), Red N Hot and the Red Chilli (Szechuan), the Middle Kingdom (Szechuan and Hunan), the Yang Sing, Pearl City and the Rice Bowl (Cantonese), the Bem Brasil (Brazilian), the Chaophraya and Koh Samui (Thai), and the Armenian Taverna.

I worked on the first draft of *Ghosts Know* at the fine Matina Apartments in Pefkos, Rhodes. Passages were also written at Hypericon in Nashville, Fantasycon in Nottingham, the Festival of Fantastic Films in Manchester, Mythoscon in Phoenix, and the Days Inn Hotel in Shoreditch.